A BIT OF A DEPARTURE:
THE FIRST LESBIAN REGENCY NOVEL

Keldyn's very own
copy
of
one of Catriona's
favorite ~~of~~ books

XOXOX

10 March 1991

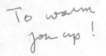

To warm
you up!

BIOGRAPHICAL SKETCH

I am a native Northern Californian, a confirmed anglophile, and a radical feminist. I spent one poverty-struck year of my undergraduate studies in Lancaster, England before graduating from Mills College in 1979.

I discovered my first love and only profession—writing—when I was twelve years old but did not start my first novel until after leaving Mills. Three novels later I fell in love again. *Pembroke Park* was written in celebration.

A recent transplant to Santa Fe, New Mexico I share my life with my lover, my typewriter, and my cat. I am currently working on a lesbian science fiction novel and have other books on the backburner including a series of contemporary novels set in Santa Fe, a series of historical novels about American women, and a sequel to *Pembroke Park* along the lines of *Molly Goes To America*.

PEMBROKE PARK

by Michelle Martin

The Naiad Press Inc
1986

Printed in the United States of America
First Edition

Cover design by The Women's Graphic Center
Typesetting by Sandi Stancil
Edited by Katherine V. Forrest

Library of Congress Cataloging-in-Publication Data

Martin, Michelle, 1957—
    Pembroke Park.

    I. Title.
PR6063.A718P45   1986   823'.914   85-82687
ISBN 0-930044-77-0 (pbk.)

To Lightning, my love and muse; for Zanah; and for Bruce,
who makes it impossible not to like some men.

It took nearly four years to write this book and see it in print. Thanks are owing to many people including: Barbara Grier of Naiad Press; Katherine Forrest who edited my manuscript wisely and well; Mary Morell of Full Circle Books who helped with the ending and thus made the book almost PC; Jane Austen and Georgette Heyer; Jo Gerlach, my inspiration and first editor; and to my mother who said, "If you like reading regency romances why not write one?" This book is not exactly what she expected, but then, neither am I.

FOREWORD

The time of this novel, 1817, is a period of social transition between the bawdy 1700s, in which women enjoyed personal and sexual freedom, and the early 1900s, when such freedom will be beyond the imagining of women forced into roles of "femininity." Demure, helpless, unsexual, with the professions closed to them, women will be allowed only those arts centered around home and family. Rigidity and propriety will become the dominating social theme until the twentieth century.

Why this transition to female repression, this growing restriction of female activity and character? Post-French Revolution Europe has become politically reactionary with social conservatism among its middle and upper class. The Industrial Revolution is in full swing, and as a prosperous middle class emerges, it will mimic the social standing and structured behavior of its noble "betters." With the rise of capitalism, women's participation in the economy will fall off drastically, and along with it, their entire sphere of influence.

England in 1817 is enjoying a flowering of all the arts. William and Dorothy Wordsworth, Byron, Keats, Percy and Mary Shelley, Scott, Austen—all are writing. Men are adorning themselves with as many "fripperies" as their female counterparts, showing off their legs in skintight breeches, padding their elegant coats to broaden their shoulders and chests, styling their hair as carefully as their neckcloths. Women of the *ton* (the nobility) uncover a good deal of their bodies, even dampening their gowns to have them cling more revealingly to their curves. Women have already become social and financial accessories, a condition which will not be effectively challenged until our own century—except by certain women. . . .

CHAPTER 1

Joanna walked down a dusty lane shadowed by large elm trees, their limbs arching across in a delicate caress of leaves and wind. Occasionally a lark called out from its perch on a bobbing twig, the warm late morning air of March holding its crystal song.

Joanna's stomach rumbled its protest at having to digest the three scones Mrs. Stempel had forced on her not an hour ago. A chubby sparrow sitting on a rock to Joanna's right cocked its head at this unexpected duet of lark and belly. Joanna promptly laughed at the stout fellow and he flew away in a huff. Joanna continued on her walk, her mind spinning away to Mr. Scott's newest novel, her thoughts fastening upon knights riding noble steeds as they galloped to the rescue of damsels in distress. Her aunt had protested more than once Joanna's enjoyment of such literature, but, her aunt conceded, at least there was proper English spirit and morality in Mr. Scott's tomes, unlike that scandalous Mr. Fielding and his *Tom Jones* of which Joanna was inordinately fond.

The dull rhythmic thud of hoofbeats brought Joanna's head up from her contemplation of her dusty shoes. Quickly she shaded her eyes, half expecting to find Ivanhoe galloping towards her.

There was no white stallion, however; only a large, powerfully built bay mare. And instead of a knight in shining armor there was a fair damsel, though hardly in distress; she seemed a superb horsewoman. She was young, perhaps of medium height, dressed in brown turkish trousers tucked into riding boots, and a dark blue long-sleeved shirt and brown vest only slightly darker than the tan of her face and throat. The rider's honey-blonde hair was caught into a thick braid that swung across her back while stray wisps floated about her face.

Stunned by this apparition, Joanna stopped in her tracks and seriously wondered if Mrs. Stempel's scones had so unsettled her stomach that she was now suffering from hallucinations.

The horse and rider also stopped and then continued towards Joanna at a sedate walk. Despite all the incongruities of costume, sex, and masculine saddle, it was the rider's face that held Joanna's rapt attention. Heart-shaped and rather plain, there was something in that face that would not let Joanna go: a strength, a sense of whimsy . . . she was not sure what it was. She only knew a sudden and compelling longing to have her oils and canvas at hand so that she might understand the swirling emotions within her by capturing them in paint.

"Hullo." The young woman greeted her with a smile as she pulled her mare to a stop. "Who are you?"

"I am Lady Sinclair," Joanna stated with caution, feeling curiously lightheaded.

"I thought so," the young woman declared as she leaned down and extended her hand which Joanna, to her surprise, found herself grasping. "We haven't been formally introduced yet. I'm Diana. Diana March. I've just purchased Waverly Manor."

"*You?*" Joanna gasped, staring up at the woman with unconcealed shock. "Waverly Manor?"

"You're not going to be needing smelling salts, are you?" Diana March asked anxiously. "I never carry them, you know."

"No, no I . . . I beg your pardon, Lady March. I was . . . daydreaming and you caught me unawares. Welcome to Heddington."

"Thank you." Diana's grin was decidedly mischievous. "You knew I had purchased Waverly Manor?"

"Oh, yes. Mr. Acton, my . . . my brother's solicitor, mentioned you only the other day."

"Whatever he said could not have been good." Diana chuckled. "Solicitors take an instant dislike to me. They do not approve of females giving them orders, I think. I doubt if they approve of our sex at all—we are always having to be provided for in wills that would be quite straightforward without us."

"On the contrary, Mr. Acton spoke very highly of you," Joanna said a trifle stiffly. She had regained her equilibrium.

"Did he? How odd. I should regard any future advice he may give you with the greatest suspicion, Lady Sinclair. His judgment seems to be faltering. There are no upcoming court battles I trust?"

"No, none," Joanna said faintly.

"Then my mind is at ease. Well," Diana said decisively as she gathered her reins, "it has been a great pleasure meeting you, Lady Sinclair. You've the honor to be the first neighbor whose acquaintance I've made after being in residence only two days. I daresay the calling cards will be streaming in now. It is a great trial being new in the district, you know. I always dread conversations about the weather. I can't tell you how grateful I am that you didn't mention today's absence of rain. Ciao!"

"Good . . . day," Joanna faltered as the bay broke into a canter and carried its unique mistress away leaving Joanna to stare after them, her body numb, her mind feverish. "Good God," she breathed.

It was several minutes before she could rouse herself sufficiently to turn and remark to the chubby sparrow who had returned to its rock: "To think that so outrageous a creature should appear in *Herefordshire!* Never have I encountered anyone who so flagrantly sidestepped every rule of social decorum!" The sparrow blinked at Joanna. She took this to mean complete agreement. "I am quite amazed," she said, and then continued on her walk.

Twenty minutes later Joanna happened to look up and saw the black iron gate on her right that signified the entrance to Pembroke Park. She turned mechanically from the elm-lined lane into the mile-long drive that led to the fifty-three room country residence of her brother, Hugo Garfield.

Though untitled, the Garfields were one of the oldest families in England. Her brother felt this heritage keenly. As did their aunt, Mrs. Frances Garfield Hampton, who, despite her marriage and subsequent widowhood, remained a Garfield to her bones. She resided at Pembroke the year round striving mightily to run the lives of all of those around her for, naturally, a Garfield always knew what was best in every situation.

The familiarity of her surroundings, the imposing edifice of her familial home looming before her, brought Joanna back to her senses.

Pembroke had been built, rebuilt, and added onto numerous times in the several centuries of Garfield habitation until at last it was an amalgam of Gothic, Tudor, and Georgian grimness, its dark walls and turrets standing out bleakly from the surrounding verdant park. During the four short years of her marriage until her husband's death, Joanna had been freed of the necessity of passing through Pembroke's massive front doors. The gentle Lord Sinclair had shared her feelings for her ancestral home: Nothing, she had remarked to him on more than one occasion, could be more dismal than the exterior of Pembroke—saving the interior, of course.

With her habitual sigh when returning home, Joanna slowly mounted the stone steps to the front door of Pembroke. She entered, ignoring the leering gargoyle above the Entrance Hall's huge fireplace; the monster had given her more than one nightmare in her childhood. She began her ascent of the Grand Staircase, removing her pelisse and bonnet despite the chill that seemed to inhabit every inch of the Garfield country home.

Joanna turned into her room on the second landing, welcoming the sunlight that streamed in through the long windows. Handing her bonnet and pelisse to Ellen, her maid, she quickly removed her walking dress, exchanging it for an empire gown of flowered silk. She brushed out her brown hair and pronounced herself ready to meet the world. She walked down the outer hallway, came to a door, rapped twice, and then entered to find her daughter lying against the pillows of her chaise lounge listening to Miss Anthony, her governess, read to her from the history of the War of the Roses.

Joanna's daughter was far too pale and thin for her eight

years; a life of continual illness had kept her indoors and often bedridden. The girl's spirit rebelled at this imprisonment but her body had continually betrayed her until she was left increasingly fretful and cross with all those around her, most of all herself. Joanna remained the only one able to laugh her out of her moods and fidgets.

"Mama!" the girl cried out.

"Hullo Molly," Joanna said as she kissed her daughter's forehead. "I didn't mean to interrupt. I'll come back when you've finished."

"Oh no, please," Molly pleaded. "I'd much rather talk to you than listen to Miss Anthony talk about those stupid Plantagenets. Please?"

Exchanging a smile with Miss Anthony, Joanna told the governess that she might safely leave Molly in her charge. Joanna then sat on the chaise beside her daughter and took her small thin hands in both of her own.

"Well," Joanna said, "what shall we talk about?"

"Anything you like," Molly replied as she happily resettled herself against her pillows. "Where did you walk today?"

"Down the front drive and out into the lane, and then down to the parsonage where Mrs. Stempel stuffed me with her dreadful scones and scolded me for going out without a parasol, assuring me that I shall be wizened and wrinkled by the time I am thirty."

"She's such a fuss-budget," Molly said, wrinkling her nose in distaste.

"That is not kind of you Molly, or polite," Joanna said reprovingly, "however true. Besides, she was quite right, you know. I can feel the freckles popping out all over my face even as we speak."

"Oh stuff," Molly giggled. "What else did you do?"

"Well, after escaping Mrs. Stempel—and her scones—I proceeded through the Franklin's north meadow, cut across our eastern pasture, and came back up the lane home."

"Is that all?" Molly asked, clearly disappointed. "Didn't you meet anyone besides Mrs. Stempel?"

"Well . . . ." Joanna said with a smile, "I did meet one person on the road."

"Really? Who?"

"Our new neighbor, Lady Diana March."

"Lady March?" Molly squealed. "Oh Mama, how lucky you are! Aunt Hampton says that Lady March has travelled all over the world. Did she tell you any stories? Did she talk about Italians and scimitars and murderous caliphs?"

"You are a bloodthirsty little devil, you know that?" As Molly giggled at this Joanna asked, "And how did Aunt Hampton learn that Lady March is a world traveller?"

"Mr. Acton told her yesterday when we were at tea and you were late," Molly replied, shoving her brown locks off her forehead. "Mr. Acton says that Lady March is a . . . a non-conformist. What is a non-conformist, Mama?"

"Someone who does not follow the rules of society."

"Like murderers and thieves?" Molly asked eagerly.

"No, no." Joanna smiled. "They are criminals. Let me see if I can explain. Do you recollect the Thorntons?" Molly nodded. "They are Roman Catholics," Joanna continued. "They do not follow the principles of the Anglican Church which is the Church of England. They do not *conform* to our national religion. You see?"

Again Molly nodded. "Is Lady March a Roman Catholic, Mama?"

Joanna chuckled. "I doubt it. No, Lady March does not conform in other ways. Her manners, her speech are too open, too nearly rude to be considered proper. Her actions don't bear talking about. She does not conform to society's views of acceptable social behavior. You see?"

Molly nodded eagerly. "What else does she do?"

"Well . . . Lady March wears—to put it delicately—

masculine clothing. And she does not use a sidesaddle as a lady, as any woman should. She sits astride her horse like a man!"

"Really?" Molly breathed, her grey eyes widening with delight. "How exciting! Tell me more, Mama. Please tell me more!"

"Molly," Joanna said reprovingly, "Lady March is not exciting. She is an embarrassment to all right-thinking women. With only our one meeting I think I may be safe in saying that Lady March is a scandalous creature!"

"But that is exciting," Molly insisted. "We've never known anyone who was scandalous or did things differently. Don't you think it's exciting to find something new?"

"Simply because something is new does not make it exciting," Joanna countered. "In Lady March's case it was rather unpleasant."

"Oh," Molly said, clearly crestfallen.

"But it was only one meeting," Joanna hastened to assure her, "and we merely introduced ourselves. Perhaps if we should meet again. . . ."

"You will find her to be exciting?" Molly eagerly concluded.

Joanna smiled. "Stranger things have happened."

CHAPTER 2

On the day following Joanna Sinclair's encounter with Diana March, her brother, Hugo Garfield, was cantering towards the long-desired goal of Pembroke Park, his friend and companion, Lord Thomas Carroll, at his side, and his luggage coach a discreet distance behind them. An hour's further travel brought him to the road his sister had traversed the day before. It was from this vantage point that he chanced to observe a great deal of unusual activity at Waverly Manor.

"I say Tom, look over there," Mr. Garfield instructed his friend, reining to a stop. "What's going on?"

'Well, from this distance I can but hazard a guess," Lord

Carroll obligingly replied, "but it looks to me as if half the laborers in Herefordshire are renovating Waverly Manor. Is there anything wrong in that?"

"There's a great deal wrong for I never authorized such work and I'm damned if I'm going to pay for it," Mr. Garfield grimly replied. "Come along. Let us investigate this . . . activity."

These two gentlemen, after instructing their coachman to wait for them, turned their horses down the side road at an easy canter. They were soon pulling in before the modest two-story house that was Waverly Manor. The lower half of the building was of ivy-covered brick, the upper half timber. Smoke emanated from two of its many chimneys while workmen hammered upon the roof, dangled from riggings at the sides of the house, and carted bricks and lumber to the stable which lay at the rear of the manor.

"For unauthorized work things seem to be moving along at a good clip," Lord Carroll observed.

"It is going to stop with even greater alacrity," Mr. Garfield seethed as he jumped from his horse and stalked up the front walk, Lord Carroll directly behind him.

"You there, Jenkins!" Mr. Garfield called to a corpulent carpenter on the roof. "Who authorized you to do this work?"

"What's that, sir?" Jenkins called back.

"Who told you to do all of this?"

"Beg pardon, sir?"

"Where is your master?" Mr. Garfield shouted, quickly reaching the end of his patience, which was never in great supply to begin with.

"Oh . . . in the house, sir," Jenkins called down.

"We shall soon see what's what," Garfield informed his amused companion as he stormed up the brick front steps of the manor and pushed open the door without bothering to knock.

They entered bedlam. A maid busily scrubbed the steps of the main stairway that rose from the small Entry Hall, while two boys of no more than fifteen vigorously scraped the varnish from the wainscotting, all three shouting at each other as if they stood hundreds of yards away, rather than a few feet. A greater din came from the left, and the two men turned and entered the main drawing room where painters and carpenters were just completing their work on the walls, panelling and ceiling. One dusty man of red face and gnarled hands shouldered past Mr. Garfield and Lord Carroll with a wheelbarrow of broken bricks while a maid, dressed in a grey skirt and blouse, a brown scarf on her head and a long plait falling down her back, stood on a ladder as she carefully hung a large painting above the fireplace. The ribald song concerning a woman of dubious reputation pouring lustily from her throat caused both gentlemen to blush, adding to Garfield's fury. The soprano made one or two minor adjustments to the painting, concluded her song, and then carefully stepped down off the ladder.

"Where is your master, girl?" Garfield demanded as he strode towards her.

"I beg your pardon, sir?" was her frosty reply as she turned to face the two men, her green eyes snapping.

"Where is your master?" Garfield reiterated between clenched teeth. "I wish to speak with him at once."

"I have no master, sir."

"Then show me to your mistress!" Garfield bellowed.

"I am my own mistress, sir. And who might you be?"

"I am Hugo Garfield and I will thank you to keep a civil tongue in your head! What is your name, girl?"

"March," the young woman replied. "*Lady* . . . Diana . . . March."

If Hugo Garfield had not been an English gentleman born and bred his mouth might have dropped open at this disclosure. As it was he could only stare at her.

"Lady?" he uttered.

"I wish to know, *sir*," Lady March continued acidly, "by what right you trespass in my home."

"What right?" Garfield gasped. "What right? I'll have you know, madam, that I own this building and the land that it stands on!"

"On the contrary. You lost all title to both the house and the estate on Tuesday last. On that date your solicitor, Mr. Acton, signed over the deed of this property to me. You gave him power of attorney for just this purpose, I believe, and he acted upon it," Lady March calmly informed her new neighbor. "I paid a fair sum for this estate and I will thank you therefore, *Mr.* Garfield, to leave my house at once."

"This cannot be," Garfield insisted. "Why was I not informed of the sale?"

"That is an issue for you to raise with Mr. Acton," Lady March replied. Noticing the inactivity and undivided attention of the workmen in the room, she said pointedly, "This is not some play for your amusement. I believe that you all have work to do?" They quickly returned to their tasks.

"We were probably already on the road when Acton sent word to you, Hugo," Lord Carroll said to his friend. "His letter will undoubtedly find you in a month or so."

"Undoubtedly," Garfield replied with some bitterness. "I apologize, Lady March, for any rudeness I may have displayed. I trust you will be happy at Waverly," he said curtly as he turned on his heel and quit the room; Lord Carroll, with a hapless grin at Lady March, hurriedly followed.

The two men remounted their horses and continued on their journey without a word between them. Reaching the iron gate of Pembroke Park, they trotted up the drive and but a few minutes later jumped to the ground, handing their reins to the grooms who ran to meet them.

With a sigh of satisfaction Garfield mounted the broad steps to his ancestral home, noting that the chip on the third step had yet to be repaired. "What do I pay them for?" he muttered as he entered the mansion. "To lie in the sun all day, eat my food, and sleep under my roof?"

"We are early, Hugo," Lord Carroll said soothingly. "The work was undoubtedly scheduled to be done before your expected arrival."

"Hmph!" was Garfield's reply as he handed his hat and gloves to the newest Pembroke butler—the third in two years—and got directions to his aunt and sister, before proceeding from the Entrance Hall into the small day parlor in the western wing.

The gentlemen entered the parlor to be greeted by a pleasing scene of domesticity. Mrs. Hampton—a woman of some fifty years possessed of pale blue eyes, a long nose and double chin, her white hair neatly hidden beneath a matronly cap—and Joanna were seated together on a small brown couch. Before them rested a tea tray on a low table. The two women sat gently stirring their cups of tea as they spoke quietly together.

"Hugo!" Joanna cried, looking up. "Thomas! You're home!"

"We are indeed," Garfield said as he advanced into the room to kiss his aunt and sister.

"We did not expect you for another week, Hugo," Mrs. Hampton said as she rang for two more teacups.

"I was able to conduct my business with greater speed than I had hoped, and a good thing, too. You would not credit what I have just—"

"Being a dutiful fellow," Lord Carroll broke in, hoping to forestall Hugo's certain tirade against Lady March, "Hugo insisted we fly back with all undue haste to insure our arrival for Wednesday tea. Good day to you, Mrs. Hampton." Lord Carroll smiled as he clasped her outstretched hand. "Hullo Joanna," he winked at Lady Sinclair.

She smiled in turn. "It is good to have you back amongst us, Tom."

"Such warmth gives me hope of a less critical welcome at the Ancestral Abode," Lord Carroll said with a grin.

"I would not view our good will as any reflection of the greeting you will receive at Crismane," Mrs. Hampton informed Lord Carroll. "I had occasion to speak to the Dowager only yesterday and she chanced to remark that she was rather put out at not having received a single letter, let alone a visit, from her only son in the last two months."

"The Dragon is spewing fire again! Sanctuary, Hugo. I beg you to grant me sanctuary!" Lord Carroll implored.

"Do give over, Tom," Garfield said wearily as he sat down opposite his sister and aunt, who kindly handed him a cup of tea. After taking a tentative sip of his tea and finding it to his liking, Garfield asked, "Aunt Hampton, did Acton tell you he had sold Waverly Manor?"

"Why yes," Mrs. Hampton replied with some surprise. "He kept us informed of the matter daily. But how do you come to know of it, Hugo? I should not have thought that Mr. Acton's letter would have reached you in Worcestershire before your setting out to return home."

"It didn't," Garfield grimly replied. "We saw activity at Waverly as we came down the road and went to investigate."

"There's a great deal of bustle goin' on," Lord Carroll remarked. "Lady March seems to be renovatin' every brick and board on the place."

"Did you meet her?" Joanna asked.

"We did indeed," Lord Carroll said, grinning. "The woman knows the most confoundedly embarrassing songs."

"You would not credit it, Joanna," Garfield said, "but when we entered the Manor we found Lady March not only dressed but acting as if she were some common parlor maid. I quite blushed for her."

"I am amazed, Hugo," Mrs. Hampton declared and even went so far as to set down her teacup. "Mr. Acton had mentioned that Lady March spent most of her youth out of the country, but her family and background are excellent. They would not lead one to expect such base behavior as you describe. She actually dressed as a *maid*?"

"Lady March certainly seems to favor a more . . . fanciful

wardrobe than most young women," Joanna ventured.

"Have you met her?" Lord Carroll asked.

"Only for a moment while I was out walking yesterday morning. You would not credit it, Hugo, but she was dressed in those turkish trousers you see in all of the travelogues, and nought else but boots, shirt, and a waistcoat. I own I was quite shocked."

"To think that such a woman should enter our neighborhood, inhabit our house," Mrs. Hampton groaned.

"And what was your opinion of your new neighbor after so shocking a meeting?" Lord Carroll inquired.

Feeling three pairs of eyes closely scrutinizing her, Joanna answered carefully. "I . . . cannot like anyone who so blatantly and heedlessly ignores those rules of society which govern us all," she replied. "She seems . . . dangerous. But I would like to paint her. She is such an original and I found her face rather interesting."

"Did you think so?" Garfield said. "I found it very plain and wholly unattractive."

"That is because she was glaring at you," Lord Carroll said, laughing. "I daresay if she had smiled you would think her more tolerable."

"I shouldn't think so," Garfield said dismissingly. "Do either of you know anything of Lady March's family?" he asked of the ladies.

"Her parents," Mrs. Hampton replied as she poured herself another cup of tea, "were Lord and Lady March of Cornwall. Apparently the family held estates and business concerns in the Ottoman Empire and Asia and so they spent a good deal of their time out of the country. Her parents, a brother, and a sister, are all dead. Her only living relation, an older brother, inherited the earldom and the bulk of the family fortune and lives out of the country. Lady March inherited a fortune totaling some thirty thousand pounds a year from her father, an uncle, and her maternal grandmother."

Hugo Garfield's teaspoon fell with a clatter into his saucer.

"She has been in England, I believe, only since November," Mrs. Hampton continued, ignoring her nephew's stunned expression, "and spent the succeeding five months looking for a small estate before finally purchasing Waverly Manor."

"How can you know so much of a woman you have never even met?" Joanna marvelled.

"I cannot like it," her brother declared, clearing his throat and setting down his teacup. "To have such a woman in the neighborhood is most discomfiting. Her fortune has clearly left her heedless of the duties and responsibilities attendant upon her position in society. The young women of this shire might easily imbibe from her the foreign fripperies and habits that now corrupt the Ottoman Empire."

"I cannot think that turkish trousers will be the downfall of that ancient civilization," Joanna remarked.

"Nor do I understand why she had to undertake renovations at Waverly," Garfield complained, ignoring her. "It was quite all right as it was."

"Hugo, she had every right to—" Joanna began.

"Lady March did not stop there," Mrs. Hampton intoned. "Only yesterday she returned all of the furnishings to us, Hugo. We received wagonload after wagonload, every piece of furniture, crockery, linens, even the pictures that have been at Waverly since well before your poor Mama took up residence—they were returned as well!"

The revenue he would have enjoyed had the new tenant at Waverly retained the furnishings for her own use had somewhat reconciled Garfield to the loss of Waverly to such a creature. This news, however, thoroughly squashed that acceptance, sealing the coffin on Lady March in Garfield's mind, as it had in Mrs. Hampton's.

Joanna, too, had been upset by yesterday's caravan from Waverly Manor, but listening now to her aunt and her brother dissect and condemn their new neighbor, she felt the old obstinancy swell within her breast. Nobody, she was convinced, not even Diana March, could be as bad as her aunt and brother proclaimed her to be.

CHAPTER 3

In the following ten days news of Diana March spread quickly throughout Heddington and its environs. While the inhabitants of Pembroke Park saw nothing further of their new neighbor, they visited or were visited by those who had encountered Lady Diana March, having gone so far as to call upon the newest addition to Herefordshire.

All had been horrified by her. She was cordial enough, even friendly, they reported. She had rung for tea and asked of their families and commented properly on the weather. But all of this was done in a most unnervingly hearty manner while dressed in the garb of a lowly kitchen maid, a kerchief actually tied on her head! She talked of her current ventures on the Exchange, mentioned the large purchase of manure she had made to fertilize some of her fields, and laughed heartily over her own tale of her eldest brother's disastrous visit to the Catholic Pope. More than one caller's nerves had been quite overset by the call.

"I was never more stunned," Mrs. Bartlett informed Joanna as they sat in the Bartlett's small morning parlor, the sun carefully screened from their delicate complexions. "She actually began to detail her *breeding* plans to improve her stable and then extolled the excellencies of her irrigation system! Angela was quite put to the blush and poor Susan was so shocked that she could not utter another word for the rest of our call!"

Joanna murmured her sympathy while struggling mightily not to smile. Mrs. Bartlett was a matron of some forty years and possessed of four daughters—of whom Angela and Susan were the eldest—and two sons, as well as a husband of startling merchantile ability, which was why Garfield permitted his family to associate with them. Garfield liked connecting himself with money.

Mrs. Bartlett had been thought pretty in her youth, but her dark hair was now swept with grey, her trim figure grown plump. She had the ability to talk on any subject and at great length, and always managed to steer the topic of conversation back to her six children who were, in their mama's opinion, "incomparable." She was the silliest woman in Joanna's acquaintance and therefore invaluable, for Joanna dearly loved to be amused.

"To think that such a woman would move into our neighborhood," Mrs. Bartlett continued after instructing her maid to bring a fresh pot of tea and a second tray of pastries. "She has a past, Lady Sinclair, be assured of it. She has a past! With such open ways she could not have helped but be ruined in her youth, nor does she seem to have profited by the experience. Think of it! No relation living with her to give her countenance. No female attendant to secure her honor and reputation. Galloping across the countryside like a man! It is too shocking for words, Lady Sinclair. Too shocking for words!"

"It *is* rather unsettling to encounter a woman who seems to delight in her . . . eccentricities," Joanna remarked, accepting another cup of tea from Mrs. Bartlett and declining a pastry. "It is a pity that she should give her every whim such free rein. If she but practiced a little restraint and gave up these oddities, particularly the trousers, I daresay she might be quite presentable. From all that I have heard, she has an affable nature and can be quite charming at times. Along with her fortune, that would assure her of finding a husband. Most men are only too eager to marry a woman of thirty thousand pounds a year, but they approach the marriage altar with a lighter step when their bride is possessed of an easy and pleasant manner."

"To think that any one woman should enjoy such a fortune." Mrs. Bartlett sighed heavily as she poured three teaspoons of sugar into her cup. "It is such a trial, her coming just now, for both Angela and Susan are on the verge of making excellent matches. I've nearly brought Lord Turnbull up to the mark for Susan, and he is possessed of two estates and twelve thousand a year, you know; while Angela has caught Mr. Ashley's eye and he is reputed to be worth eight thousand a year. I could not ask more for my dear girls. Yet now all is threatened. How can they, with all of their beauty and wit and talent, compete against thirty thousand pounds a year? It is too vexing for words. Lady March will undoubtedly have every marriageable man in the county dangling after her inside of a week!"

"I shouldn't think that such a thing will come to pass," Joanna assured her, "for Lady March, without any apparent ill will, is too assertive in her manner. Men, as you know, quickly develop disgust for any woman who displays such strength of character as Lady March continually demonstrates. Her fortune is certainly a lure, but I think both Angela and Susan may rest easy for their . . . beauty and wit and talent must triumph over the defects of Lady March's character."

Mrs. Bartlett gave these words a bit of thought and then declared that Joanna must be right; indeed, she was certain of it. She called Joanna a godsend, a great comfort in such trying times as these, and then helped herself to a fourth pastry.

"But what are we to do with the creature?" she demanded. "Her fortune and family require civility towards her yet I quite dread the acquaintance. Think how mortifying it would be if she came calling in those dusty boots of hers and those *trousers*. I would lose all face in the neighborhood, I am certain of it."

"My dear Mrs. Bartlett," Joanna replied, restraining a smile, "it is not a certainty that Lady March will return your call, for her manners are quite lamentable by all reports. Indeed, in the twelve days she has been in residence, I have not heard that she has left Waverly Manor save for her morning gallops. And there is no saying that if she did call she would not be dressed in an appropriate costume. More to the point, Mr. Acton informs us that the Marches used to call upon the English Ambassadors in Alexandria and Constantinople with great frequency, and appeared in several foreign courts as well. Knowing of this, I am convinced that Lady March does at least know how to conduct herself properly."

"You are a balm to my poor nerves," Mrs. Bartlett declared with great feeling. "I only hope that you are right. The Heddington May Ball is but five weeks away and those of us on the organizational committee are quite at a loss in deciding whether we should invite Lady March."

"I think it best if she were invited," Joanna said slowly.

"It would be a frightful set down if she were excluded and one that she does not deserve for, though her manners and costume are ill-judged, she has thus far neither done nor said anything to give deliberate offense or cause harm."

"I daresay you are right, dear Lady Sinclair," Mrs. Bartlett replied, sighing heavily once more. "But only think if she should extend her Turkish costume and come dressed as a harem girl!"

Joanna choked on her tea and spent the next several moments struggling to subdue her coughing fit. Recovering, she turned the conversation to less turbulent topics. Taking her leave of Mrs. Bartlett some thirty minutes later, Joanna returned to her curricle in a contemplative frame of mind. Her groom helped her into the vehicle and then settled himself beside her as she gathered the reins and urged the black gelding forward.

The day was warm and clear and Joanna usually relished driving in such conditions, a soft breeze teasing her hair, the strong horse responding to her every command. But today her mind was preoccupied, revolving around the knotty issue Mrs. Bartlett had raised: What was she to do with Lady Diana March? Do something she must, for the Garfields were the leading family of Heddington, and indeed the entire shire, and Lady March had purchased an estate previously theirs. She could not be ignored. Nor could her acquaintance be cultivated, for Propriety was the true Garfield god.

Yet civil relations were required. To date they had not been forthcoming. Hugo continually put off calling on Lady March, claiming business concerns; while Mrs. Hampton flatly refused the office of family emissary, declaring that she saw no need to pollute her acquaintance with the addition of Lady March to her circle. So the role had fallen to Joanna. And Joanna had balked.

Ruminating upon this reluctance, and being of an honest nature, she realized that she was disturbed by Lady Diana

March—and rather afraid of her. For one who had known not the slightest trepidation upon her presentation at court, Joanna was startled to discover such an emotion ruling her actions now. How should Lady March be dangerous? What was there to fear?

Joanna puzzled over these difficult questions but could come to no certain answer. She was left feeling even more unsettled, and rather put out at feeling such discomfort because of a stranger. Not used to behaving in an incivil manner, her inability to bring herself to call upon Lady March was, to Joanna, the very height of incivility. A guilty conscience was the inevitable result of so glaring a lack of action.

Unused to both guilt and procrastination, thus becoming even more disturbed as she turned the curricle into the elm-shaded lane that led to Pembroke Park, Joanna found her gaze turning in the direction of Waverly Manor. What was Diana March like off that great bay mare of hers? Were trousers and kerchiefs her only wardrobe? What odd twist of mind could bring her to discuss her stable with Mrs. Bartlett? What exactly was this March woman doing to Waverly Manor?

Not having formed any firm decision to do so, Joanna turned her curricle into the road that led to Waverly Manor and Lady Diana March.

CHAPTER 4

As Lady Joanna Sinclair pulled her gelding to a stop before the front brick steps of Waverly Manor and allowed her groom to help her down from the curricle, she knew she had committed her first mad act. She stared at the house, her stomach knotting with tension. Madness was new to her.

"Wait for me," she commanded the groom, and then marched up the front walkway as any true Garfield would: head high, shoulders back, her steps purposeful. Coming to a stop she pulled the bell. After some moments the door was opened by a short, greying woman in her late forties dressed in a black gown with lace, the style proclaiming her to be one of the more titular servants.

"Good afternoon," Joanna said in a clear, firm voice. "I am Lady Sinclair. Is Lady Diana March at home?"

"She is," the somber-faced woman replied. "I am Mrs. Pratt, Lady March's housekeeper. If you will follow me, I will then inform Lady March that you have called." Mrs. Pratt took Joanna's card, led her to the large Drawing Room, and then went to fetch her mistress.

Given this brief respite, Joanna quickly took stock of her surroundings. Quite amazed, she wandered around the room with growing pleasure. Where once there had been dark, rather oppressive wallpaper, there were now walls painted in a light yellow. A thick Persian rug of tans and golds covered the dark wooden floor. The furniture, which Joanna knew on the best Heddington gossip to have just been sent up from London, was designed in the simplest manner to afford comfort and beauty. Joanna saw, with some relief, that Lady March had elected to use ash rather than the simulated bamboo the Prince Regent had insisted be the current rage.

Statuary, vases, figurines and assorted knick-knacks from as far afield as the Mediterranean, Asia, and Arabia, rested on tables, stands, mantles, and sideboards. Each one, however small or unobtrusive, was a masterpiece of line and beauty. But the paintings held Joanna's rapt attention. Indeed, the design of the room, the colors and lines, all seemed to lead one's gaze to the artwork hanging on the walls.

Rather than the dismal family portraits, amateur watercolors, and poorly executed landscapes that filled most English homes, Lady March had hung paintings by Botticelli, Vermeer, Velazquez; and a magnificent still-life adorned the mantle of the room's large fireplace. Joanna could not place the artist but this hardly mattered as she took in the play of light and shadow, the perfection of a crystal goblet, the succulence of a freshly cut lemon, the purity of. . . .

"Magnificent, isn't it?" a voice inquired.

Joanna whirled to find Lady March smiling at her from the doorway. Joanna realized with surprise that Lady March was a little shorter than herself and dressed in a plain gown of pale green muslin that gently molded itself to the soft swell of her breasts and the curve of her hips; her dark blonde hair was brushed and curled into a thick luster that fell to her shoulders and partially down her back.

"It is lovely," Joanna heard herself reply, her heart unaccountably beginning to increase its pace. "Never has a still-life caught and fixed my interest as this one does. But I fear I must confess to not knowing the artist."

"Anne Vallayer-Caster," Lady March replied as she advanced into the room, "a Frenchwoman of consummate skill. She was highly regarded in her own lifetime I'm happy to say. How many women can claim such an honor? I think her superior to Chardin but most would quarrel with me there. They're all quite wrong of course. She is a constant source of delight to me. I've another still-life of hers in my bedroom."

"Do you paint?"

"Alas, no. I've the eye and the love but not the skill. My lot in life is to collect, not to create. But this is a poor greeting for you indeed! Lady Sinclair, I am very pleased that you have come," Lady March declared heartily as she captured one of Joanna's hands and firmly shook it. "Won't you sit down? Mrs. Pratt will be bringing the tea tray in at any moment and will be quite cross with me if she finds that I've kept you standing all this time."

"Thank you," Joanna murmured uneasily as she sat in the chair indicated to her.

A silent tension pulsed between them until Joanna cleared her throat and said, "I fear that I have been most remiss in my duties as a neighbor. I should have called upon you much sooner than this to welcome you to the neighborhood."

"It takes time to work up one's courage, I know. From the stunned faces that have left this house I've no doubt Waverly Manor has been reported as a veritable lion's den. I commend your bravery for calling at all."

Mrs. Pratt, having entered during this speech, placed a tea tray before Lady March, frowned severely at her mistress, and then departed, closing the door quietly behind her.

"I am glad you waited, Lady Sinclair," Lady March blithely continued. "I know this was the Dowager's home for many years until her death. Seeing it in a muddled state of renovation might have been painful for you. To see it now is to see a butterfly, not a caterpillar. It is so very different that I hope it stirs no memories at all. Sugar? Honey? Milk? Lemon?"

"Milk only, thank you," Joanna replied, receiving the teacup from Lady March's hands.

"I hope you are not horrified by what my disrespectful whims have wrought," Lady March said, foregoing all additions to her own tea.

"On the contrary," Joanna replied, "I heartily approve of the changes I have seen so far and think Waverly much the better for them. My mother, the Dowager, indulged her mourning of my father, I fear. To enter the Manor was to enter some dank crypt. This room used to be so dark and cold that I dreaded coming into it. Now I find it warm, welcoming, quite beautiful."

"You are very kind. I've a decided abhorrence of dark rooms. I am glad the changes please you."

"I understand that you were in residence during the whole of the renovations."

"Yes."

"I would think the hardships entailed by such difficult conditions would have been quite untenable."

"When one has huddled in a tent in the Sahara during a three-day sandstorm with eight people, two dogs, and a goat, anything else is like a stroll through Mr. Wordsworth's lyrical countryside."

"Still," Joanna said, unable to keep from smiling, "it seems like quite a bother."

"I am one who needs to supervise. Since this was to be my home I wanted to insure that all of the work was done properly."

"Surely your housekeeper could have overseen the work while you enjoyed the rustic charm of one of Heddington's inns. Or you might have stayed in London. Mrs. Pratt seems a very capable sort of woman."

"This was to be my *home*," Lady March quietly reiterated.

Having no other reply to make, Joanna took refuge in her tea. "Do you plan to make renovations in the rest of the estate?" she asked at last.

"Only a few. The stable has been repaired and extended; the orchard needs a bit of work; and I want to convert some pastureland and use it for crops— corn, wheat, vegetables—you know the sort of thing. The majority of the work, however, will be at the front and rear of the house. I'm having a hedge put in to surround the manor. Having lived in nearly every inhospitable country on earth I find that I long for lush green gardens all around me. There has clearly been an attempt at gardening at Waverly in the past, but I intend to greatly extend it. I've a need to see life burgeoning around me."

"Will you spend your winters in London and partake of the Season with the rest of the upper echelons, our all too fashionable *ton*?"

"Oh yes," Lady March replied. "But only as a convenience for my friends. Several in my acquaintance will not admit the pleasures and beauty of country life and therefore steadfastly refuse to rusticate with me. Thus, the only hope I have of enjoying their company is to visit them myself or to take a house in London. Since I dearly love to entertain, I shall opt for the latter, adding an occasional visit to the more stubborn and distant of my friends."

"Shall you entertain at Waverly Manor as well?" Joanna asked, amused and interested in spite of herself.

"I've already sent out the announcements of my new domicile. I am expecting my friends to descend on me at any moment, like vultures spying Prometheus's liver."

Joanna shivered. "I do not know if I would like such friends."

"It is not that they are not excellent company," Lady March replied with a grin. "They simply have a highly developed appreciation of my pantry and my kitchen. Specifically, they adore my cook. Juan Carlos has been with me for five years and at each dinner party I give he receives the most outrageous bribes to leave my employ. Fortunately he is a loyal fellow. Loyal to me at least. When I informed Tony, my brother, that Juan Carlos chose to accompany me to England rather than remain behind with him in Alexandria, Tony took it rather badly. Refused to speak to me for a week."

"Herefordshire can surpass that easily," Joanna declared as she wondered fleetingly what had become of the discussion of the weather appropriate to first visits such as this. "The Stanwycks and the Harcourts were once engaged in a twenty-year feud because Lady Maud Harcourt hired away the Stanwyck's cook. These noble families cut each other at every opportunity, refused to allow their friends to inter- mingle, and on one occasion threatened a display of arms. The affair died only two years ago when the poor cook died. Now both families enjoy mediocre chefs and once again are on the best of terms."

"Ah England, England," Lady March sighed rapturously, "how I have missd thee!"

Joanna forgot herself enough to chuckle.

"Would you like more tea?" Lady March inquired.

"No, thank you," Joanna replied, embarrassed by her unseemly levity.

"Well then," Lady March said, "my renovations are a *fait accompli*. Would you like a tour to see what my whims have wrought at Waverly?"

"Tour?" Joanna said faintly. She had expected perhaps a discussion of gelding methods, but certainly not this.

"Yes," Lady March said brightly. "You'd be the first. Aren't you just the slightest bit curious about the wondrous transformation a bold and daring mind can create?"

Joanna stared at her hostess. "You are quite mad," she thought.

"Don't be alarmed, Lady Sinclair. Everyone thinks so, but it's only partially true."

Joanna jumped and then blushed furiously as she realized she had spoken aloud. "I . . . I beg your pardon, Lady March! I didn't mean . . ." she stammered.

Lady March smiled. "Come, there's no need to be embarrassed. I like honesty in a person. It seems a very rare article in England. Would you like that tour?"

"Yes please," Joanna replied, overwhelmed, appalled by her own behavior.

"Wonderful! We're off then," Lady March declared.

She led Joanna into an adjoining salon of a size similar to the Drawing Room. Joanna quickly lost all traces of embarrassment in the wonder of Lady March's renovations. The salon's walls had been painted a light blue, the panelling and wainscotting scraped, cleaned, and revarnished to bring out their natural beauty. Two fireplaces faced each other from opposite walls. In the center of the room were two parallel cream-colored brocade couches with matching chairs. The walls held more artwork: Rubens, Raphael, Chardin. Lady March kept up a running commentary on how she had acquired this painting or discovered that figurine, and Joanna found herself relaxing as her fascination grew.

They went next into a library staggeringly different from what it had been in the Dowager Garfield's day. Gone were the dark leather sofa and chairs, the grim panelling, the severe portraits. Instead there was bright, gay wallpaper, white curtains, a cheerful floral print upholstery on the chairs opposite the fireplace and at the rosewood desk and secretary. A royal blue satin settee rested against one wall and looked out the windows along the opposite wall to the eastern side of the house. Two walls were lined top to bottom with shelves bearing books of every age, size, and national origin.

"This is lovely," Joanna breathed.

Lady March smiled at her. "It is nice, isn't it?" The smile became fixed and Joanna suddenly realized that her hostess was staring at her with the oddest expression in her green eyes. Joanna's heart began to pound, just as it had when Lady March first greeted her.

Her hostess seemed to recollect herself, turned abruptly, and next showed Joanna into a small sitting room done primarily in reds and browns. A breakfast room adjoined, and beside it was a large, airy dining room whose decor, consisting chiefly of green plants and brightly painted lattice work, reminded Joanna irresistibly of the Hanging Gardens of Babylon. In no way, certainly, did it resemble any dining room she had ever seen.

The only other parlor on the floor had been turned into a music room, and this amused Joanna, for her mother had never had anything but contempt for young women who dabbled on the pianoforte and then insisted, at the slightest provocation, on demonstrating their mediocrity. Despite her mother's prohibitions, a pianoforte, harpsichord, troubador harp, lute, guitar, and three different recorders were now in evidence.

"Do you play all of these?" Joanna asked as she wandered around the room.

"A few," Lady March admitted, "although I keep most of these for the amusement of my guests. Idle hands would continually wander in a very improper manner if I did not provide a more appropriate means of entertainment. Come," she said, apparently oblivious to Joanna's flaming cheeks, "I'll show you the upstairs."

Recovering slowly, Joanna followed her hostess to the second floor. Each of the eight bedrooms possessed that same light airiness that Joanna had observed below. Each was decorated in its own color scheme and possessed all the amenities any guest could ask for.

And throughout the house, on the walls, in the bedrooms, on a myriad of tiny stands, rested artwork of the most arresting skill and beauty: statues and figurines by Bernini and Cellini and anonymous artists from Hellenistic Greece, from Egypt and Asia; paintings by Jan Van Eyck, Leonardo da Vinci, Boucher, and many others, including, in the sitting room that adjoined Lady March's bedroom, one work that seemed to present the shadows of the soul.

Lady March, noticing Joanna's riveted gaze, moved beside her. "It is lovely, isn't it?" she said quietly.

"Magnificent," Joanna sighed. "Who is the artist?"

"Rosalba Carriera. I am glad you like her, she is one of my favorites. She was particularly praised in her lifetime for her pastels and her allegories, though she is virtually ignored today. When I look at any one of her works I am always made a little sad, for at the height of her career she went blind and spent her last years unable to do that which gave her happiness and the world beauty."

"I would end my life if fate betrayed me in so cruel a manner. To be unable to paint. . . . How she must have suffered."

"Do you paint?" Lady March inquired, her green eyes studying Joanna with a lively interest.

"A little," Joanna conceded. "It gives me great pleasure. I paint when I can and flatter myself that I am not so bad as the Bartlett daughters."

"They are a rather dismal lot, aren't they?" Lady March chuckled.

"Oh, they're quite sweet and very kind and everyone in Heddington is very fond of them. It is just that the Bartletts are so remarkably foolish."

Lady March burst into a delighted ripple of laughter that Joanna found oddly attractive. This disturbed her for she had not intended to find anything about Lady Diana March attractive. She had been prepared to be appalled, outraged, horrified, and insulted. She had not expected to be lulled by a beautiful and charming house and the open friendliness of its mistress into a liking of the new owner of Waverly Manor. She had not expected to drop her own reserve so far as to actually joke with what was, after all, an adventuress!

Something about Waverly Manor, something about its mistress, seemed to drain off all propriety of thought and action until one was left to the mercies of one's own nature and the whims of Lady March.

This was the danger, Joanna realized, that she had sensed from the very beginning.

She felt out of control—a new and terrifying sensation. Lady March had done something—Joanna was not quite sure what—to throw her off balance. She felt a little naked and very, very frightened.

Soon after their return to the main floor of Waverly Manor Joanna made her excuses to Lady March and fled her new neighbor. Knowing she must appear foolish, but no longer caring, she hurriedly climbed into the waiting curricle before her groom could jump down to assist her. Gathering up the reins, she set the tall gelding off at a vigorous trot, only drawing a full breath into her lungs when a bend in the road obscured her view of Waverly Manor and Diana March's view of her.

Slowly the tension left her breast and a new fear touched Joanna's heart. What if Lady March returned her call? What could Joanna do? How would she act after behaving so foolishly with Lady March at Waverly Manor? Even worse, what if Lady March should draw from Joanna that lightness of manner her brother and aunt found so appalling? What was she to do?

And what if Lady March did not call? What would she do then?

CHAPTER 5

Joanna stared critically into the full-length mirror of her dressing room. She studied her dark brown hair which had been pulled back from her forehead and carefully braided and looped *a la Grecque* at the back of her head; smoothed the line of her silk gown; observed the play of light in the sapphires that hung from her ears and the large sapphire pendant that glowed on her breast. "What do you think?" she asked her daughter.

"You will be the most beautiful woman at dinner," Molly declared. "No one could look prettier than you do in that rose gown, not even . . . Caroline Humphrey."

"There is nothing like loyalty in one's children. Thank you, darling," Joanna said, kissing Molly's cheek.

"May I *please* come downstairs with you?" Molly pleaded, pushing her hair off her forehead.

"Was your praise intended as a bribe, then?"

"Oh no, you are very pretty, Mama," Molly hastened to assure her mother, "but I do long to go down with you."

"Not tonight, my love. You know your Uncle Hugo's rule: children must not be seen after six in the evening."

"But just this once. . . . To meet Lady March?" Molly wheedled.

"Oh ho, so that is it."

"Just to see her?"

"Lady March looks no different from anyone else."

"Oh, but she does!" Molly insisted. "She is very scandalous, everyone says so, especially Aunt Hampton, and I've never seen a scandalous person."

"Nor would this be an appropriate occasion to do so."

"Oh but Mama," Molly said crossly.

"I shall invite her to tea someday and then you may meet her," Joanna compromised.

"Tea?" Molly cried, brightening instantly. "When?"

"I don't know. In . . . a week or so perhaps."

"But that is so very far away," Molly complained as Joanna led her out of the dressing room and into the hallway.

"Lady March is a very busy woman."

"But she'd be willing to come to tea at any time, I know it!"

"We shall see." Joanna smiled as she pushed open the door to Molly's bedroom. "Now into bed with you. You are late already and our guests will be arriving at any moment."

Having safely tucked Molly into bed, Joanna left her daughter's room and began her slow descent of the Grand Staircase, a hand trailing behind her on the railing. As reluctant as Molly had been to go to bed, that was nothing to what Joanna felt as her imagination swept over the coming party.

How could she have been so crackbrained as to have actually invited Diana March to a dinner where a dozen of the most important personages in Herefordshire would gather? Joanna was convinced that Lady March would undoubtedly shame herself and therefore her hosts.

Joanna groaned with a fresh stab of guilt. Why hadn't she told her brother of some of Lady March's more outrageous comments when she had visited Waverly Manor a week ago? And why had Hugo decided to mend the rift with his new neighbor, to support Joanna's decision to invite Diana March to this dinner over the staunch objections of their aunt? Hugo was one to hold a grudge, not offer an olive branch. So great a shift in Hugo's attitude left Joanna feeling rattled and wholly unsure about the coming dinner party.

With a sigh Joanna joined Hugo and Mrs. Hampton in the cavernous Entrance Hall as their starched and immaculate butler opened the front door to reveal Mr. and Mrs. Bartlett, Miss Angela Bartlett, and Miss Susan Bartlett. Lord Cyril Palmerston, Lady Amelia Palmerston, and Mr. Roger Palmerston arrived soon after in tandem with Mr. and Mrs. Frederick Willoughby, Mr. Gerald and Mr. Terrence Willoughby, and Colonel Huntington-Firth, who was seventy-three and had frequent complaints of the gout. The next to enter were Lord and Lady Chesterfield, their sons Harold and Ian, and their daughter Mary; Lady Caroline Humphrey and her brother, Lord Franklin Humphrey; Mrs. Harriet Hornby; and, finally, Lady Diana March.

It was with a vast and secret sigh of relief that Joanna greeted this last guest, for Lady March had come dressed in a simple, decorous, dark beige evening gown, her honey-blonde hair a mass of carefully arranged curls, a miniscule emerald necklace at her throat with matching earrings dangling from her earlobes. She greeted her hosts with great cordiality, despite Mrs. Hampton's critical stare; brushed aside with a laugh Hugo's apology for his earlier boorish behavior; thanked Joanna for the invitation to dinner; and then seemed mesmerized by the gargoyle above the large fireplace in the Hall.

"Fascinating," Joanna heard her murmur before Lady March advanced into the large Drawing Room where the rest of the guests had gathered.

With some amazement Joanna observed her brother approach Lady March in his dark brown coat and breeches, slip her arm through his, and then lead her around the room, introducing her to those personages she had not yet met. Whence came so much civility to a woman who had outraged him but a fortnight ago?

"How kind of Hugo to take the poor girl in hand," Mrs. Hornby, a silver-haired matron, remarked at Joanna's side. "Her acceptance in Heddington is now assured."

"It's put Caroline's lovely nose out of joint, though," Mr. Ian Chesterfield noted as he joined them, resplendent in breeches of the palest yellow, his shoulders carefully padded beneath the yellow and white frock coat, his cravat so intricately knotted that he could scarcely turn his head in either direction. "I've a suspicion dear Caroline is taking an instant dislike to your new neighbor," Mr. Chesterfield added with all seeming innocence.

Joanna turned to gaze at Lady Caroline Humphrey, the acknowledged beauty of Heddington and an heiress worth some twelve thousand pounds per annum. Lady Caroline was tall, perfectly rounded, noble in her bearing. She possessed a wealth of glossy black hair, long and beautifully arched black eyebrows, blue eyes sparkling now with suppressed emotion, and alabaster skin. She held herself with all the superiority of beauty, fortune, and family. Looking at Caroline's brittle smile as she conversed with Mr. Terrence Willoughby, her blue eyes never leaving Hugo and Diana March, Joanna had to agree with Mr. Chesterfield: Caroline did not seem overfond of Lady Diana March.

"But Hugo is acting with the greatest propriety," she could not help but protest. "As host it is his duty to introduce our guests to each other, and Lady March is the only newcomer here tonight."

"I'm sure that don't matter a fig to Caro," Mr. Chesterfield said with a grin, despite the confines of his cravat. "In the past it was always she who claimed Hugo's arm."

"Caroline Humphrey has more sense than to be jealous of Lady March," Mrs. Hornby declared. "She is superior to Lady March in every respect and Hugo knows it."

"Superior in everything but fortune," Mr. Chesterfield pointed out.

Joanna stared at the laconic Mr. Chesterfield and then at her brother.

"Don't be absurd, Ian," Mrs. Hornby commanded.

"And yet, nothing is settled between Hugo and Caroline," Joanna said faintly.

"It was settled in Caroline's mind by the time she was thirteen and you know it, Joanna" Mr. Chesterfield retorted. "She has not, however, settled Hugo's mind lo these seven years, and I think she has just suffered a severe setback. Hugo's mind appears quite unsettled by Lady March's fortune."

"I will not listen to such foolishness," Mrs. Hornby declared and moved off to find more convivial company.

"Is it foolishness, Joanna?" Mr. Chesterfield inquired, arching one brow.

"I . . . I know not what to think," was all Joanna could reply.

"I daresay this evening's festivities will give you plenty of food for thought." Mr. Chesterfield ambled off with a grin, leaving Joanna in an increasingly distrought frame of mind.

Diana March felt none of Joanna's qualms about the evening. Retiring to the main Pembroke Dining Room (there were three in all), she had quickly sized up her dinner partners and felt some reason to hope that she would be tolerably amused. The many-chinned Colonel Huntington-Firth seemed garrulous and full of fight; and Lord Humphrey, magnificent in midnight-blue coat and white breeches, his black hair glistening in the chandelier light, seemed so very ridiculous in his vanity that Diana thought he would undoubtedly provide good sport.

Diana listened, during the first course of the meal, to the Colonel's rabid account of the American War for Independence, making comments such as "Really?" and "My word!" at appropriate intervals. During the second course as he began to rail against Lord Byron, Lord Humphrey on her right began to ask her the usual civil questions: How did she find Herefordshire? Had she no relatives in England? What did she think of the weather?

At the beginning of the third course the Colonel's attention was captured by Mrs. Hornby on his left, who had been so unfortunate as to make a complimentary remark about Yorkshire. Diana would have been perfectly happy to eavesdrop on this altercation, but her attention was claimed by Lord Humphrey who quickly directed their conversation to his favorite topic: himself.

During the next four courses of the meal, which to Diana became interminable, Lord Humphrey regaled her with his youthful exploits at school and on the Grand Tour; his favorite hunting stories; and his many close calls on the Marriage Mart. In this same period he grasped her hand on five different occasions; gazed steadily into her eyes with an intensity Diana found laughable; and set up a continual round of sliding his left foot, and frequently his knee, against

Diana's own leg and foot. "Sir, you forget yourself," and "I have a fondness for my right hand. Please return it," were uttered by Diana often, but to no avail. Lord Franklin Humphrey was persistent and oblivious to these efforts.

At the end of the seventh course Diana had grown so bored by Lord Humphrey that she decided she had tolerated quite enough. She hailed Mrs. Bartlett from across the table and quickly engaged her attention by mentioning how well Angela and Susan looked this evening. Lord Humphrey, however, was not at all chastised by this snub. He joined in their conversation and frequently sought confirmation from Mrs. Bartlett of the many compliments he made Diana.

"Is Lady March not a charming addition to the neighborhood?" he demanded of Mrs. Bartlett. "I have never before found such wit and grace in one woman. Note how beautifully her hair is arranged. Have you ever seen so rich a color? How jealous all the young women of Heddington must be." All the while his left foot was fondly stroking Diana's.

Flashing a brilliant smile at this gross irritation, Diana stomped upon Lord Humphrey's offending limb and was rewarded by hearing a small groan escape his lips. Quickly he turned his attention to Lady Palmerston on his right and Diana was freed from his obnoxious conversation and his even more obnoxious advances for the rest of the meal.

The dinner ended at last with many a sigh of pleasure and hearty praise for the Garfield cook. The men and women then separated: the gentlemen retiring to Mr. Garfield's study for port and cigars; the ladies returning to the Drawing Room for wine and conversation. Quickly Joanna found her way to Diana's side.

"Lady March, I am so very sorry," she gravely declared. "I could not prevent Aunt Hampton from placing you between the Colonel and Lord Humphrey. They must have greatly tried your patience."

"There is no need to apologize, Lady Sinclair," Diana

replied. "I found the Colonel a delightful conversationalist. I was well entertained. As for Lord Humphrey, he was nought but a mosquito in my ear."

"What's that?" Mrs. Bartlett said as she bustled up to them. "Lord Humphrey? Oh, a charming man. Charming! So kind, so considerate, always so well dressed, and such a fortune! Ah, if only one of my girls could manage to catch his eye."

"Mrs. Bartlett, you cannot be thinking of what you say. Lord Humphrey is a . . . a scoundrel!" Joanna protested. "His reputation amongst the women cannot even be spoken of in polite society."

"The follies of youth, my dear. The follies of youth," Mrs. Bartlett replied good-naturedly.

"A gentleman of seven and twenty can hardly be termed a youth, Mrs. Bartlett," Joanna said severely, blushing for what Diana March must think of them.

"Ah, but when you reach my age, my dear, you will think differently, mark my words. Come, Lady March," Mrs. Bartlett said in rallying tones, "did you not find Lord Humphrey everything that is congenial? Such flattery, such praise! I'll wager he's smitten with you, Lady March. Smitten! Shall wedding bells be tolling?"

"I found Lord Humphrey to be a most well-practiced lecher," Diana calmly remarked as Joanna paled. "If I had any intention of taking a husband, which I do not," Diana continued, "I would sooner marry Colonel Huntington-Firth. At least I would never need wonder whose foot he was fondling at dinner."

"The Colonel?" Mrs. Bartlett exclaimed. "How absurd! You must be funning. Ah, that is it! You have been tweaking my nose and I did not even know it! Oh la!" Mrs. Bartlett cried. "You are a wit, Lady March! Not marry? Oh la, how absurd! Why, with your wit and your fortune you are certain to find a husband. In fact—oh, I have just had the most famous idea!—I shall take you under my wing, my dear. You shall be my protege! Mark my words, Lady March, I shall have you married by Michaelmas!" Mrs. Bartlett beamed at the two women and then bustled off.

"If I discover a line of cow-faced swains at my door tomorrow I will have to shoot her," Diana remarked.

Joanna promptly forgot her horror and burst into laughter. Such indecorous mirth startled Joanna as much as it did her guest. "I . . . beg your pardon," Joanna stammered. "I don't know what came over me. You must think me very ill-mannered."

"On the contrary," Diana replied, "I think you should laugh more often. It becomes you."

Joanna stared at Lady March but was fortunately saved from making any reply by her aunt who called her away to attend to those duties of a hostess so numerous on such occasions.

Diana's green eyes followed the path of her hostess longer than was perhaps proper, and then she once again began to wander around the Pembroke Drawing Room. She spent several minutes with the Miss Bartletts agreeing that it would be quite infamous if there was not at least one waltz at the Heddington May Ball. She passed quickly through a desultory conversation on the subject of cucumber versus hartshorn compresses for the headache with Lady Palmerston and Mrs. Willoughby; decried with Mrs. Hornby the scandalous habit of dampening one's gown which the current crop of London misses seemed to have adopted to show off their figures; and then found herself standing before Lady Caroline Humphrey, a fate she had hoped to avoid.

"My dear Lady March," the beautiful creature murmured with deadly intensity, "I am so glad you could come tonight."

"As am I," Diana replied.

"I trust you are enjoying the evening. Already you have a

bevy of beaux. My brother cannot sing your praises enough and Mr. Hugo Garfield seemed to admire you excessively."

"He was merely being polite."

"Not at all," Lady Caroline countered. "He seemed most solicitous of your well-being. We all remarked it."

"He is an excellent host."

"Indeed. Mr. Garfield comes from a long and proud heritage. There is no greater family in England. You have spent most of your life abroad, I believe, and cannot, therefore, be aware of the intricacy and importance of English family connections. I, for example, have known Mr. Garfield all of my life. We have shared many such evenings as this. Indeed, on three different occasions in the last four hundred years our families have been linked by marriage."

"And I daresay such links will be forged in the future," Diana replied.

"When there are two old families such as the Humphreys and the Garfields there must inevitably spring up a similarity of taste, education, and opinion. Such are the true foundations of any union."

"An admirable viewpoint."

Receiving no satisfaction from this conversation, Lady Humphrey changed the subject. Knowing herself to show to advantage on horseback she said, "Heddington is renowned for its excellent game. Perhaps you would care to join one of our hunting parties? I can assure you of only the best society: the Garfields, the Palmerstons, the Fitzroys, the Chesterfields."

"It sounds enchanting, but I do not hunt."

"No?" Lady Humphrey said, arching one beautifully shaped black eyebrow. "How very odd."

"Not very. I'm a vegetarian."

"How fascinating," Lady Caroline replied, stifling a yawn.

All further conversation was ended by the expeditious

return of the gentlemen to the Drawing Room. Diana quickly separated from Caroline Humphrey but could not enjoy her newfound freedom for Hugo Garfield quickly bore down upon her. With an inward sigh Diana greeted the gentleman politely, assured him that the dinner had been excellent, the company exemplary. All the while she sought some means of escape, for she had seen that mercenary gleam that now glowed in Mr. Garfield's brown eyes in the eyes of too many men in her acquaintance. But escape was not forthcoming. For his sister's sake Diana struggled to converse with some degree of civility.

"You must find our little community quite tepid after seeing so much of the world," Mr. Garfield declared with the smile which he knew made him appear quite handsome.

"On the contrary," Diana replied, unmoved by his beauty, "Heddington and its society delight me. I enjoy the quiet of the country and seek no more adventures in my life."

"So few young women of our era enjoy such wisdom. They seek only excitement in their days and would, I believe, become Amazons if they could."

Struggling not to smile, Diana declared that she found this report to be most disturbing.

Mr. Garfield quickly agreed. "The women of today," he proclaimed, "are too volatile for their own health and peace of mind. Witness the sad case of that Mary Wollstonecraft creature of a few years back, not to mention the heinous Lady Caroline Lamb. My own sister foolishly insists upon maintaining homes in Kent and in London for the majority of each year. If she resided at Pembroke Park year round she could share the arduous duties of a parent with her aunt and her brother and know financial ease as well. She is obstinate, however, and will not yield."

"Lady Sinclair is, I believe, well past her majority and must be trusted to know her own mind," Diana pointed out.

Mr. Garfield smiled condescendingly. "I thought you would be her advocate for you have led a life quite out of the ordinary and must defend any woman of independent stance to support your own character. Yet you have the luxury of a large fortune to support you, whereas Joanna does not. She will, I trust, understand this critical point in the near future. One cannot enjoy an adventurous independence if one does not have the financial reserves to promote it."

"Very true," Diana answered as she sipped her wine.

"I understand from Mrs. Hampton that you will be attending the Heddington May Ball," Mr. Garfield said.

"Yes," Diana replied, "the good ladies of the organizational committee have very kindly invited me although I am still a virtual stranger to the neighborhood. I shall have a small party staying with me and am hopeful that I will be permitted to bring them as well."

"Heddington is always eager for new society, as am I. You will, I hope, honor me with two dances at the ball, Lady March?"

Cursing herself as a blind fool for not seeing this request coming, Diana could only accede to the invitation with all the civility her mother had ever hammered into her. Mr. Garfield beamed, thanked her for so gracious a reply, and then left her, having succeeded fully in his intentions toward Lady Diana March for that evening.

Diana's relief at Mr. Garfield's departure was shortlived for she quickly found herself trapped near the main door of the Drawing Room by the amazingly persistent Lord Franklin Humphrey.

"You have been sorely missed, Lady March," he declared without preamble. "I think it a barbaric custom to separate the men from such charming company as yours after dinner, don't you?"

"I have always found the company of women immeasurably preferable to that of men," Diana bluntly replied.

Lord Humphrey smiled at her. "Now you are teasing me."

"Why is it that men think it impossible for women to find any pleasure in their own company?"

"Come now, Lady March," Lord Humphrey said with a grin, "you cannot mean to tell me that you find a discussion of the newest fashion in petticoats preferable to a circle of doting male attendants?"

"But I do."

Lord Humphrey chuckled. "Ah Lady March, you are too clever to reveal your real desires. Mustn't let men swell up with their own importance, eh? I commend you. Women gushing about one's manly features can be quite wearying."

"Had I known that, I would have been a geyser of praise," Diana replied.

But the remark apparently went over her tormentor's head. "You are a delight, Lady March," he declared.

"And you, my lord, are amazingly obtuse."

Lord Humphrey began to laugh. "What will you say next?"

"I doubt if you would like to hear it."

"Any gentleman would be eager to hear the opinion of so lovely a lady."

"Your eyes decieve you, my lord," Diana said frostily. "I am remarkably plain. It is my fortune that is handsome."

"Nay, I'll not stand by and allow you to deprecate yourself in such a fashion," Lord Humphrey solemnly protested. "You are but toying with me, Lady March," he continued, drawing uncomfortably close. "You see that I have been caught by your beauty and you seek to punish me for such presumptuousness. Alas, I am but a humble moth caught by your brilliant flame. Do with me as you will."

With a cheerful smile up into Lord Humphrey's unappetizing face, Diana calmly poured her glass of wine over Lord Humphrey's pulsating abdomen.

"Oh my, what have I done?" she said mildly as she stepped away from the stunned lord. "My hand must have slipped. How unforgivable of me."

"Not . . . at all, Lady March," Lord Humphrey managed to reply. "Accidents will happen. If you will excuse me, I will see what can be done to repair this . . . discomfiting situation." He moved rigidly away.

Diana gazed after her opponent with quiet satisfaction. Then her ears caught the unmistakable sound of girlish giggling coming from behind the partially closed Drawing Room door. Quickly handing her empty wine glass to a passing footman, Diana slipped quietly from the room only to be met by a pale, thin, chuckling creature clad in a nightshift and dressing gown and slippers, her light brown hair tumbling about a round face possessed of a nose that was most decidedly pug.

"You must be Puck come to make an ass of me," Diana said.

"No, I'm Molly Sinclair and that was wonderfully done." Molly grinned at her engagingly as she brushed her hair off her forehead. "I never saw such a silly expression on anyone's face before and I'm so glad it was that horrid Lord Humphrey's face. He calls me a cherub."

"The beast!" Diana grimaced.

"He is very odious, isn't he?"

"Very," Diana agreed. "Shouldn't you be in bed?"

"Oh yes."

"Your invitation to dinner was not missent through the post then?"

"No." Molly grinned, totally entranced.

"Then what are you doing down here?" Diana whispered.

"Well, I wanted to see what you look like," Molly said, brushing back her hair once more. "I've never seen a hunchbacked hoyden before."

"Ah."

"You're not at all hunchbacked are you?" Molly asked disappointedly.

"I'm afraid not. Whoever said that I was?"

"My Uncle Hugo and Aunt Hampton. Are you at least a hoyden?"

"Some people think so, yes," Diana admitted with a grin.

"Well, that's something," Molly said with obvious satisfaction. "What is a hoyden?"

Diana was forced to put her hand to her mouth to stifle a hoot of laughter.

"Well?" Molly demanded as she struggled to retie the sash of her dressing gown.

"A hoyden," Diana replied in a quavering voice, "is any woman who does not treat men with the respect and reverence they feel is due them by virtue of their sex."

"Oh."

"You're disappointed."

"Oh no," Molly said hastily. "It is just that. . . . Well, you look so ordinary."

"I do beg your pardon," Diana said gravely. "I thought it would be wisest to appear as nondescript as possible tonight. I've been the greatest rattlepate with your mother at our previous meetings. I did not wish to cause her or myself any further embarrassment."

"That was very good of you," Molly replied, clearly let down.

"I tell you what," Diana said. "I shall invite you to tea at Waverly Manor and I shall wear the most outrageous costume in my wardrobe strictly for your benefit."

"Would you?" Molly gasped. "Would you really?"

"On my honor."

"Oh you are wonderful!" Molly exclaimed. "I knew that you would be."

"How remarkable. Do you, by chance, have any Gypsy blood in you?"

"When may I come to tea?" Molly demanded, triumphantly completing the bow on her dressing gown sash.

"Whenever you like," Diana promptly replied.

"I shall have to talk Mama around," Molly said, suddenly growing doubtful. "I don't go out much."

"By choice? Or do they keep you chained in your room and feed you only bread and water?"

Molly stared at Diana in some amazement, adjusted her bow, and said, "It's just that I'm not very strong."

"Slander!" Diana declared. "What utter rot. I tell you now, Miss Sinclair, that you've the look of a lion's cub about you."

"Really?"

"I've seen lions' cubs and I know what I'm talking about," Diana said with the greatest authority.

"I wish Mama thought I was a lion's cub. She's always afraid I'll catch cold and then get pneumonia and then die in the very bloom of life."

"Did she tell you so?" Diana asked, thoroughly captivated.

"Well . . . not exactly," Molly conceded. "It was my Aunt Hampton who said it, but I know Mama feels the same way."

"Your mother loves you very much and wants you to get healthy and strong."

"I know, but it is so awfully dull getting healthy and strong," Molly complained. "I have to take potions."

"Poor little cub," Diana sympathized. "I daresay it is just as dull as having to listen to Lord Franklin Humphrey."

Molly forgot herself so much as to laugh. This was her undoing for her mother's quick ears caught the sound and she soon tracked it to its source. "Molly! Why aren't you in bed?" she demanded as she stepped into the hallway, closing the Drawing Room door behind her.

"Lady Sinclair, it was I who lured your innocent daughter into this secret assignation," Diana stoutly declared, all intentions of foregoing rattlepated behavior swept away with this unexpected confrontation. "The evil Count Leopold has thwarted our every effort to effect Molly's escape from his malevolent clutches. You see how pale and thin she is?" Diana demanded, tilting Molly's face into the lamplight. "The treacherous Count has held this poor child chained in his dark, dank dungeon and fed her nothing save bread and water! Oh, we had such hopes of winning Molly's freedom tonight. But now, alas, all is lost. We are discovered. Poor Molly!" Diana cried, feverishly clutching the girl to her breast to smother Molly's laughter. "Will you never be free to watch the rabbits frolicking with gay abandon in the green fields?"

Joanna stared at Diana as if she had just had a glimpse of those very rabbits frolicking in her hallway. She quickly recollected herself, however, and gravely informed Molly that it was several hours past her bedtime. A footman was summoned and charged with seeing Molly back to her room.

"Goodnight Miss Sinclair," Diana called. "Don't forget our rendezvous." Molly flashed her a quick smile before ascending the stairs. "Ah Youth," Diana sighed wistfully.

"I hope she didn't make too much of a nuisance of herself," Joanna said with some stiffness.

"On the contrary," Diana replied, turning towards her with a smile, "I found her to be the most delightful conversationalist I've yet encountered in England, saving yourself of course."

"Thank you, Lady March. Now if you will excuse me, I must return to my other guests. I have a great many obligations to fulfill."

"Someday we really must sit down and dispel all these absurd notions of yours."

Joanna turned back. "What notions would you dispel?" she asked in spite of herself.

"Well," Diana said, surprised at the question, "first of all I would do away entirely with the notion that Molly is but a hair's breadth from being an invalid. I know you will think me presumptuous, but I find Molly to be a very robust child, particularly when I consider that she has obviously been confined indoors all her life."

"You sound like Dr. Baker, a physician I consulted in London last year," Joanna could not help but remark. "He thought Molly only needed a romp in a Herefordshire meadow to recover."

"May I ask, is here anything clearly wrong with Molly?"

"She has suffered through every childhood illness imaginable, leaving her frail and sickly."

"But she survived unimpaired?"

"Yes, but very weak. She is susceptible to every draft."

"I see." Diana paused a moment. "My sister Rebecca had a similar history. My parents were very protective of her health and would not permit her to go out of doors either, and she remained sickly and peevish. One day my father hired a German governess who promptly tossed Rebecca out of the house and ordered her to learn how to garden. From that day forward Rebecca's constitution rapidly improved until she was just as strong as any of us. You see my point? Doctors and pills and potions were of little use. But when left to Nature and to her own resources Rebecca grew in strength and health."

"I daresay there may be some truth in what you say," Joanna said slowly.

"Bearing that in mind," Diana said with a grin, "I have taken the liberty of inviting Molly to tea. I promise to have a roaring fire in the grate and a hot pot of cocoa waiting for her."

"That is very kind of you, Lady March, but there is no need."

"Oh, but there is! Molly is the first fast friend I have made in Herefordshire. She invited me to a secret assignation. It would be rude of me not to return the honor. You could even come, too, if you like."

"You are too generous." Joanna could not help but smile.

"I might be presumptuous but I am always magnanimous. What say you, Lady Sinclair? May Molly come to tea?"

"I shall insist upon it," Joanna replied with sudden decision.

"Excellent creature!" Diana cried happily. "Oh what fun we shall have! I have promised to wear my most outrageous costume, you know."

"Perhaps I will come anyway," Joanna replied, and Diana was promptly overcome with laughter.

"I think I shall like you, Lady Sinclair," she said, still chuckling. "Yes, I am almost certain of it."

"I beg you consider what you say. I would not have you be overhasty in this decision for the world."

Diana regarded her hostess with frank pleasure. "You are far more formidable than first appearances would allow," she said with quiet decisiveness.

Joanna, who had never in her life been called formidable, could only stare.

"Come," Diana said, taking Joanna's arm, "let us return to the Drawing Room. I am anxious to discover which of the rest of your guests will try to make love to my fortune."

CHAPTER 6

Joanna twisted and untwisted a dark brown curl around a finger as she stared out the Breakfast Room window on a scene of natural splendor. The Breakfast Room at Pembroke Park faced east towards a large stand of budding trees towering up towards the dark blue sky dappled with occasional white clouds like over-rich dumplings, floating lazily, pushed gently on by a breeze that was more an afterthought than any concerted effort towards a wind. It was bucolic perfection and Joanna was not at all pleased by it.

Tea at Waverly. . . . What an astoundingly foolish thing to agree to! Some madness must have prompted her last night for now she had no desire whatsoever to pay a second call on Diana March. So unreserved a nature, so ready to act on a whim, was too unsettling.

Her elbows resting on the table, her chin cupped in her hands, Joanna felt the soul of misery. Her upbringing had not prepared her for Diana March. Left to rely on her own resources, she felt certain that they would betray her in some ghastly way. She had agreed to take tea at Waverly Manor—worse was certain to follow.

"Joanna! Do not sit there like some uncouth farmboy dreaming of his cornfields!" Mrs. Hampton commanded as she entered.

Startled, Joanna jumped and then hurriedly put her hands in her lap. Mrs. Hampton had the discomfiting ability to reduce Joanna to the status of an eight-year-old with one sentence.

"It is no wonder Molly's manners are so lamentable when you are her example," Mrs. Hampton declared as she took her place at the table.

"Molly behaves very well," Joanna protested before she could think better of it.

"Molly behaves without thought or propriety. I have remarked it more than once. You have chosen, it seems, not to act on my advice."

"I have chosen to raise Molly without that formality of behavior you prefer, certainly. She is my daughter and I must teach her those things I deem to be of greatest importance to her youth and her future," Joanna replied with more stridency than she knew was prudent.

"You had just this same headstrong independence as a child," Mrs. Hampton remarked as she poured herself a cup of tea. "I said then that no good could come of it and here is the proof. You are ruining your daughter."

Joanna's outraged gasp was checked by the entrance of her brother. "I have just received a note from Lady Diana March," he declared as he seated himself at the head of the table, oblivious to the tension simmering in the room. "She thanks us in a most pleasing manner for last night's entertainment. It is very prettily done, saying no more than it ought. I begin to see how ill-formed our first opinion of her was, how unwise it is to listen to the wild gossip that so easily springs up in a small country neighborhood. We should be on our guard in the future."

"I will not pretend to understand you," Mrs. Hampton stated as she rang for their breakfast. "Lady March's character is known to all in Heddington. One pretty note cannot change what she is."

"You base your opinion on what you have heard. I base mine upon what I have seen. Lady March's conduct last night was exemplary," Mr. Garfield declared.

"Throwing her wine all over poor Lord Humphrey was hardly exemplary," Mrs. Hampton retorted.

"It was an unfortunate accident. Franklin told me so himself," Hugo replied.

The maid entered with the first course, bringing all conversation to a halt. At her departure Joanna heard herself mention the upcoming tea at Waverly Manor.

"You did not agree to such a scheme?" Mrs. Hampton cried.

"Yes, I did," Joanna admitted. "But I have begun to think better of it."

"I see no reason to reconsider," Hugo said. "I think it an excellent idea for you to call on her again."

"Hugo! Of what can you be thinking!" Mrs. Hampton gasped, setting down a forkful of fish.

"Indeed Hugo," Joanna said with far less emotion than her aunt, "I find Lady March not at all what you would desire for an acquaintance. She is quite irreverent and without that propriety of thought and action you so admire in our sex. It may not be wise to pursue her friendship."

"For shame, Joanna," Hugo replied. "For over a fortnight you have pressed me to establish civil ties with Lady March. You have reminded me of her family, her position, her close proximity to Pembroke Park. None of these things have suffered any alteration. Having won the point, why do you give it up?"

Joanna searched for some argument that would sway her brother, but could find none she might utter aloud. How to explain that she found Lady Diana March dangerous? How to say that their neighbor stirred long dormant emotions within her that were best left undisturbed? Facing this impasse Joanna remained silent and it was left to Mrs. Hampton to voice her objections. This she did with some acidity and great volubility, but to no avail. Joanna and Molly were to go to tea at Waverly Manor.

* * *

Feeling very much as if she were preparing to face Monsieur Robespierre's guillotine instead of Lady Diana March's tea tray, Joanna allowed her coachman to gravely hand both she and Molly into the Sinclair barouche on the following afternoon.

"Mama, what's a vegetarian?" Molly asked as they moved swiftly down the Pembroke drive.

"I beg your pardon?" Joanna said distractedly as she pulled herself away from her anxious thoughts.

"Veg-e-tar-ian."

"Ah. Someone who does not eat meat. But why do you ask?"

"The other night, when Lady Humphrey asked Lady March if she hunted Lady March said no, she was a vegetarian. But I saw Lady March eat the mutton, the venison, and the salmon at dinner, so she can't be a vegetarian, can she?"

"It doesn't seem likely," Joanna replied, tactfully ignoring this overwhelming evidence of youthful eavesdropping.

"Then why did she tell Lady Humphrey that she is a vegetarian?"

"I daresay Lady March was only funning."

"Oh," Molly said, a reply she used whenever she had a great deal to think over. "Mama?" she said at last. "I don't think she wanted to hunt with Lady Humphrey."

"I wouldn't be at all surprised."

Molly had not been out of doors since their arrival at Pembroke Park in February. With the countryside now open to her eager gaze, she became increasingly animated as she discovered the many advances that spring had already made. By the time they pulled to a stop before Waverly Manor Molly was pressed against the door of their coach so that she might not miss anything. When their driver opened the door she tumbled with a squeal into his arms, which set them both laughing. Barking could be heard from the stableyard.

"She has dogs, Mama. She has dogs!" Molly cried. "And oh Mama, smell the wisteria." She drew her thin shoulders back and breathed in great gulps of air as the coachman handed Joanna out. "The air is so thick with their scent. I wish we had wisteria."

"I will tell your Uncle Hugo that you said so." Joanna smiled as she looked up at the plump purple vines beginning to bloom on the oak and elm trees around the Manor, and drew their heavy sweetness into her lungs. She felt a lessening of the tension that had plagued her all day.

Upon reaching the front door Joanna was prohibited from ringing the bell by their hostess, who opened the door without warning and beamed cheerfully at them.

Both Sinclairs gaped at her.

"You've arrived! Oh, I am so glad you could come,"

Diana declared as she swept them into the house.

"What *are* you wearing?" Molly demanded.

"What? Oh, this? I found it in Egypt. It's the sort of thing I fancy Cleopatra might have worn when she sailed down the Nile on her barge."

"What is *that*?" Molly asked, pointing at the large, glittering jewel in Diana's navel.

"That, my dear child, is a diamond," Diana replied.

"But how do you keep it in?" Molly asked, agog.

"That is a riddle which has puzzled the greatest philosophers throughout the ages. Do you approve of my costume? I wore it just for you."

Mother and daughter stared at the bare feet; the dark gold harem trousers clinging tenaciously to rounded hips; the matching vest that revealed far more of Diana's full breasts than it covered; the navel with that very disconcerting diamond. Garnet bracelets hung at her wrists while golden coils, like snakes, clung to her bare upper arms. She wore a garnet chained headband and earrings while her blonde hair, parted in the middle, spilled freely across her shoulders and down her back. And everywhere there was smooth skin: arms, back, midriff, breasts.

Molly declared that it was wonderful. Joanna, her blush increasing in intensity, would have chosen a far different adjective. With great unconcern for Joanna's discomfort Diana led both her and Molly upstairs, swung open a door, and ushered them into a sunlit room. What Joanna saw as she stepped in convinced her that in a lifetime that had known too many heinous errors in judgment, accepting an invitation to this tea was the worst idea she had ever had.

A thick green Persian carpet covered the whole floor of the small room. In its center was a large, low mahogany table bearing three plates and napkins and a large vase of daffodils. Around this table lay nearly a dozen cushions and pillows of varying colors and fabrics. In the corner nearest the room's only window rested a huge potted palm. On the white walls paintings and two enormous tapestries depicted the more opulent courts and exotic peoples of the East. Upon the mantle of the room's fireplace, and on several small stands stood statuary that Joanna could only term erotic, the embraces and poses held by the various figures too passionate to be considered platonic, too sensual to be innocent, too disturbing to be viewed philosophically. As promised, a warm fire burned cheerfully in the small grate.

"This . . . was not here a week ago," Joanna managed to say.

"It wasn't finished yet," Diana replied as she tugged on the bellrope. "I felt the need of a little haven of decadence. The English mania for propriety and decorum becomes too much for me at times. This room is reserved for only my most special guests. You're the first ones I've had in here."

Joanna said nothing.

"Are we going to have tea at that table? On those cushions?" Molly asked.

"Yes," Diana replied, turning her piercing gaze from Joanna to give Molly her full attention. "I thought we'd be indolent today. I hope you don't mind."

"It will be wonderful!" Molly declared as she ran to a large, overstuffed paisley cushion at the head of the table and plopped herself down.

"An excellent choice," Diana commended her. "And which shall you have, Lady Sinclair?" she asked with far less warmth.

"I? I do not think, Lady March, that we should. . . ." Joanna stopped, realizing that there was no polite way to extricate herself from this horrendous situation. "The blue satin to Molly's right will suffice," she said woodenly.

"You are too kind," Diana said before advancing to the table. "I shall lounge on your left, Molly, upon this pink silk monstrosity."

Molly applauded this decision as Joanna reluctantly lowered herself onto the blue satin cushion. No sooner was she settled than a caravan of servants led by Mrs. Pratt entered bearing trays of succulent cornish game hens; steaming bowls of savory pilaf and curry; golden braided loaves of bread; serving dishes of steamed garden vegegtables; and a large silver bowl of fat hothouse strawberries, a pitcher of cream standing at the ready. There was even a large China pot of tea and a smaller pot of cocoa for Molly. Mrs. Pratt secured a large square of linen around Molly's neck, tsked at Diana's costume, and then led the servants from the room as Diana announced that all the food was to be eaten with their fingers.

Interrupting Joanna's horrified protests, Diana ruthlessly tore apart one of the loaves of bread and handed the pieces to her guests. She then placed liberal heaps of pilaf, curry, and vegetables on their plates before handing round the platter of cornish game hens which her guests had to claim with their bare hands, a novelty that sent shivers of delight down Molly's spine and a barely suppressed shudder of horror through Joanna. Molly and Diana fell to this feast without a thought to maidenly decorum, Diana remarking that she would have to use some discretion if she did not want her diamond popping out and being lost forever. This last comment utterly destroyed the last vestiges of Joanna's appetite.

Molly sampled the curry, decided that she rather liked it, and helped herself to more as Diana poured a second round of tea. As Diana reached across the table to hand Molly her cup of cocoa Joanna's vision was filled with her hostess' soft breasts. Her blush returned with added force. How could any decent woman expose so much of herself, even in the privacy of her own home? Joanna's eyes strayed unwillingly towards Diana's naked midriff, gently rounded and so feminine. Her head began to pound. Lady March was everything that was objectionable, every shocking report she had ever heard was proved true by this encounter. As soon as she was able Joanna would get Molly and herself out of this room, out of this house, and they would never return again.

Molly scooped a handful of pilaf into her mouth and declared it good.

"I got that recipe from an old Arab sheik after I had smuggled myself into his camp in the Sahara," Diana said.

"You didn't!" Molly said suspiciously.

"I most certainly did."

"Why did you sneak into his camp?" Molly demanded.

"His men had captured my maid and intended to use her for their own nefarious purposes. I wanted her back."

"What did you do?" Molly's grey eyes had grown very round.

"I managed to get safely into the sheik's camp, but then I bumped into his favorite camel and the wretched creature set up such a ruckus that I was instantly captured and taken to the sheik."

"What happened then? Were you made a serving girl or a harem dancer? Did they flog you or leave you staked out in the desert to die a hideous death?"

Diana studied this grimly imaginative little girl with some amusement and then replied in a melancholy voice, "I wish my fate had only been half that romantic. The sheik had known my father for years," she sighed, "and had every intention of returning my maid to us unharmed. He laughed heartily at my little escapade, gave me my maid, two camels and a goat for my efforts, and then asked if I wanted anything else of him. Having dined on his pilaf when we had last visited him in Alexandria, I naturally asked him for the recipe."

"Have you ever ridden a camel?" Molly asked as her mother tentatively sampled the chunk of bread Diana had given her.

"On several occasions," Diana assured the girl. "I've also ridden on elephants, been up in a balloon, and swum in the Caribbean."

"Girls can't swim," Molly declared with great superiority.

"Can too," Diana retorted.

"Cannot," Molly insisted.

"Says who?"

"Mama, girls can't swim, can they?" Molly asked, appealing to a higher authority.

"I daresay if Lady March claims that she can swim then she can," Joanna replied, guiltily swallowing a bite of bread.

"In the Caribbean?" Molly said dubiously.

"Can you think of warmer water in which to learn?" Diana returned. "I suppose you would take lessons in the Atlantic."

"I wouldn't take lessons at all. Girls don't swim."

"Do so."

"Do not."

"Who taught you how to swim?" Joanna asked in an amused attempt to end this argument.

"My brother, Sam," Diana replied in some surprise as she turned to face her guest. "We were staying on a tiny sunbaked island and I browbeat him into it."

"What was it like . . . swimming?" Molly asked.

"It was like being free and knowing the ease of a fish."

"What kind of fish?" Molly demanded.

"Sturgeon," Diana replied. It was all Joanna could do to keep from laughing. "My body," Diana continued, "stopped having to work to remain upright, to be poised and graceful and all those things mothers say you have to be. I remember there was a stand of seaweed and it slithered across my body and tickled me and felt very strange, and a little dangerous. But when you swim, or just float on the water as the sun is sinking into the sea to join you, you discover what true physical grace and peace really are."

"It sounds wonderful." Joanna sighed without realizing it.

"Mama, can I learn to swim?" Molly asked eagerly.

"I will see what I can arrange," Joanna replied with a smile as she tried delicately to pull apart her cornish game hen.

"One must pretend to be a Viking invader when one eats with one's hands," Diana advised. "Ruthlessness is everything." She demonstrated by inserting her thumbs into the breast of her own hen and, with one sharp tug, pulling it neatly apart. Joanna, a trifle squeamishly, followed this example; her hen gave way but not without squirting her in the eye. Molly and Diana promptly collapsed with laughter, Diana falling off her cushion and onto the floor, her arms clutching her aching midriff.

"Be careful . . . your diamond!" Joanna cried anxiously. This only caused Diana to shriek with more laughter which set Molly to laughing all the harder so that she, too, toppled off her own cushion and became tangled in her bib. It was some time before Joanna could restore a modicum of order to the room. "I think we should have more tea," she said with some severity as Diana and Molly resettled themselves and tried not to giggle whenever they looked at each other.

"Tea, yes tea," Diana replied, clearing her throat. "An excellent suggestion. Nothing restores a sense of English propriety like a good cup of tea."

Joanna, with a forbidding frown at Diana which won a lopsided grin and a wink in return, refilled their cups as she struggled not to give way to her own chuckles.

"What is that?" Molly demanded, pointing towards a large blue-grey cat that had just emerged from behind the potted palm and was now stretching languorously in the sunlight.

"That is Aphrodite," Diana said as the cat strolled over to Molly, uttered one *Mowr!* and fell down on her side, raising her head to be scratched. Molly quickly obliged. "The most indolent creature I've ever met," Diana continued. "She will remain at your side for as long as you've strength enough to pet her and when you are exhausted, will fall asleep and not awaken until it comes to her attention that she might be hungry."

"She's wonderful," Molly breathed as she reverently stroked the cat who was so obliging as to purr.

Joanna smiled. "Dogs, cats, elephants, camels, fish . . . I am amazed that you don't have a peacock strolling through your garden."

"What a brilliant idea!" Diana exclaimed. "I wonder where one might procure such a bird?"

"Would you not be afraid of Aphrodite stalking the poor creature?" Joanna asked.

"Look at her, Lady Sinclair." Joanna watched the cat roll onto its back and stretch so that Molly might rub its round belly. "Does that look like an animal who has the vaguest idea of what dinner on the hoof looks like?"

Joanna had to agree that Aphrodite did not. "But what of your dogs?" she asked. "Surely they would be only too happy to devour an innocent peacock."

"They are not permitted into the gardens," Diana triumphantly replied as she scooped some strawberries into a small bowl, poured thick cream on them, tilted her head back and dropped one of the succulent fruits into her mouth. "God, I love decadence!" she sighed rapturously and this set Joanna to laughing. "Well, don't you?" Diana demanded.

"I do not know. I have never witnessed decadence, let alone indulged in it before."

"You poor, deprived creature," Diana said with a look of sympathy. "It is a good thing that we have met so that I may instruct you in the proper way to conduct life."

"Decadence is of some importance in your scheme of things, is it?" Joanna inquired.

"Of paramount importance," Diana affirmed, dropping another strawberry into her mouth.

"I see." Joanna smiled. "You must disapprove of me very much, then. I'm not at all decadent, you know."

"For an intelligent woman you do not know yourself at all."

"I know that I am not at all like you."

"On the contrary, you are very much like me. That is what you find so terrifying. 'Sisters we are, yea twins we be, Yet deadly feud 'twist thee and me.' "

"And what, praytell, do you mean by that cryptic quote?"

"Only that it seems to me that we are forever defending ourselves from the pleasure of each other's company," Diana said.

"*You* wore that atrocious costume," Joanna said.

"And *you* couldn't see the fun of it," Diana retorted.

"You take a perverse delight in shocking people," Joanna contended as Molly watched this interchange with great interest.

"Of course I do," Diana cheerfully agreed. "It's great fun."

"I do not like shocking people," Joanna declared self-righteously.

"That is because you have never done it before. I daresay you would enjoy yourself immensely if you but tried it once."

Joanna gave it up and began to laugh. "You are incorrigible."

"Of course I am, but I'm right," Diana replied. "Have a strawberry."

To her surprise, Joanna found herself opening her mouth which Diana promptly filled with a fat strawberry.

"Good?" Diana inquired.

Joanna could only nod, her hostess' luminous breasts

once again filling her gaze as Diana leaned towards her over the table.

"We shall be friends in spite of ourselves," Diana warned.

"An ominous fate indeed," Joanna said, smiling, "to exemplify Mr. Johnson's 'endearing elegance of female friendship.' "

"I am not at all elegant," Diana said.

"But you are—on some rare occasions—endearing." Joanna smiled, and for the first time in their acquaintance Lady Diana March blushed. Thinking this quite a coup, Joanna helped herself to another strawberry.

At last the Sinclairs rose to go. Reluctant goodbyes were said all around and the Sinclairs finally departed Waverly Manor, stuffed and satiated and simmering with a host of insidious new ideas.

Diana, after waving them off, slowly wandered back into the house, moving aimlessly from room to room as she noticed how oppressively quiet Waverly Manor had become.

CHAPTER 7

One week to the day after her tumultuous tea at Waverly Manor, Joanna retired to the private sitting room adjoining her bedroom, and sat down with her sketchpad and pencil. But she found that her thoughts and emotions were too agitated to permit a flowering of creativity; they created an insurmountable wall between herself and her art.

She threw down her pencil in disgust. It was one thing to have Hugo and Mrs. Hampton fritter away her time with useless projects and petty errands, it was quite another to turn upon and deny herself that which gave her the greatest pleasure and comfort in her life. She could not draw now.

She felt not the slightest connection with the picture that had been forming in her mind these last three days. "Blast Hugo!" she muttered.

A quarrel with her brother over her finances had become a weekly occurrence. He would summon her into the masculine domain of his study, remind her of the one thousand pounds yearly income left her by her husband, and the drain her homes in Kent and London, her own carriage and team of horses, and a staff of servants made on these funds. She, in turn, would remind Hugo of the income she derived by letting out both homes during much of the year, and the quarrel would escalate from there. It went against the grain for Hugo to humor the independence of a sister who should be relying entirely upon his largesse. It infuriated him that Joanna's brother-in-law should administer and greatly increase the trust fund Joanna's late husband had established for Molly. It was not the present Lord Sinclair's place to insure the future of Hugo's niece, let alone aid and abet the independent stance of Joanna.

For her part, having endured the same quarrel for the four years since her husband's death, Joanna had grown bored and had recently begun to chuckle during the more impassioned passages of Hugo's tirades. This did not at all serve to endear her to him. The argument she had just left, brought about by her purchase of her first new ball gown in two years, Joanna had won; and she had again not given in to Hugo's demands to live year round at Pembroke. But she had lost the peace of mind she had enjoyed upon awakening that morning and that particular tingle a woman feels when she knows that she will be attending a ball in the evening.

Wearily Joanna walked into her bedroom and gazed at the blue-green gown she would wear that night. She had agreed on the design of the gown in a mad, daring fit that now left her with an evening dress totally devoid of sleeves or anything resembling a bodice. It would create an argument with at least Mrs. Hampton, and probably Hugo as well. Joanna could hear them: "You are dressed as shockingly as Lady Diana March!" they would cry. "At least I have not a diamond in my navel!" she would retort.

Joanna began to chuckle and then to cast about in her mind for some way of preventing her relatives from ever seeing her in the ball gown.

* * *

That evening, when nearly half those invited had arrived, Joanna—safely hidden in her cloak—and Hugo and Mrs. Hampton made their entrance into the Heddington May Ball. They were inconspicuous amid the press of revellers eager to make their own entrance into the ball and partake of the many bowls of excellent Herefordshire punch, and sup from the many tables overburdened with every delicacy Heddington had to offer. Those desirous of working up an appetite to fully appreciate these refreshments made their way to the dance floor where they might show off their finery to fullest advantage.

Soon after entering the ballroom Mrs. Hampton found herself hailed by Lady Chesterfield and so deserted her nephew and niece. Joanna, approached by a maid, could remain within her wrap no longer and thus, with a deep breath, gave up her cloak. Hugo, fortunately, was having a few words with Roger Palmerston and Joanna might have missed his scrutiny all together, for she had begun to slip away, when Mr. Ian Chesterfield caught sight of her and boomed: "B'gad, Joanna, if that ain't the most smashing gown I've ever seen you in. . . . Or should I say, almost out of?"

This had the effect of drawing the attention of nearly half the occupants of the room to Joanna's costume. She found herself swathed in a rosy blush. "I'm glad you like it,

Ian," she muttered in the teeth of Hugo's outraged glare before she managed to make good her escape. She did not get far, however, before Lord Carroll stepped up to her, neatly attached her to his arm, and then led her to the dance floor.

"You are breathtakingly beautiful tonight, Joanna," Lord Carroll began their conversation.

Joanna sighed. "Please Tom, I wish you would not. You know that I detest flattery."

"Nonsense! Why else did you wear so alluring a gown? Why else did you arrange your hair in so tempting a fashion, and adorn yourself with so alluring a perfume if you did not wish my praise and the admiration of every man in the room?"

"I wanted to feel daring. I wanted to enjoy myself and your making calf-eyes at me is *not* enjoyable, Tom."

"Very well," Lord Carroll conceded, and directed their conversation to Diana March and her guests who had arrived at Waverly Manor not two days before the ball. Upon Joanna's assuring him that they were indeed expected that night Lord Carroll replied: "From all that I have heard, a Heddington ball seems far too prosaic an entertainment for any friends of hers."

"She is not half so top-lofty as some people seem to think."

"Why Joanna, I believe you like her!"

"I wouldn't be at all surprised," was Joanna's sanguine reply.

With the end of the dance Joanna refused Lord Carroll's offers of refreshment and escaped with a murmured excuse. She tucked herself into the handiest corner and from this vantage point watched the brilliantly costumed crowd stroll and sweep past her.

The Humphreys entered the ballroom. Joanna watched with growing dismay as Hugo not only did not go up to Caroline, but actually turned his back and walked in the opposite direction. Joanna blushed for the boorish behavior of her brother. Much as she detested Caroline Humphrey, the woman had done nothing to deserve so open a snub. She had just formed the intention of going to Caroline and apologizing for so unkind a cut when she was accosted by Mrs. Hampton.

"Joanna, how could you? How could you?" that appalled woman cried. "How *could* you wear so indecorous a gown at a *public* ball?"

"Because there aren't enough people to shock at a *private* ball," Joanna retorted, her aunt's vehemence fueling the fire of irritation which seemed to swell Joanna's breast.

"I will not tolerate such impertinence from you," Mrs. Hampton declared. "Have you no thought to the feelings of your own relatives? Think of the humiliation I have had to suffer as one friend after another has commented upon the hideous impropriety of such a gown. Think of my shame as I have observed every man in the room ogle my own niece. Why, you are dressed as shockingly as Lady Diana March!"

"At least I have not a diamond in my.... Good heavens!"

Mrs. Hampton, along with everyone else in the ballroom, directed her gaze to the ballroom door. "That can't be Lady March," she sputtered.

"But it is," Joanna breathed.

Diana was dressed in a sleeveless gown of white silk, with an overgown of golden gauze that fell to her knees. Her blonde hair was pulled back from her face and hung down her nearly naked back in a shower of curls. At her side was the most delectable specimen of manhood Joanna had ever seen. He stood well over six feet in height and was dressed in a cavalry officer's red uniform that did everything possible to show off his lean, muscular form. His black hair was formed into carefully arranged Greek curls. His brown eyes were particularly fine, his smile devastating.

"Lady Diana March and Colonel Geoffrey Hunt-Stevens!"

the herald announced.

Behind them stood an exquisite young man, as like unto Adonis as any golden creature could be. The royal blue of his coat was mirrored in his eyes. His pantaloons revealed the most perfectly shaped masculine legs Joanna had ever stared at. His partner was a young woman of no more than twenty years, her black hair and eyes a stunning contrast to his glowing beauty.

"Miss Jennifer Hunt-Stevens and Señor Jorge Morales!" the herald declared.

Behind them advanced a silver-haired grande dame of perhaps fifty-five years whom the herald introduced as Lady Hildegarde Dennison. She surveyed the room with a haughty air, whipped out her fan, and then swept into the ballroom while the rest of the guests broke into near hysteric conversation.

Colonel Hunt-Stevens led his hostess into the country dance that was playing and drawled, "We seem to have brought a breath of life to this dull little country affair."

"Don't be catty, Geoff," Diana chastised, "it doesn't become you."

"My dear Diana, *everything* becomes me. I am a paragon, haven't you heard?"

Suppressing a grin, Diana admitted that she had heard a good deal about him, mostly from his own lips. "Now do try to be on your best behavior tonight," she implored. "These are my neighbors, after all, and it won't hurt me to get along with them."

"You grow more conservative with each passing year," the beauteous Colonel said with a sigh.

"This is called maturity, Geoffrey. The accumulation of wisdom. You could use a little of it yourself, you know. Trying to seduce Prince Sergei, really!"

"You heard about that, did you?" The Colonel grinned with no visible trace of maturity.

"Tales of your misconduct colored my mail for weeks. I can't remember when I last was so well entertained by my correspondence."

"Darling Diana." The Colonel beamed as he kissed her hand. "I knew you could not be so very severe. I wonder," he mused as his brown eyes scanned the ballroom, "if some lowly farmer with dirt under his fingernails might be able to hold back my ennui."

"Geoff, you wouldn't dare!" Diana gasped, missing her step.

"I would dare anything to escape boredom!"

"Geoff this is *England*. They could hang you for what you're considering."

"But Diana, what is life without challenge?"

"Prolonged by a good forty years," Diana scathingly replied. "Honestly, Geoff, why can't you be satisfied with Jorge Morales?"

"He is very beautiful, I know, but not at all open to experimentation. In short, my love, he is dreadfully dull."

"I suppose Richard Danby bored you to tears after a year of loving him."

"That is ancient history."

"Why must you nip from masculine flower to masculine flower like an overheated hummingbird?" Diana said in exasperation.

"Without variety there is no renewal of one's vital life force," the Colonel solemnly declared.

"Geoffrey," Diana said with her severest frown, "there is more to life than lust."

"Oh my dear," the Colonel laughed, "you *are* innocent."

"I am serious, Geoff. What will you do when you are old and no longer handsome enough to attract lovers?"

"I shall shoot myself as any self-respecting mortal should."

"I don't know why I like you," Diana remarked as she

went into her final curtsy. "You are so very shallow."

"But I dance divinely."

"Too true," Diana said, laughing.

"Mrs. Pratt informs me that you've taken in another stray."

"Annie is not a stray, she is an excellent maid."

"And one growing big with child," the Colonel pointed out.

"Have you any objections?" Diana inquired dangerously.

"None whatsoever," the Colonel hastily assured her. "I simply do not understand why you feel compelled to play Lady Bountiful once again."

"Then attend me well, my fair ignoramous. Annie was most brutally raped by one Lord Franklin Humphrey while in his employ. When he saw her belly growing he cast her out. Her family spurned her, even the most Reverend Stempel turned her away from the church door. Annie is not the first, apparently, to suffer his lordship's violence. Mrs. Pratt found her on the road to Ludlow in Shropshire where Annie intended to seek out a doctor of ill repute to help rid her of the child. Fortunately, Mrs. Pratt ordered her into the gig and brought her to me and I was able to put her to some easy work. I'll not turn my back on any girl so ill-used by the world. But for our births, I might have been in a similar situation."

"Slander!" the Colonel cried. "That blade you keep strapped to your leg would run through the first man that tried to roger you."

"Perhaps," Diana conceded with a grin.

With the end of this conversation came the end of Mrs. Bartlett's patience. Unable to stem the tide of her curiosity, she bustled up to the couple exclaiming: "My *dear* Lady March I am so glad you could come. What a magnificent gown, you *must* give me your dressmaker's address. And those pearls! Divine! I was saying to Lady Palmerston only the other day that these modern young women do not fully appreciate the beauty and propriety of pearls. They must needs have something *spectacular.* But who is your charming escort? I don't believe that I have seen him in the neighborhood.''

With an amused sidelong grin at her ashen partner who knew a Matchmaking Mama when he saw one, Diana quickly performed the introductions. Geoffrey bowed slightly, murmured that he was delighted, and was prohibited from saying anything further for Mrs. Bartlett once again burst forth.

"This is such an honor, Colonel! We have so few young men of quality and distinction in our little community that you are positively dazzling all of the young women in the room. Oh, the hearts you have captured tonight, Colonel! *Everyone* is longing to meet you. Do you stay long in Heddington?''

"No more than a fortnight," the Colonel said, searching the room for some means of escape. "I've family business to attend to in Surrey."

"Only a fortnight?" Mrs. Bartlett exclaimed, thoroughly distressed. "My dear Lady March you must speak to the Colonel. You must implore him to stay! Convince him of the many pleasures of Heddington. A fortnight is not a proper visit at all. Colonel, you should be ashamed of yourself! I daresay you've not seen Lady March in over a year, and to leave her after only a fortnight? Unthinkable! Persuade him to stay, Lady March. I know that you can."

"Then you know more than I do, Mrs. Bartlett," Diana replied, trying to suppress a chuckle. "Geoffrey is a stiff-necked fellow and seldom attends a word I say. Perhaps, however, if you introduce him to your . . . acquaintances here tonight he might be induced by a word or a smile to remain a while longer."

Mrs. Bartlett hurriedly declared that she would follow

this advice to the letter and looped the hapless Colonel's arm through her own and led him away, proclaiming that he must and would remain in Heddington. The one glance that Geoffrey was able to cast at Diana before the Heddington revellers hid him from view assured her that he would have his revenge.

Shivering with delight at her own audacity, Diana nevertheless found herself answering for her sins much sooner than she had expected. She was accosted by Hugo Garfield, his silver coat and white pantaloons modestly displaying his handsome figure, his brown locks done with modish conservatism. Diana might have thought him handsome if he did not continually succeed at turning her stomach.

After a variety of compliments regarding her appearance, Mr. Garfield reminded her of the two dances she had promised him and instantly led her onto the dance floor. Ascertaining that Colonel Hunt-Stevens had no claims upon her, Mr. Garfield spent the whole of both dances declaring that he found every word Diana uttered, every step she took, to be utterly entrancing, even going so far as to smile fondly when Diana heatedly denied that her opinion of the Corn Laws was "charming." Mr. Garfield wagged his finger at her and led her to the punch bowl.

Lady Hildegarde Dennison, meanwhile, demanded of her companion, "Who is the proud-looking young man so assiduously courting Lady March's favor?"

Mrs. Hornby, an acquaintance of ten minutes standing, replied, "Mr. Hugo Garfield."

"Garfield . . . Garfield . . . I believe that I met his father once. He had just that same sneer of self-satisfaction."

"The Garfields are a very proud family, and . . . acquisitive. Although we are but recently acquainted, Lady Dennison, I hope that you will not be offended if I just put a word in your ear regarding Mr. Garfield."

"And why should I be concerned with Mr. Garfield? I

have not even met the fellow and hope to be spared the honor."

"Your hostess, however, is becoming well acquained with the gentleman," Mrs. Hornby pointed out.

"Ah. There is some danger in this?"

"Only for Lady March. I will speak plainly, Lady Dennison, for I sense that honesty will not offend you."

Lady Dennison bowed.

"For the last several years it has been believed, and with good reason, that Mr. Garfield would marry Lady Caroline Humphrey, a young woman whose pride is the equal of Mr. Garfield's and whose fortune surpasses his somewhat," Mrs. Hornby continued. "But since Lady March moved into Waverly Manor he has cut Caroline on every social occasion and now, as you see, dances attendance upon Lady March."

"A young man's affections may wander, at least in my experience," Lady Dennison observed.

"Be under no illusions, Lady Dennison. Mr. Garfield has no affection save for money."

"And why reveal Mr. Garfield's appalling lack of character to me?"

"I am concerned that Lady March might be taken in by Mr. Garfield's solicitous attentions on her behalf."

"Well, Mrs. Hornby, my hostess is an amazingly perspicacious young woman in such matters. But I will take care to have a word with her when we are alone."

Mrs. Hornby commended this sensible decision and the two women soon parted on the best of terms. Diana and Hugo also parted on the best of terms, Hugo pleased with all that he had accomplished that evening, Diana pleased to be out of Hugo's company at last. Her intention being to lose herself in the crowded ballroom so that Mr. Garfield could never discover her again that evening, she buried herself amid neighbors, entering into perfectly desultory conversations and thinking herself very fortunate indeed.

Hailed by a feminine voice, Diana turned to discover Joanna Sinclair approaching her. Having caught only glimpses of her neighbor thus far in the evening, Diana could now only stare, her cheeks growing indecorously warm as Joanna drew before her.

"I have found you at last. How glad I am that you came tonight. That was a very impressive entrance you made. Heddington will be talking of it for weeks to come," Joanna declared.

"Thank you." Diana smiled despite the thundering of her pulse. "We practiced it for hours."

Joanna laughed. "I don't doubt it."

The combination of Joanna's gown, her perfume, and her easy levity left Diana feeling increasingly lightheaded. "I . . . trust Molly suffered no ill effects from her tea at Waverly," she managed to say.

"On the contrary, it seems to have done her a world of good. In fact, I remembered the story you told me of your sister and I bundled Molly up yesterday and the day before that *and* the day before that and took her for a walk in the Pembroke gardens."

"Bravo! What had Molly to say to such unaccustomed exercise?" Diana asked, regaining her equilibrium.

"Yesterday she asked Hugo if she could help Jenkins, our gardener, plant a new bed of flowers. My brother was, of course, horrified by the proposal. Ladies may pick flowers, but not plant them apparently. Molly thinks that very unsatisfacory and has been sulking ever since."

"Poor little cub. Gardening would do her a world of good."

"I begin to agree with you, but Hugo is adamantly opposed."

"Mr. Garfield would be opposed to any scheme not of his own devising," Diana replied with some heat.

"True," Joanna said with a grin, "but what can be

done?"

"Oh, now you should *not* have asked me that, Lady Sinclair, for my mind is of a devious bent and will undoubtedly come up with an unsuitable, but thoroughly brilliant, idea."

Joanna laughed. "Such as?"

"What Mr. Garfield does not know will not hurt him. Let Molly garden at Waverly Manor. I would not tell him about such exercise, and I am certain that you would not. . . ."

"Waverly Manor? Oh, I could not allow it!"

But Diana cajoled and pleaded and an appointment was finally made for Molly to appear at Waverly Manor at nine o'clock on the following morning.

"We've bagged her at last, Hildy," a gleeful feminine voice declared behind them.

The two women turned to find Jennifer Hunt-Stevens and Lady Hildegarde Dennison.

"I do not approve of these elusive tactics of yours, Diana," Lady Dennison informed her hostess. "I find them too exhausting. Who is your companion? You have failed to introduce us."

"Oh you are cruel, Hildegarde, to chastise me twice in one breath," Diana complained.

"Cruelty and propriety are often synonymous," Lady Dennison declared. Joanna stared at her in amazement.

"I must write that down in my diary tonight," Miss Hunt-Stevens exclaimed. "It sounds so very profound."

"I am always profound, Jennifer," Lady Dennison intoned. "I am surprised you have not remarked it before this."

"But I have!" Miss Hunt-Stevens hastened to assure her. "My diary is simply littered with your profundity."

Diana only just managed to suppress a hoot of laughter and even Joanna found her own self-control sorely strained.

"Well?" Lady Dennison demanded of Diana.

Introductions were hastily made. Before the women could enter into a cozy *tete-a-tete*, however, Lord Carroll drew up to remind Joanna that she had promised him the next dance. Wishing that she might find some excuse to put him off so that she could remain with so entertaining a trio, Joanna found herself instead being led to the dance floor.

"Diana she is divine!" Miss Hunt-Stevens declared when the couple was out of hearing.

"Indeed," Lady Dennison said, "with those brown eyes—"

"They are hazel," Diana tersely corrected.

"As I was saying, with those hazel eyes and full mouth, the thick lustre of her hair, and the glow of her skin, Lady Sinclair reminds me forcibly of one of Raphael's Madonnas. She is amazingly beautiful, in fact. I am most put out with you, Diana, for not mentioning this before."

"Ye gods, yes!" Miss Hunt-Stevens exclaimed. "You've treated us very shabbily, Diana. I was expecting some fat country matron, not that delightful creature. She is perfect for you. I am infallible in my opinion of others, despite my relative youth, and I tell you, Diana, she is perfect."

"Jennifer, you are reading far more into this than exists!" Diana protested.

"Bah!" Lady Dennison retorted.

"Lady Sinclair is my neighbor and the first friend I have made since returning to England. That is *all*!" Diana insisted.

"Mm-hm," Miss Hunt-Stevens replied.

CHAPTER 8

At precisely nine o'clock on the morning after the Heddington May Ball, the sky a dark blue above the newly leafed trees of Waverly Manor, Diana March advanced across the front lawn to greet her guests. She was dressed in brown, baggy trousers, a man's white workshirt, its sleeves rolled up to her elbows, and boots that Joanna decided had never known a clean moment in their life. A peacock quietly trailed behind her. Joanna's sudden burst of laughter drew Diana's attention to this interloper and she quickly shooed the creature to the back of the manor.

"Joy and Harmony will have Peacock Fricasse for supper

tonight if that stupid creature isn't careful," Diana muttered.

"Why on earth did you give your dogs such odd names?" Joanna inquired as Waverly's newest addition haughtily swished its long tail around the corner of the house.

"I chose them because they are the qualities I want most in my life," Diana replied. "I thought if I called them often enough they would come to me."

"Your head is filled with the most nonsensical notions," Joanna said admiringly.

"You are not the first to remark it."

Mrs. Pratt advanced down the front steps of the manor, gravely greeted Joanna and Molly, and then proceeded to pull a large blue-grey smock over Molly's dress, buttoning it in the back. She received Joanna's effusive thanks with a grave nod and then returned to her duties inside Waverly.

With Molly tugging eagerly on Diana's hand, the trio made their way to the back of Waverly Manor, chatting in a comfortable manner as if they were all friends of long standing. With a resolute squaring of her shoulders Diana led them to a gnarled old man, browned by the sun, impossibly wrinkled, who was methodically applying his spade to the rich earth.

"I want you both to meet my gardener, Bert Smythe. Bert, this is our new assistant, Miss Molly Sinclair, and her mother, Lady Sinclair," Diana said.

Bert touched his cap at Joanna and then looked grimly at Molly. "I'll not be coddling young whipper-snappers and so I told ye, Lady March, he announced.

"I'm *not* a whipper-snapper," Molly declared in an injured voice.

"And we want no coddling, Bert," Diana added, suppressing a smile. "Molly is here to learn how to garden. She will work very hard, I promise you."

Bert returned to his spade without comment, doubt emanating from every fiber of his aged being. Joanna herself began to doubt the success of this venture, but before she could speak her reservations Diana had begun to lead Molly around the garden, showing her the dozens of flowers that were already peeking up through the earth, discussing her plans for furthur cultivation as if Molly were a horticulturist of some eighty years. Molly hung on her every word.

Joanna gave up all hopes of intervention and retired to a shaded marble bench where she watched the progress of her budding gardener. Diana March displayed far more patience with her young charge than Joanna would have thought possible in one of such eccentric habits. Indeed, Diana and Molly seemed perfectly content with each other's company as they began to transplant the seedlings of fruit trees Diana had chosen to grace the southeastern corner of her property, and Joanna was perfectly content to watch them work. After an hour's labor, the work accomplished, Diana and Molly moved onto a bed where pansies were to be placed. They settled onto the ground and, after a few instructions, Molly was happily transplanting the flowers. Deciding that her assistant needed no further supervision, Diana rose and walked to where Joanna was seated.

"This is marvelous. This is truly a most momentous day!" Joanna exclaimed as Diana sat down cross-legged on the ground before her. "Look at her! Never have I seen Molly so animated, never have I seen her concentrate on one thing for such an extended period of time. Why, she is mesmerized by the work! Oh how I wish I could paint her as she bends to smell the earth."

"Why can you not do so?" Diana inquired, mesmerized herself by the sunlight that occasionally flitted through the leaves and lit Joanna's hair or mouth.

"I do not keep my paints at Pembroke."

"But I thought that you had told me that you painted and that you enjoyed it immensely," Diana said, perplexed.

"I do. But my brother and my aunt cannot tolerate my

working on a canvas. They do not approve of my passion for painting and think that I am idling my time away. Rather than argue with them as I have done in the past, or continually tear myself from my easel to attend to their errands which they deem of greater importance, I give up painting during the time I am at Pembroke Park."

"Oh, that is monstrous!" Diana said in a choked voice.

"No, no! It is only the Garfield dislike of art."

"How can you tolerate so wretched a disregard for your needs and desires?" Diana demanded, her face flushed with anger.

"This is my family, Lady March. I am used to such disregard."

Diana was prohibited from a further retort by the sudden appearance of Geoffrey Hunt-Stevens and Jorge Morales, who strolled arm in arm from around the side of the Manor, and made their way to their hostess' side. Both were immaculately dressed in riding breeches and coats, their hair tousled, their cheeks red from recent exercise.

"I can only commend your stable, Diana," Señor Morales declared. "The gallop this morning was most exhilarating."

"You are too kind, Jorge," Diana replied.

"But who is the fair damsel perched so charmingly upon this humble garden bench?" Geoffrey inquired.

"You are such a cad, Geoff," Diana said admiringly. "Dear Rogues, this is Lady Joanna Sinclair. Lady Sinclair, the fellow with the flowery verbosity is Colonel Geoffrey Hunt-Stevens. His companion is Jorge Morales, an extraordinary guitarist of the Spanish royal court."

The two gentlemen bowed, each claiming Joanna's hand in an admiring kiss. "So you are the fair neighbor of whom Diana speaks so well," Geoffrey said.

"Does she indeed?" Joanna smiled mischievously, glancing at the red-faced Diana.

"Oh! Have we let the cat out of the bag?" the Colonel

said with no trace of remorse. "Diana cannot stop speaking of you, Lady Sinclair, and your apparently delightful progeny. Having met you at last, it is easy to understand the reason."

"We have been most eager to meet you, Lady Sinclair," Jorge Morales assured Joanna, thus saving Diana the necessity of making some sort of retort. "The Lamberts, who are the most amusing of American acquaintances, made the bet with us that Diana would never gain the friendship of a member of the *ton.*"

"I fear I am only on the fringes of the *ton* nowadays," Joanna confided.

"Geoffrey, she is lovely," Jorge declared, studying Joanna who quickly blushed.

"I quite agree," his companion replied.

"Diana, you must write a concerto to Lady Sinclair's eyes. They are exceptional," Jorge announced.

"Is he mad?" Joanna asked.

"He is Spanish," Diana calmly replied.

"I would prefer a concerto to her hair, Diana," Geoffrey countered.

"I will take that into consideration,"Diana said.

"He is not Spanish," Joanna said.

"No, Geoff is quite mad," Diana replied.

"But I am delightful company," the Colonel added and Joanna had to laugh.

Before she was able to give him the set down he deserved, Diana was called to Molly's side to admire the work she had done. Half the bed of pansies had been planted and tomorrow, Molly declared, she would complete the other half. Diana applauded this resolve. "Then you may tell everyone that this is your flower bed," she said. "Your mother will be very proud."

"She will be stunned," Molly declared.

"I daresay she will." Diana smiled. "Good heavens, look

at you, child! You've more dirt on you than you've left for the flowers. I think it best that you run into the house and ask Mrs. Pratt to help you clean up before your mother sees you and faints dead away."

"Mama never faints," Molly said stoutly.

"There is always a first time. Run along now." Molly quickly obliged and Diana was able to return to her other guests.

"Diana, your neighbor is a delight," Jorge declared. "She, too, is bored by Haydn."

"All my friends have only the best taste in music, art, and fashion," Diana averred, sitting down once again on the well-trimmed lawn.

"It is a pity you have not a similar good taste in your own wardrobe," Geoffrey said, his nose wrinkling.

"Practicality is never fashionable," Diana retorted.

"But it needn't be so gauche," the Colonel said with a shudder.

"Diana!" Lady Hildegarde Dennison trumpeted as she swept down the steps of the back terrace and advanced upon them with grim purpose. "There is a small, muddy creature running through the house screeching for Mrs. Pratt!"

Diana grinned. "Yes, I know."

"You cannot mean to just sit there?"

"Mrs. Pratt and Molly will find each other soon enough."

"Molly?"

"My daughter," Joanna broke in.

"Lady Sinclair I am most disappointed in you," Lady Hildegarde said, turning to Joanna. "To have a child is bad enough. To have a child who actually goes out amongst company is worse still. But to have one that screeches is inexcusable."

"I will speak with Molly most firmly, I do assure you, Lady Dennison," Joanna replied, struggling not to smile.

"Your brother is Hugo Garfield, is he not?" Lady Hildegarde demanded.

"He is."

"That explains everything."

Diana forgot herself so much as to laugh out loud and even Joanna could not help but chuckle.

"Mr. Garfield is the too-proper gentleman who clung so tenaciously to our Diana last night?" Jorge inquired.

"The very same," Lady Hildegarde replied.

"Then you malign the poor child, Hildegarde, for to screech is a very improper thing to do and something I do not believe Mr. Garfield would think to undertake," Jorge said.

"That is very true," Hildegarde mused. "I daresay the child might be presentable . . . in ten years' time."

Molly emerged from the back of the Manor just then and dropped breathlessly down beside Diana on the cool lawn, all evidence of her morning's labors erased.

"Goodness, why are you out of breath?" Diana inquired.

"I ran all the way from the back terrace," Molly puffed.

"But that is only thirty yards," Diana exclaimed. "I am horrified, Molly. A big, strapping girl like you huffing and puffing like this. I daresay you could not even run once around Waverly Manor."

"I could!" Molly said hotly.

"Could not."

"Could too!"

"I doubt it." Diana's voice dripped with skepticism.

"I'll prove it to you." Molly struggled furiously to her feet. "I shall run *all* the way around Waverly Manor and *that* will show you!" So saying, Molly ran off on the path leading to the right of Waverly Manor. Diana, thoroughly pleased with herself, leaned back on one elbow.

"Lady March," Joanna said dazedly, "why do you want my daughter to run herself into exhaustion?"

"Running and walking are the best things in the world for strengthening a body," Diana placidly replied. "I can promise you that if we can but keep Molly at this, you will not recognize her in a month's time."

"If you do not run her into her grave first, you mean," Joanna said with some heat.

"She is stronger than you think," Diana replied.

"I say, Diana," Jennifer Hunt-Stevens declared as she trotted up to the little group, "did you know that there is a pug-nosed elf gasping for breath outside your library windows?"

"This is Diana's newest amusement for her guests," Geoffrey explained.

"And very clever of her, too, to rid us of youth's presence," Hildegarde added.

"Dear Diana, that is why I like visiting you so very much," Jennifer cooed. "I always feel a little mad in your company."

Molly chose this moment to emerge from around the far left side of Waverly Manor.

"Good God she did it!" Joanna cried, rising to her feet in the excitement of the finish. The others burst into applause as Molly ran straight into her mother's arms.

"I ran all the way around Waverly Manor, Mama!" she gasped for it was all that she could do to drag air into her lungs. "See," Molly said, looking defiantly at Diana, "I *told* you I could do it and I did."

"So you did," Diana replied with a bland smile. "But how often did you have to stop to catch your breath?"

"Only a few times," Molly said defensively.

"A few?"

"Six or seven. But at least I ran all the way around!"

"Very true," Diana agreed, "and I commend you for it. Such a feat required a great deal of determination. But why stop with this one success?"

"What do you mean?" Molly asked, instantly suspicious.

"Why be satisfied with one run around the house that leaves you drooping with exhaustion? Why not see if you can improve upon your performance? I had in mind your running all the way around Waverly Manor without stopping to catch your breath. We could make the exercise into a wager if you like. I could make it very much worth your while."

"What sort of a wager?" Molly asked, a larcenous gleam in her grey eyes that nearly sent her mother into convulsions.

"If you could accomplish the feat I have laid before you in, say, four weeks time, you would win . . . Ah! I have it! You would win your very own harem costume!"

"Really?" Molly squeaked, setting Hildegarde's teeth on edge.

"Oh now wait a minute . . ." Joanna began, half-amused and half-horrified.

"And if you can't run around the house without stopping for breath you would have to keep running for another four weeks after that," Diana blithely continued. "Agreed?"

"Agreed!" Molly eagerly affirmed.

"But a harem costume!" Joanna protested. "What will Aunt Hampton say? What will Hugo say?"

"They will say that she looks very fetching indeed," Diana replied. "Ah, Mrs. Pratt, how good of you to think of refreshments," she said to the housekeeper soberly advancing towards them with a tray, the sun sparkling on the cameo at her throat.

"I thought Miss Sinclair might want a restorative after her morning exercise." Mrs. Pratt set the tray down on the bench Joanna had so recently vacated. "I hope you like lemonade, Miss."

"I adore it!" Molly declared, promptly sitting down on the lawn. "And look! Cinnamon muffins!"

"You are a most discerning woman, Mrs. Pratt," Joanna said with a grateful smile.

"My many years of experience have given me some insight into the needs of active young ladies," Mrs. Pratt replied before turning and making her way back into the house.

"What on earth did she mean by that cryptic remark?" Joanna demanded as Diana handed around the frosty glasses of lemonade.

"It was a subtle reference to the many trials and tribulations Pratt has suffered in Diana's employ," Hildegarde replied.

"Diana was a right little hellion in her youth," Geoffrey offered.

Joanna chuckled. "I don't doubt it."

"I am not yet in my dotage, Geoff," Diana retorted as the Colonel pinched the delectable derriere of Señor Morales, "although you will undoubtedly make me old before my time."

"Geoffrey will make us all old before our time," Hildegarde declared.

"You reckon without Mrs. Bartlett," Joanna, who had not observed the Colonel accost Jorge, broke in. "She will reduce your friend to a quivering mass of docile married manhood before a fortnight has passed."

"Heaven help us all," Diana said.

CHAPTER 9

In the heat of midafternoon Diana lay naked beneath cool silk sheets, the Alexandrian street noises a distant murmur. She knew only this room, the drawn curtains leaving it shadowed, expectant. The sheets caressed her thighs, her belly, her breasts; she hungered for the hands, so like silk, yet skilled in the art of passion.

The door opened. A woman entered clothed only in a white chemise. Diana could not see her face in the dusk of the room, but she knew the woman. Wanted her. Needed her.

"Please," she whispered, holding out her hand. She felt but did not see the woman smile. The chemise slipped lazily to the ground allowing Diana to feast on the sight of those full breasts and large brown nipples, the rounded belly, the curling mass of dark hair that set her heart to shuddering. Slowly the woman came to her. She took Diana's outstretched hand and kissed the palm, allowing her tongue to circle the fevered center. Diana's need poured from her throat in a strained moan. "Please," she whispered again, "it has been so long."

Diana slid to the center of the bed, the silk teasing her body. She felt the woman raise the sheet and lower herself onto the bed, moving closer, ever closer. They met at last beneath the cool silk. Yet what Diana felt was not soft warm flesh—but dry, hard bones. She looked up and saw a hollow-eyed skull smiling at her as the bones spread themselves upon her. . . .

* * *

Diana tore and kicked the bedclothes off her. A hand at her mouth to silence her terror, she sat up in her bed at Waverly Manor, knees drawn tightly to her chest. Shudder after shudder rippled through her body as her heart thudded in her breast. Finally she remembered to draw long, slow breaths into her, and this, at last, brought her fully out of the dream.

Trembling, realizing that she was cold, then taking one last shuddering breath, Diana pushed herself out of her bed, pulled on her thick blue velvet robe, slid her feet numbly into her slippers, and stood in the center of her bedroom, her arms wrapped around her torso, the white waxing moonlight pouring in on her as she tried to get her mind to start thinking again. But she knew only fear.

The library as sanctuary came to Diana as a feeling, rather than a rational thought, and she found herself leaving her bedroom and walking downstairs, images from her nightmare pursuing her down the staircase and across the hall. Desperately she pushed open the library door and entered to find a lamp lit, the fire crackling in the grate, and Hildegarde Dennison, her silver hair tumbling down her back as she stood in the firelight clothed in a jade green Chinese robe, an arm outstretched to Diana, her hand offering a glass of amber liquid.

"Brandy?"

"Yes, please," Diana whispered, taking the brandy snifter in both hands and quickly downing half of the liquid fire. She shuddered once and then a calm slowly filtered through her. "Oh God," she said, and then looked at Hildegarde. "What are you doing up at this hideous hour, Hildy?"

"I am, as you know Diana, a notoriously light sleeper," Hildegarde replied as she poured herself a small glass of madeira. "I heard you cry out and thought you might be in need of some company."

"Oh."

"Come," Hildegarde said gently as she slid an arm around Diana's waist and led her to the royal blue settee against the far wall, "let us sit down like civilized people. I doubt if you can remain standing for very much longer."

"Yes," Diana murmured and obediently sat down beside her friend.

"Drink your brandy," Hildegarde commanded and again Diana obeyed. Observing the chalky pallor leave her young hostess' face, Hildegarde took a sip of her wine and said, "I didn't know you had started having your nightmares again."

"I haven't . . . I mean I hadn't," Diana managed to reply. "This was the first in nearly a year."

Several pertinent questions flooded Hildegarde's mind at this disclosure but she held them back, knowing how precarious was Diana's hold on her present state of calm. "Which one was it?" she asked instead.

"The . . . skeleton." Diana quickly took another sip of

brandy.

"The same one you had so often when you stayed with us in Vienna?"

"Yes. . . . No. It was . . . different."

"How so?" Hildegarde watched Diana closely.

"I couldn't see Gwen's face, not even in the beginning. It was out of focus, hidden. And her hair was darker than it should have been and her body was . . . fuller. It was Gwen. That is, I knew her, Hildegarde. But she had changed."

"Reality in dreams is often distorted."

"Yes." Diana took another sip of brandy. "I don't understand!" she burst out. "It has been almost a year, Hildy. A whole year without those damned nightmares. And now they've come back."

"You have only had one, Diana."

"They are like hiccoughs. Once you get them they keep coming back," Diana said grimly. "What am I going to do?"

"You could always come back with me to Vienna and allow Celeste and me to undertake to cure you once again."

"And have your whole staff threaten to quit because of the screaming *Anglaise?* No thank you, Hildy. I'll spare you that difficulty at least. Besides, I like being in England. I like living at Waverly Manor. I don't want to leave."

"It is most puzzling. I do not understand why you have had this nightmare tonight when you say you are happy in England, happy at Waverly, and, by all appearances, had a perfectly enjoyable day today."

Diana sighed. "I am at a loss as well."

"Perhaps you have hidden reservations about teaching that child who has such an affinity for mud and high-pitched shrieks."

"Molly?" Diana smiled. "I adored having her here today and you know it, Hildy."

"And Lady Sinclair as well?"

"Oh yes! It is odd, Hildegarde, but I feel that despite all our differences Lady Sinclair and I will be great friends."

"Not so many differences, Diana. Indeed, there are a great many similarities. It is not so very odd at all."

"She is still a little shocked by me I think."

"I would not be surprised. You were always outrageous, Diana, but never have I seen you behave in quite so mad a fashion as in this last week. You used to have more sense than to ride about a conservative countryside in trousers, for example. I would caution you against these frequent displays of eccentricity, you could easily offend or antagonize your neighbors and that will only cause you grief in the end. Indeed, I am surprised that Lady Sinclair, a very proper young woman, has been so persistent at maintaining a connection with you."

"But she is lovely, isn't she Hildy?"

"That she is, my dear."

"And very lonely, too, I think."

"Then that is another similarity between you."

"I am not lonely, Hildegarde! I have literally hundreds of friends—"

"Whom you love very much, yes, I know," Hildegarde broke in. "But there is still an emptiness within you, a need unfulfilled. And Lady Sinclair, as you have said, is the first friend you have made in England. I voiced my concern in Vienna and I will voice it again. It is not good for you to bury yourself in some English backwater away from all society and friendly ties. You are one who needs to have loved ones around you, whether that be your brother, Jennifer, a lover, or even me. It is not good for you to live alone like this. Perhaps that is why the nightmare came tonight."

"But I was the farthest thing from being alone today!"

"Precisely."

Diana stared at her friend.

CHAPTER 10

Two days after the Heddington May Ball, Diana March and Jennifer Hunt-Stevens sat in the main Waverly Drawing Room laughing heartily over letters each had just received from one Mr. Peter Elliot, who seemed to fancy himself a Falstaff. He had written two passionate, and identical, love letters addressed to a Daisy and a Penny who were, apparently, serving girls in a Lancashire tavern. Mr. Elliot, however, had erred in that he had placed these *billet doux* in envelopes addressed to Diana and Jennifer. As both had known Mr. Elliot for several years and were well-schooled in his wit, they read on eagerly, hoots of laughter escaping their maidenly throats. Their mutual hilarity was interrupted, however, when Mrs. Pratt entered and announced that Mr. Hugo Garfield had come to call.

"Oh good God," Diana groaned.

"I knew it! I knew it!" Jennifer crowed. "Shall I slip out the other door so that you two can have a nice private *tete-a-tete*?"

"Take one step towards that door, Jennifer, and I shall be forced to wreak violence upon your person!"

Chuckling gleefully, Jennifer settled herself on the gold sofa beside her irate hostess.

"You may show Mr. Garfield in, Mrs. Pratt," Diana informed the housekeeper. "And we will have the usual sort of tea tray."

Mr. Garfield entered a moment later dressed in dove grey trousers and matching coat, his shirt white, his black waistcoat adorned with small silver flowers, his brown hair gleaming, his air purposeful. He bowed gravely over each woman's hand; took the chair Diana indicated to him; and then proceeded to enter into a very proper discourse on the late spring weather, the newest guests to visit the Palmerstons, and, of course, the Heddington May Ball which Mr. Garfield declared had provided him with exceptional pleasure due solely to Diana's charming company and kindness in dancing with him twice that evening. Tea was brought in, poured out, and duly sipped.

Diana, who had been well-drilled by her mother, replied politely to all Mr. Garfield's comments and even initiated a discussion of the local flora and fauna which Jennifer found unaccountably amusing, giggling on several unremarkable occasions.

Twenty minutes after he had arrived Mr. Garfield rose, bid the ladies good afternoon, and strode from the room, bowing and wishing good day to Lady Hildegarde whom he encountered in the doorway.

"Diana," Hildegarde announced as she entered the room, "Mrs. Hornby wished me to warn you against Mr. Garfield. Am I too late?"

Mr. Garfield repeated his call on the following afternoon while Diana was seated in conversation with Jorge Morales. On this occasion Mr. Garfield stayed thirty minutes; commended the renovations Diana had made at Waverly; drank two cups of tea; and then departed. On the day after that he again stayed thirty minutes, this time in company with Diana and Lady Hildegarde who remained silent as Diana struggled to retain her patience during a conversation concerning the lamentable forwardness of certain young ladies of the *ton* who had been so unfortunate as to openly pursue Mr. Garfield during the preceding London Season.

These visits did not go unremarked at the Waverly dining table.

"I can see the wedding now," Geoffrey Hunt-Stevens rhapsodized over the cucumber soup, "Diana in shimmering white silk with lace dripping all over her and orange blossoms floating down upon her in the chapel."

"Charming," Diana said, and grimaced.

"The man is clearly besotted with you . . . or should I say your fortune?" Jennifer offered.

"I would rather you said nothing at all," Diana retorted.

"His eyes never leave you," Jennifer continued, unchastened, "and his face, on two separate occasions, actually became animated as he discussed his most recent successes on the Exchange."

"The man is a money-grubbing peon," Jorge Morales muttered as he tore apart a loaf of bread. "The gall of the English! If I were not a member of the royal court of Spain I would remove his sneer, I would run this man through with my rapier like *that*!"

"I have never observed this blood-thirsty side of your

nature before, Jorge!" Geoffrey marvelled. "You've started tingles going up and down my spine."

"For my part, I am appalled by Diana's behavior," Lady Hildegarde intoned.

As Hildegarde was frequently appalled by her behavior Diana was not surprised by this pronouncement. Nevertheless, she felt compelled to ask the reason behind it.

"You see Lady Sinclair in the morning and her brother in the afternoon and to neither do you indicate that you have no desire for the latter's company," Hildegarde replied. "Worse still, you make no attempt to discourage what is obviously a courtship on Mr. Garfield's part."

"I have done *everything* to discourage Mr. Garfield!" Diana protested in righteous indignation. "I show him no warmth, no affection, no partiality. I avoid all personal conversation and, in fact, am boringly civil during his calls."

"But Diana, that is just the sort of behavior Mr. Garfield seeks in a young woman," Jennifer pointed out with a grin.

"To be fair," Geoffrey volunteered, "I heard Diana refuse Mr. Garfield's invitation to take part in a hunting party he is planning. And she resolutely refused to grant him more than one dance at Mrs. Bartlett's ball next week."

"Nevertheless," Hildegarde said, "Diana has steadfastly refused to enlist Lady Sinclair's aid in turning aside Mr. Garfield's attentions."

"I am perfectly capable of fighting my own battles, Hildy," Diana retorted, viciously slicing into her mutton. "I have given the heave-ho to more suitors than I care to remember. I do not need Lady Sinclair's intervention."

"That is what has amazed me," Jorge said. "Often I have seen Diana dismiss even the most boorish of louts with but a single word or look. But this she will not do with Mr. Garfield."

Geoffrey said in a stage whisper, "There are extenuating

circumstances."

"If you are speaking of Joanna Sinclair then you have it exactly," Diana said heatedly. "I have no wish to lose her friendship by cutting her brother."

"Diana, Lady Sinclair understands her brother's character all too well," Hildegarde said. "She will not be offended at your turning Mr. Garfield off. Indeed, I believe that she secretly yearns to see him properly set down."

"There is also Mr. Garfield's position to consider," Diana countered. "To offend him is to earn his enmity and to cause a great deal of succeeding trouble for myself in the neighborhood."

'You need not antagonize the wretched fellow,' Hildegarde replied. "Simply behave in your usual outrageous fashion when in his company and he will quickly develop a disgust of you and depart of his own accord."

"You are the one who advised me not to behave outrageously while in Hereforshire," Diana pointed out in exasperation.

"Our hostess is being deliberately obtuse," Hildegarde announced. "I suggest that we ignore her until she has recovered some of her quicker wits."

"Since you seem determined to have the fellow," Geoffrey offered, "I think it only fair that you tell him of your intemperate romance with the glorious Gwenyth McFadden."

"I am *not* going to have Hugo Garfield," Diana shouted, "and Gwen is none of his damned business!"

"Poor dear," Jennifer sighed, "she just can't make up her mind whether to have or dismiss Mr. Garfield. Try some more zucchini, Diana. It should settle you down in no time at all."

Neither the zucchini nor her friends' solicitous attentions were efficacious in settling Diana on anything save the resolve to have her revenge on guests who were made so merry at her current misery.

And still Hugo Garfield called upon her.

He began to discuss his family with Diana, including its lamentable lack of a title which he put down to poor timing. The Garfields apparently had had a knack for choosing the wrong side in a royal struggle, or for offending their king just as a preferment was to be conferred. This appalling state of affairs Mr. Garfield was firmly determined to correct in his lifetime. Diana understood this declaration all too well.

He asked for a tour of her gardens and insisted on taking her arm. He asked to see her library and brought her his own copy of Milton's *Paradise Lost* to read at her leisure. Mr. Garfield's speech, too, altered. He began to compliment Diana at every opportunity: on her household, her economy, her gardens, her wardrobe, her eyes, her hair. He spoke with some warmth about her fingers and wondered aloud that she had not yet a wedding band to grace her left hand.

Having grown desperate, Diana took to avoiding Waverly Manor altogether in the afternoons so that when Mr. Garfield called she was regrettably "out." After the second day of this stratagem, however, Diana was forcibly reminded of a frying pan and a fire.

Mr. Garfield called in the morning.

The people of Waverly Manor had gathered on the back terrace with the completion of their morning's activities; Molly and Diana had cleaned themselves and now wore morning attire of the utmost propriety as they earnestly discussed the work they would undertake on the morrow; Joanna sat between Geoffrey and Jorge, both of whom, to her intense amusement, had entered a duel of flirtation to capture her company at lunch; Hildegarde and Jennifer were arguing over *Lysistrata*. None of them were prepared when Mrs. Pratt appeared in tandem with Mr. Garfield. Conversation came to an abrupt halt.

Jennifer, Geoffrey, and Jorge were entertained by his arrival; Hildegarde was intrigued; Molly was frightened;

Joanna was momentarily discomposed; Diana, in true English tradition, was determined to muddle through . . . somehow.

"Mr. Garfield, how good of you to call," she murmured. "You know everyone, I believe?"

Hugo bowed over her hand. "I confess," he said, "that I am surprised to find my sister and my niece here as well. Joanna, I thought you were out for your morning drive with Molly."

"We undertook the exercise and then called upon Lady March before returning to Pembroke," Joanna calmly replied. "We occasionally stop here. Molly is particularly fond of Lady March's dogs."

"They're wonderful, Uncle Hugo!" Molly chimed in, hoping to add a breath of realism to the tale.

"That will do, Molly," Mr. Garfield said reprovingly, for he did not approve of children speaking when in adult company.

"Will you join us in a glass of lemonade, Mr. Garfield?" Diana inquired.

"Yes, thank you," Mr. Garfield replied as he took a seat beside the golden Jorge Morales.

Conversation seemed hopelessly stalled, Diana's guests eager to see what Diana would do next. For his part, as Hugo considered the matter, he was glad to find so large a company. In particular, he was glad to find Joanna at Waverly Manor. A friendship between his sister and Diana March was all to his advantage. A fondness for Joanna was but one more means of inclining Lady March in his favor. Unperturbed by the silence, Hugo sipped his lemonade.

He began a stilted conversation concerning the many uses that a well-trained dog might be put to. Despite the silence that greeted these remarks Hugo seemed quite happy and determined to stay right where he was and so, with a resigned sigh, Diana handed Hugo the plate of oatmeal cookies and agreed that yes, some dogs made excellent companions.

CHAPTER 11

The Sinclair barouche had scarcely pulled to a stop before Molly burst through its door and began her morning run around Waverly Manor, calling a breathless greeting to Diana who had just emerged from around the side of the house.

"That child is bristling with energy," Diana commented as Joanna, carrying a case, stepped from the barouche to join her on the front lawn.

Joanna replied with a wry smile, "She has only been gardening and running for a fortnight and already she has exhausted me."

"You have opened Pandora's box, Lady Sinclair."

"I begin to know it."

"What are you carrying?" Diana asked as they began to stroll to the back of Waverly Manor.

"Several sketchpads, charcoal, and my pencils. I can resist no longer. I am going to at least draw Molly gardening, even if I am prohibited from painting her."

The two women entered the back gardens and Joanna took up her habitual position on the shaded marble bench, making only one comment regarding the astounding lack of her brother's presence, before permitting Diana to rejoin Bert in the tulip bed.

As Joanna slowly drew out her sketchpad and a stick of charcoal her eyes lazily scanned Diana in her hopelessly unfashionable gardening togs, her blonde hair a thick plait down her back. What would Hugo say if he could see Diana as she was now, on her knees carefully tending a patch of red tulips? Diana made some remark to Bert which Joanna could not hear, and he made his reply. Diana stopped her work and sat back on her heels as she looked up at the ancient gardener, attending every word he said, her face open and rapt. There was such peace and honest beauty there, and a too transient joy that made Joanna's heart begin to pound with a longing to keep that joy in Diana's face forever.

"Someday," she quietly vowed, "I shall paint you as well."

Molly emerged from around the side of the house just as Mrs. Pratt stepped out onto the back terrace, Molly's gardening smock draped over one arm and a glass of lemonade in her hand.

"You are getting faster, Miss Sinclair," the housekeeper noted with obvious approval as she helped Molly into her smock.

"I only stopped three times today," Molly panted.

"You shall win your wager with Lady March, I am

convinced of it. Remember to drink your lemonade slowly now," the housekeeper cautioned before returning to her duties within the Manor.

Molly walked towards Diana and Bert, careful not to spill her lemonade and to catch her breath without being discovered. She greeted her mother without really seeing her and then joined Diana and Bert in the tulips, listening worshipfully to the instructions of the crusty old gardener.

Three quarters of an hour later Diana suddenly peered up at the sun, cried "Oh good God, Hildy will hang me!" and dashed to the house.

"What on earth?" Joanna wondered aloud.

"Hildy has threatened Diana with desertion if she is forced to gaze upon her gardening wardrobe one more morning." Jennifer Hunt-Stevens grinned down at her. "Good day to you, Lady Sinclair. I'm off for my morning constitutional."

"Has Lady Dennison such power over Lady March that she can pull our hostess out of her eccentric costumes?" Joanna smiled up at the dark-haired young woman.

"Heavens, yes. Diana adores Hildegarde. She'd sink into a decline if Hildy really got angry with her. Diana is amazingly headstrong for her five and twenty years, I know, but even so Hildy can still cow her."

"I would never have thought it possible."

"The irrepressible Diana March, eh?" Jennifer smiled. "You would be surprised at the shadows in our Diana, Lady Sinclair. Well, I'm off to commune with nature."

Joanna stared after the young woman as she strode towards the woods at an unfeminine gait. What on earth had she meant by her cryptic remark? Impatience nagged Joanna. She was left perpetually in the dark about Diana's past, and present. With a dissatisfied sigh Joanna returned to her sketchpad.

Diana emerged from the house ten minutes later dressed

in a red and white striped dress, her honey blonde hair tumbling in waves on her shoulders and down her back, held from her face by a red ribbon tied near the top of her head. "Hullo," she said cheerily. "How is it going?"

"Pretty well," Joanna conceded. "I'm just doing a variety of preliminary sketches to see which viewpoint I want to use."

"Mind if I spy?"

Joanna smiled. "Not at all."

Diana stood behind Joanna and peered over her shoulder without a word while Joanna continued to draw. After another quarter hour's work Joanna declared herself satisfied with her morning's labors, placed her charcoal back in the case, and began to wipe off her smudged fingers with a rag she kept for just that purpose. Diana, meanwhile, had picked up the sketchpad Joanna had set aside and was slowly leafing through the five sketches Joanna had done. Caught by the intensity of Diana's expression, Joanna stopped and watched her, waiting. Diana closed the sketchpad and stared at Joanna.

"Well?" Joanna said a trifle uneasily, although she tried to maintain a self-assured facade.

"These are brilliant," Diana breathed. "Brilliant!"

"Oh come now," Joanna scoffed in relief, "I know that I have some skill but. . . ."

"Joanna," Diana growled.

". . . you musn't let the rules of civility cloud your judgment. These are only rough drawings after all—"

"Joanna, will you stop all that twaddle!" Diana said, her ferocity astonishing Joanna. "I have studied the masters, the mediocre, the talented obscure, the new geniuses. I can't draw a straight line to save my life, but I *know* art and I tell you these are brilliant! My God. The power and the beauty that you achieved in just one hour with charcoal and paper . . . I am staggered." There was a pause as Diana looked wonderingly at the sketchpad. Then she exploded, "Why didn't you *tell* me you were this good?"

Joanna could only stare at her.

"Diana, what are you going on about?" Lady Dennison advanced on them, upright and invincible beneath the morning sun. "You sound like a fishwife in a summer squall."

Diana thrust the sketchpad at the older woman. "Look at these," was all that she could say and so finally Hildegarde complied.

"My word," she murmured.

"And she says she has some skill," Diana said. "*Some* skill!"

"My dear Lady Sinclair, these are magnificent," Lady Dennison said. "You have a great deal of talent with a sense of style and line presented with an originality few can match."

"She wouldn't believe me," Diana said wearily as she sank down upon the marble bench Joanna had vacated. "She would not believe me."

"I daresay Lady Sinclair is a modest young woman and because she has been surrounded by country boors who have no appreciation of truly fine art she has had no means of accurately judging her own work. My dear," Lady Dennison said to Joanna, "you should be exhibiting."

"She said she painted a little," Diana said. "I assumed a few bad watercolors, perhaps an abysmal landscape or two. The noble young widow dabbling in paints."

Chuckling, Hildegarde drew Joanna away from the bench. "You have shaken Diana, my dear, as no one else has done these last two years," she declared. "Diana has a passion for art and she is, as you have no doubt observed, a very passionate young woman. A discovery such as this is a little difficult to comprehend and wholly unnerving and has momentarily upset her equilibrium. It is rather like some cynical athiest suddenly coming upon a burning bush."

"Am I really that good?" Joanna asked in wonder.

"If I have to break into your home and steal all your paintings myself I shall see that you have an exhibition," Lady Dennison declared. "Now finish putting your things away and cleaning yourself up and I will go see if I can bring Diana down off her cloud." She went to the bench where Diana was sitting and slipped a comforting arm around her.

"I'm being very silly, I know," Diana confessed before Hildegarde could utter a word. "It is just that this has never happened to me before. Undiscovered genius . . . and I've discovered her!"

"Let the trumpets sound!"

"She must think me the greatest ninny," Diana moaned.

"Nonsense," Hildegarde said. "She was a little taken aback, perhaps, by your effusiveness and candor. She will recover. Go over now and demonstrate that you can converse in a normal, rational manner."

Diana obediently gained her feet and ventured somewhat timidly towards Joanna, who had just finished fastening the lock on her case.

"Um," Diana said, clearing her throat, "I would like to apologize for . . . shouting at you and . . . all that."

Joanna smiled. "No apology is necessary."

"It is just that you gave me such a turn!"

"The one and only time that I have been able to do so during the entire course of our acquaintance. This is an historic moment indeed," Joanna declared.

"You've every right to laugh at me, Lady Sinclair. I am ridiculous."

Joanna laughed. "Only on occasion, and I will not permit you to revert to such stuffy propriety. You called me Joanna in your recent fevered state of mind and I much prefer that to Lady Sinclair this and Lady Sinclair that. You have slipped and must pay the piper."

"Very well," Diana said with a blushing grin. "But if you call me Lady March one more time I shall bloody well scream! I am Diana."

"How do you do, Diana?" Joanna said, giving her hostess a hearty handshake.

Diana chuckled. "Very well, thank you, Joanna. Have you any of your work at Pembroke?"

"My paintings? Only a few small pieces that can easily be carried in our valises."

"I would deem it a great favor if I could see them sometime," Diana said with quiet sincerity. "You have whetted my appetite and I must be satisfied."

"Done." Joanna laughed again. "You are wreaking havoc with my vanity, Diana."

"It can be no worse than what you have done to my nerves, Joanna."

"I have written my brother-in-law of all my adventures at Waverly Manor, but none will amaze him more than this day. To receive such acclaim from a few sketches. . . . I will write him as soon as I return to Pembroke. And tomorrow I promise to bring you a few tidbits from my collection and thus enjoy your fullsome praise for at least one more day."

True to her word, on the following morning Joanna brought her three paintings, each no taller than six inches. After their separate morning's labors had been completed Joanna called Diana to her side on the bench and then drew out her paintings.

Diana stared unabashedly. The first was of a tudor house, fronted by a thick green lawn, flowers and shrubs growing in profusion at the base of the house. Morning sunlight streamed onto the dwelling, making it appear magical, a fairy cottage.

"What is this?" Diana asked.

"Hetchley Place," Joanna replied, "my residence in Kent. I keep it with me to remind myself in the more trying moments of my life that I do have a place of sanctuary."

"Your use of light and color is staggering."

Flustered, Joanna handed her the second painting. Diana gazed at a young man with light brown hair and grey eyes, round spectacles perched on his long, narrow nose. His face was a little thin, his cheeks pale. Lacking robustness, he had instead a gentleness and grace that Joanna's deft brush had somehow captured even on so small a canvas.

"My husband, Colin."

Diana stared at the painting. This man had won her hand? He did not seem at all the sort the Garfields would approve. He lacked authority, power.

"When I first came out I was beseiged by fortunehunters and the most abysmal poets who wrote the most hideous odes to my beauty," Joanna replied to Diana's bemused expression. "Colin, however, was blessedly blind as a bat without his glasses, which were broken during the first month of our acquaintance. When he finally did get them repaired he refused to believe that I was the same Joanna Garfield who had danced with him every night for a month at Almacks, and the Palmerstons, and the Hornbys. . . . He had no idea if I was rich or poor, wrote me not one poem, and actually listened to me when I spoke. I got him to marry me three months after we met."

"How very wise of you," Diana murmured, studying the picture once again. Yes, she could understand the marriage now. Joanna, at eighteen, had fled Pembroke with its gargoyles and autocratic father and boorish brother into the gentle arms of a man who loved her as she was and saw no need to change her. "Your ability to create such honest humanity on canvas is amazing," Diana said softly. "I feel as if I had known Lord Sinclair all of my life simply by looking at his portrait."

"Do you really think so?" Joanna asked eagerly. "That is what I strive for. To present the soul of my subject, not its facade."

"You succeed beautifully," Diana assured her. "Did you love your husband?"

"I was very fond of Colin." Joanna smiled. "And he gave me Molly."

"But you did not marry Lord Sinclair in the throes of a Grand Passion?"

"I shall tell you a secret. I have never been in the throes of a Grand Passion. I have read about them, of course. But the men described in the novels in the circulating library do not seem to have crossed my path. Even if they had I doubt if I would succumb as their literary female counterparts always do with such decorous glee."

"Heresy!" Diana chuckled.

"It is very awful of me, I know," Joanna said with a grin, drawing out her final painting.

Four-year-old Molly sat cradled in her father's arms as he read her a story from the large book propped before him. Neither father nor daughter seemed aware of the artist. Molly gazed intently at the book while Lord Sinclair looked tenderly down upon his daughter's pale face.

"Lovely," Diana breathed.

"I finished that just two months before Colin died of pneumonia. Every time I look at it I think myself fortunate for having insisted they pose for me."

"How I wish we had had an artist in the family. I should have liked to have their portraits around me," Diana said softly, but then seemed to recollect herself and continued with her usual bluffness, "But none of us had any skill with a brush and none could be persuaded to stay in one place long enough to be captured on canvas. We Marches must always be doing, you see."

Joanna smiled. "So I had gathered."

"You must go to the Caribbean!" Diana announced.

"I beg your pardon?"

"It is an absolute necessity," Diana insisted. "The colors there are staggering, and the light, and the water . . . . Oh, you must go! Think of what you could do with the sensual caress of sea upon sandy beach. No artist yet has been able to bring the Caribbean fully to life on canvas. But you could do it, Joanna, I am convinced of it. Your work there would be magnificent. With the paintings you've got hidden away in Kent, and the work you could do in the Caribbean, you would set the art world on its ear!"

"But I don't want to set the art world on its ear," Joanna protested.

"Of course you do."

"Well . . . maybe I would enjoy a little fame," Joanna conceded with a smile.

That smile played again upon her lips late that night as Joanna slid beneath the covers of her bed and eased her head onto her pillow. The Caribbean. How she had longed to travel as a girl, to see the world as her brother had, and to appreciate it as he had not. To paint the sensual play of sea upon sand. To brave all and dip her toes into the warm waters of the Caribbean. Perhaps even to have Diana teach her how to swim. . . .

Joanna dreamt of a sky without end, a blue canopy above a green sea that licked and teased at a white sandy beach. She arched beneath the heat of the sun and walked slowly into the warm water, feeling it permeate every hidden crevice of her body. She sighed happily as the waves pulled her down and down until she was entirely submerged in a world without weight or form.

Joanna stroked forward lazily, her hair streaming behind her as she relished the easy movement of her body clothed only in the salty wetness of this sea. All thought had left her, only sensation remained as she came upon a mass of pale green tendrils undulating in the gentle current. The seaweed called to her and she glided towards it. Her arms brushed a silken tendril of kelp and she shivered with the pleasure it gave.

Wanting more, needing more, she let herself be pulled deep within the bed. Satin tendrils caressed her body, teased her, lured her deeper into this dark forest. Joanna swam on and on, held by the seaweed, loved by it, her body warmed by its touch, and then inflamed. The tendrils slithered over every inch of her naked body, finding secret places of heat, her body caressed by a hundred different salty fingers; they lapped at her, exploring every opening until within this wet world Joanna burned and shuddered from a fire she had never known.

On and on it went, her heart pounding, her breath coming in gasps as she arched into this sea forest, her body hungering. Her arms reached out, hoping to clutch a form, a weight to her breast; but there was nothing save this mad trembling and need that drove through her until at last she was crying out again and again into this ocean, her body suddenly rigid as arms enfolded her and a head rested itself upon her breast, legs entwining themselves in hers as Joanna slowly began to drift with the tide once more.

"At last," Diana's lips murmured against the pulse of her heart.

CHAPTER 12

"I see that you have escaped Hugo's clutches at last."

"Joanna, would you be very upset if I informed you that I do not enjoy your brother's attentions?"

"Diana, I would be amazed if you did."

The two women had come together before a potted palm lurking in the corner of the Bartlett's ballroom, the roar of some two hundred guests swirling around them as they caught their respective breaths from the recent vigorous exercise each had endured upon the dance floor.

"There you are, Joanna!" a masculine voice declared on

their left. "I've been searching for you this last half hour."

The women turned to behold a gentleman of medium height, his hair a light brown, his eyes grey, his nose long and narrow.

"Richard!" Joanna gasped. "Richard, how on earth did you get here?"

"I've been traveling around on business and, being a dutiful sort, I stopped off at Pembroke to pay my respects. That new butler of yours said you were here. Mrs. Bartlett, kind soul that she is, very graciously let me enter without an invitation. By all the stars and planets, Joanna," the gentleman exclaimed as he kissed her on both cheeks, "you look smashing! I've never seen you in such beauty."

"Richard, please. . . ." Joanna said with a blush.

"Good heavens! Lady March is that you?" the gentleman cried upon discovering Diana. "Fancy meeting you in Mrs. Bartlett's ballroom of all places, and after so many years."

"It is odd, I grant you, but so my life goes. How are you, Mr. Danby?" Diana said with a smile that hid a vast confusion.

"Marvelous, thank you. But I must tell you that I haven't been Danby for years. It's Sinclair now. Lord Sinclair."

The color fled Diana's cheeks as she stared at the gentleman. Of course! He was more muscled than his brother, in fact he fairly bristled with masculine health, but the resemblence was all too apparent. Another thought struck Diana and for a moment she actually felt faint.

"You're. . . . You mean. . . . Oh you can't be . . . " she said, looking helplessly between Joanna and Lord Sinclair.

"Diana, are you all right?" Joanna asked anxiously.

"I'm fine," Diana lied.

"But this is astounding! How do you come to know my brother-in-law?"

"We met five years ago," Lord Sinclair replied in Diana's

stead, "in Rome through a mutual friend: Geoffrey Hunt-Stevens."

"What? Do you know Colonel Hunt-Stevens as well?"

"Intimately," Lord Sinclair replied.

Diana felt herself sway and quickly placed her hand on the marble wall for support.

"Is he here tonight?" Lord Sinclair asked.

"But of course. Mrs. Bartlett insisted." Joanna laughed. "Wherever you see a large group of adoring females you will be bound to find the Colonel at its center."

"I shall search him out then," Lord Sinclair declared. "Joanna, I shall see you later. Lady Diana, it was a pleasure meeting you again."

"Isn't that amazing," Joanna said as her brother-in-law moved away, "that Richard should know both you and the Colonel? I wonder why he never mentioned it in his letters?"

"Is there any champagne close at hand?" Diana said weakly.

Lord Sinclair, meanwhile, had taken his sister-in-law's advice and soon discovered a bevy of languishing females around the stunning figure of Geoffrey Hunt-Stevens, the light from the ballroom's large chandelier glinting with equal brilliancy on his black boots and his intricately curled black hair. While Geoffrey had always enjoyed an admiring throng, he did not enjoy a female throng, and his frustration was revealed in the abrupt way he tossed down a glass of wine and in the boredom that clouded his brown eyes.

Had he not just handed his empty goblet to a passing footman, the Bartlett's ballroom would have been startled by the sudden shattering of glass upon the highly polished floor as the Colonel's brown eyes met the grey eyes of Lord Sinclair. Geoffrey paled as Diana had paled, he even swayed a moment before a woman's particularly scratchy laugh returned him partially to his senses. What excuse he made he cared not as he broke free from his admirers and stumbled to a halt before Lord Sinclair.

"Hello Geoff," Lord Sinclair said easily, despite the pounding of his heart.

"Richard. . . . My God, what are you doing here?" Geoffrey managed to say.

"Looking for you, of course. Joanna said I might find you here."

"Joanna?"

"Joanna Sinclair. My sister-in-law."

Geoffrey stared at Lord Sinclair and then began to laugh, a note of hysteria coloring the edges. "Sister-in-law," he said, shaking his head. "It is too perfect. Too utterly. . . ."

Lord Sinclair smiled. "Yes, I thought so."

A trembling suddenly seized Geoffrey. "Oh God, Richard," he whispered, his hand stopping before it reached Lord Sinclair's cheek, "why have you come?"

"We can hardly discuss this in the middle of Mrs. Bartlett's ballroom," Lord Sinclair pointed out. "Come, let us go outside. You look in need of some fresh air."

Still stunned, Geoffrey allowed himself with unusual docility to be led out onto the Bartlett's back terrace, and from there into the carefully planned abandon of the Bartlett's garden. The cool night air finally returned Geoffrey to his senses. He pulled Lord Sinclair to a stop near a thicket of blackberry bushes and, with more force in his voice, demanded once again to know why Richard Sinclair had come. Richard replied with a soft kiss upon his lips that sent the blood surging into Geoffrey's ears.

"I came because I can no longer live without you," Richard stated calmly.

"Don't be trite, Richard, it is too boring for words," Geoffrey said harshly as he again struggled to recover his equilibrium.

"True emotion is never trite," Richard countered with a smile. "I love you, Geoff. I've loved you for five years. I haven't stopped wanting you in all that time. And you still want me, don't you? Don't you?" Richard demanded, leaning against Geoffrey who, despite his best intentions, found his arms going around his tormentor and pulling him close. "Don't you?" Richard whispered before their mouths met with a hunger that left them both shaken.

"No!" Geoffrey seethed, pushing Sinclair away. "Damn it, Richard, why are you doing this?" He drew a ragged breath. "It's no good. It can't work. Every time we've come together we've ended agreeing it's impossible between us."

"No, *you* said it was impossible and I didn't want to hold you against your will. I thought you'd learn to come to me of your own accord. I'm tired of waiting, Geoff. I won't play the patient Griselda any longer. We belong together and I am going to convince you of it."

"Give it up, can't you?" Geoffrey raged, his hands clenching Richard's shoulders. "You know I can't be faithful. I tried with you and failed miserably. My heart just isn't large enough. It has no room for fidelity."

"It *is* large enough, Geoff," Richard softly replied, his eyes capturing Geoffrey's. "It has held my love safely all these years. You do not trust your own ability to remain faithful, but even more, you fear that *I* will not be able to love you over a lifetime. You could not be more wrong. Whatever it takes, *mon amour,* I shall convince you of the truth and longevity of my regard."

"Damn it, Richard, I love someone else!"

"Who? Jorge Morales? Don't make me laugh. He is *papier mache.*"

"Your vanity amazes me. Do you think I can love no one but you?"

"You have it exactly. How clever of you to take my meaning so quickly. I warn you Geoff, I am tired of pursuing you across two continents. I will chase you no longer. Now you will come to me. I want you on your knee before me within the week declaring your undying love. You may even present me with a bouquet of violets," Richard informed his stunned companion before strolling back towards the Bartlett's ballroom.

As Richard re-entered the ballroom and liberated a glass of wine from a passing footman, Jennifer inquired of Diana, "I say, isn't that Richard Danby?"

"Sinclair. He is Richard Sinclair now. He inherited his brother's title. He is Joanna's brother-in-law," Diana replied in a strained monotone. Jennifer went off into a peal of laughter. Diana regarded her with little love. "You are going to be a great lot of help, I can just tell," she said bitterly.

"*Au contraire,* Diana. I shall sit very demurely and watch the world come crashing down upon our ears. Oh, if only Peter were here. How he would laugh!"

"You are doing very well by yourself," Diana said with some disgust. "Do give over, Jen. We're in the devil of a fix."

"Nonsense, Diana! Where is your sense of fun? This little affair will rock Heddington to its toes. We shall have a marvelous time."

"Jennifer, this is England," Diana said sternly. "This is *rustic* England. Rustic Englishmen do not take kindly to the cavorting of two men in the throes of a Grand Passion."

Jennifer sighed. "You're right, I suppose. It seems we will all have to take turns standing guard over them to ensure that they at least behave properly in public. . . . Joanna's brother-in-law," she gurgled with renewed mischief, "it is too delicious, Diana. How I should love to see her face when she discovers the true state of Richard's regard for Geoff!"

Diana shuddered. "The saints preserve us all."

"Nonsense! She will handle it beautifully, I'm convinced of it. And that would give you the perfect opportunity to tell her about Gwen."

"I am not going to tell Joanna about Gwen," Diana said in amazement. "I am never even going to mention Gwen to her. There is no reason—"

"Of course there is," Jennifer retorted. "To get her used to thinking of you in that way and thus encourage her own feelings for you to flower. Besides, it is just not cricket to hide one lover from another."

"Joanna is *not* my lover, she will never *be* my lover, and if you do not stop these absurd innuendos I shall have to throw you out of Waverly Manor, burn all of your letters, and order the servants never to mention your name in my presence again!"

Jennifer shrugged. "Have it as you will. I still say you're missing out on a cracking-good opportunity, though."

* * *

Thoroughly inebriated, swaying slightly on his feet, and intent upon seduction, Lord Franklin Humphrey scanned the ballroom and then gladdened Mrs. Bartlett's heart by selecting her third daughter, sixteen-year-old Prudence, as his dancing partner. Prudence, who perfectly understood the makings of a good catch, permitted Lord Humphrey to clasp her much too firmly, allowed him to praise her figure with too much familiarity; and then agreed to partaking of a breath of fresh air with him in the back gardens.

Their very separate hopes were quickly dashed, however, by Mrs. Harriet Hornby, who successfully blocked their exit at the garden doors and proceeded to rake them both over the coals with such violence of emotion that poor Prudence began to blush and stammer and beg Mrs. Hornby's pardon, and swear that she had meant no harm, only the ballroom was so very stuffy and Lord Humphrey had said. . . .

Lord Franklin Humphrey, for his part, had ceased to hear Mrs. Hornby. She had nipped this current affair in the bud, but there were other possibilities. . . . He once again scanned the ballroom and this time a face arrested his attention, the face of a woman in her fifties bearing no real beauty, but a good deal of strength. He recognized that face, but he could not recall where he had seen it, and this, in his soused state, so irritated Lord Franklin that he interrupted Mrs. Hornby in mid-bombast to ask the identity of the silver-haired grande-dame. Startled, Mrs. Hornby replied that it was Lady Hildegarde Dennison.

"Dennison, Dennison," Lord Humphrey muttered. "Why do I know that name? Where have I seen that face? . . . Of course!" he suddenly cried. "Hildegarde Dennison the Ladykiller. Old Waldo Dennison's Turkish divorcee!"

To Prudence these cryptic phrases meant nothing, but Mrs. Hornby stared at Lord Humphrey with growing horror. She gasped, "Can it be? Are you certain?"

"Of course I'm certain," Lord Franklin said impatiently. "I saw her myself driving openly through Constantinople with her female paramour. The whole town talked of nothing else."

Recollecting her recently acquired duties as guardian, Mrs. Hornby ordered Lord Humphrey home to his bed to sleep off his obvious inebriation before she pulled Prudence back across the ballroom floor, ordering her not to repeat a word of what she had heard.

"But what did I hear?" the poor girl cried, utterly bewildered. Mrs. Hornby, however, did not deign to make a reply. She dragged Prudence to her mother's side, informed Mrs. Bartlett of the necessity of instructing her daughters in the skill of detecting the Lecherous Male, and then went in search of Lady Diana March.

Trapping her prey in the middle of the ballroom, she demanded without preamble to be told of Lady Dennison's lineage and husband.

Alarm bells clanging in her head, Diana was nonetheless

forced to admit that Lady Dennison's husband had been the English Ambassador to Turkey until his death six years earlier.

"How could you? How *could* you bring that . . . that *woman* into polite society?" Mrs. Hornby cried with the utmost horror.

"She is my friend."

"She is an abomination! To leave her husband for the arms of a French *woman*. To actually set up housekeeping with her in the very city where her husband represented the King and England!"

The stridency of Mrs. Hornby's voice drew a small circle of onlookers around them, including Mr. Ian Chesterfield. "Who's this you're talking of?" he asked amiably and, when informed by Mrs. Hornby, he clapped a hand to his forehead. "But of course!" he said. "The source of one of Europe's greatest scandals! Living right under our noses and we didn't even know it! You remember, Tom," he said to Lord Carroll at his side, "Ambassador's wife leaves husband for another woman. French as I recall. What was her name?"

"Celeste Marie-Therese Sauvatin," Diana calmly supplied.

"Yes, that's it!" Mr. Chesterfield cried happily. "The daughter of a first cousin to the King of France. Oh this is marvelous!"

"Surely, Lady March, you cannot have known of this unclean alliance?" Lord Carroll intoned.

"I could not help but know," Diana replied steadily. "Hildegarde and Celeste sought sanctuary in my parents' home on the day Hildegarde left her husband."

"You speak with pride of such atrocious behavior," Mrs. Hornby stated. "How can you condone such actions? How can you harbor that wretched creature?"

"As I said, Lady Dennison is my friend," Diana said coldly. "She is also a very powerful and highly respected member of Viennese society. Her salons are considered quite *de rigeur.*"

"Are they, b'gad?" Mr. Chesterfield exclaimed, thoroughly entertained by this small drama.

"I shall see to it, Lady March, that all doors are closed to Lady Dennison," Mrs. Hornby declared. "And as long as you continue to defend so base a character you leave me no alternative but to do all that I can to bar you from Heddington society as well."

"A pox on your Heddington society, Mrs. Hornby," Diana snapped. "If it is filled with small minds and cold hearts such as yours I am well quit of it."

"You are ruined in Herefordshire, Madam," Lord Carroll intoned.

Diana laughed. "Sir, I have been ruined in every other country, why not Herefordshire?"

"You will not be so glib in a week's time, I think," Lord Carroll stated.

"Slander!" Mr. Chesterfield cried. "I daresay Lady March was born glib and will remain glib until the day she dies!"

"A champion!" Diana marvelled, laughing. "My God, a champion standing in the middle of Mrs. Bartlett's ballroom in the midst of Herefordshire in stately England upholding my fair honor. Whoever would have thought it?"

Mr. Chesterfield, far from being embarrassed by this speech, was charmed and immediately asked Diana for the next dance to which she readily agreed.

At the end of the Quadrille, at which Mr. Chesterfield was particularly adept, every one of Mrs. Bartlett's guests knew of the history of Lady Hildegarde Dennison, and each secretly rejoiced that Heddington should be so blessed with so delicious a scandal.

CHAPTER 13

Diana was immersed in a thin volume of Anne Bradstreet's poetry when Mrs. Pratt entered, announced Hugo Garfield's presence, and then withdrew from the parlor, allowing Hugo to enter before Diana could utter a protest.

Mr. Garfield was dressed with a formality unwarranted by a morning call—his coat dark blue, his white breeches unsullied by the merest speck of dust, his cravat intricately tied in the Mathematical, his dark brown hair carefully arranged, his fingernails gleaming. Diana's dismay increased with her survey of him, two things particularly distressing her: Mr. Garfield had found her alone; and he had, this morning, an air of decision about him that seemed to have to do with her. Diana wanted Hugo Garfield to make no decisions about her whatsoever.

"Good morning, Mr. Garfield. How good of you to call," Diana said politely as she set down her book and rose to greet him.

"The goodness is yours in receiving me, Lady March," Hugo replied as he took her hand and, to her horror, kissed it. "You are particularly lovely today," he continued, refusing to give up her hand as he gazed fervently into her eyes. "I like you in that shade of lavender. You should wear it more often."

"Thank you, sir," Diana replied as she succeeded at last in freeing her hand. "Won't you sit down? I'll ring for tea."

"Thank you, no. I've no desire for tea today."

"No?" Diana said with a worried frown.

"Nor can I sit. I cannot be still for my emotions are of too tempestuous a nature. Lady March . . . Diana," Hugo uttered in ringing tones, once again taking her hand in both of his, "how glad I am that I have found you alone at last. I have called on you every day this last fortnight. My attentions have been noted by all of Heddington. My feelings cannot be unknown to you."

"I . . . believe that I understand you very well, Mr. Garfield," Diana replied uneasily.

"How can you not when I have not the strength to hide my true sentiments from you?" Hugo said. "Your beauty and your grace have overset all reason until I seem not myself. You have undone me, my dearest Diana. I am no longer Hugo Garfield but your slave to do with as you like. I must say it, my heart will deny expression no longer. I love you with every fiber of my being. Say that you will make me the happiest of all mortal men. I beg you to marry me, Diana, as soon as it may be arranged."

Wondering how this innocent morning could bring such

unmitigated disaster, Diana attempted to reply to this fervent declaration. "I . . . am grateful for so kind a regard, sir, but fear I cannot grant what you ask," she said, freeing herself from his grasp with barely concealed relief.

"But you must! You shall!" Hugo insisted in the complacent voice of one used to having his own way. "I will not leave this house until I have won your hand and your heart."

"I am expecting more guests at any moment, I have no room to put you up as well." Diana sighed at his blank expression. "Mr. Garfield, you have known me scarcely three months! That is hardly time to know your true—"

"Three months or three years, I know that you are the woman I want as my wife," Hugo stoutly declared as he studied himself in the mirror above the mantle.

"Oh, I have no doubt of that, Mr. Garfield." Diana could not help but smile. "But you are not the man I want as my husband. Indeed, I want no husband at all. I enjoy my independence and have vowed never to marry, so I beg you give up this scheme and let us part on civil terms."

"Nay, madam, I'll not leave for I shall be the one to change so foolish a vow," Hugo declared with utter certainty.

"Mr. Garfield, do not force me to be blunt."

"You need a man to take care of you, Diana, and I am that man," Hugo replied.

"I need no man's care."

"But you are a woman and have a woman's need to rest safely in the harbor of her husband's arms."

"I am not some ship, sir, for you to command. I seek neither your protection nor your love. I desire not your regard. I do not and cannot care for you and therefore will not marry you," Diana said with an intensity that could not be misunderstood.

Mr. Garfield took a sudden turn around the room, a flush of anger rising in his cheeks as he came to a stop before Diana once again. "How is this possible?" he demanded. "You have given me every reason to believe that you welcomed my advances, and now you spurn me as you would some lowly laborer."

"I have treated you with the common civility of a neighbor, Mr. Garfield. You chose to misconstrue both my words and my actions in your blind pursuit of my fortune and my title!" Diana had grown quite as furious as her enraged suitor.

"How dare you think me a common mercenary!"

"I dare, sir. It is easily done. Your motives are all too common. I know my face to be plain. I know that my independence disgusts you; my manners offend you. My opinions oppose yours at every turn. The only thing that can attract so proper and avaricious a gentleman as yourself is thirty thousand pounds a year."

"That is quite enough, Lady March," Hugo seethed.

"No, Mr. Garfield, it is not!" Diana retorted, her fury holding full sway. "*My* heart will no longer deny expression. I call you mercernary for that is what you are. You have spun lies and flattery with equal abandon in an attempt to deceive me of your true motives, but you have failed miserably, sir. I have understood you all too well. You play the role of a lover admirably, Mr. Garfield, to someone uncaring of honesty and integrity in her life's partner. I suggest that you try your wiles on Caroline Humphrey. Perhaps she will be more receptive to your entreaties. They only disgust me."

Overcoming the desire to strangle these pointed words in Diana's slender throat, Mr. Garfield turned on his heel and stalked from the room and thence from Waverly Manor, leaving Diana to stare after him, her hands clenched, her breast heaving with rage.

For his part, Mr. Garfield jumped into his gig and with a vicious crack of his whip set his bay gelding off at a violent canter away from Waverly Manor and Lady Diana March. As his gig careened down the road his mind churned with the indignities he had suffered. Disgust her, did he? Mercenary, was he? It would give him great pleasure to wipe that superior expression from Diana March's homely face once and for all. "By God!" he growled between gritted teeth, "I shall have my revenge!"

He turned the gig into the lane that led to Pembroke Park, caring not that his horse was lathered from the sudden exertion and the terror his whip inspired. His mind whirled with every possible means of shaming Diana March publicly, to wound her as she had injured him. He heard not the many birds chattering in the elm trees on either side of the lane, the deep blue May sky made no impression upon him. He would have passed without a glance the curricle coming towards him had not a familiar voice called out, the second time quite sharply. Hugo recognized Tom Carroll, and reluctantly pulled his horse to a stop. He was in no mood for polite conversation, even with this, his oldest friend.

"Hugo, are you mad driving your horse like that? You'll kill the poor beast!" Lord Carroll declared, drawing beside him.

"What I do with my own cattle is none of your affair!"

"Now what has put you in such a high dudgeon?"

"It is none of your concern, Tom," Hugo replied, staring straight ahead.

"You've heard about Lady Dennison and Lady March, I suppose. It is a pity that your hopes should be dashed by so foul a tale, but at least you need not endure the humiliation of having a wife with so vile a connection, Hugo."

"What? What are you talking about, Tom?"

And so it was that Hugo Garfield was made cognizant of Mrs. Hornsby's staggering discovery at the Bartlett's Ball on the previous evening. He stared at Lord Carroll, scarcely able to comprehend the horrific scope and implications of the tale. He questioned his friend on every detail. Every word uttered that fateful night was repeated; and at last Hugo was convinced of the truth of the report.

"But this is monstrous!" he breathed. "To think that *I* should be the instrument of that woman's entrance into Heddington society, and to think that she, in turn, would introduce so foul a female into common acquaintance. Tom, this cannot continue. They must be removed at once from Heddington, from Herefordshire, from England if possible!"

"I agree wholeheartedly. But how is it to be done?"

Hugo gave the matter careful consideration. He had not dared hope that he would have his revenge so soon after being so grievously injured. "I shall break the sale of Waverly Manor," he announced.

"Don't be absurd, Hugo. It can't be done. You've no legal precedent for—"

"Acton shall find one. Why else do I pay him?"

"And if you cannot reverse the sale?" Lord Carroll demanded.

Hugo was silent for some moments. Then a smile played about his lips. "I am going to London, Tom."

"But why?"

Hugo's smile grew. "If Lady March and her family are as cosmopolitan as everyone claims then I will be most likely to get information of them in town."

"Yes, but what information are you seeking?"

"I'm not sure," Hugo replied slowly, his brown eyes glowing with a secret excitement. "But from what you have told me, it seems reasonable to believe that Lady March and her . . . friend have committed other deeds that they would not want published to the world. I shall find them out, Tom, and, if necessary, blackmail these women into removing themselves from Herefordshire and hopefully England itself! I shall ruin them, Tom." He brushed a speck of dust from his coat sleeve, squared his jaw, and looked across at his friend. "It is my duty to do so."

CHAPTER 14

"Hard at work, I see."

Diana looked up, squinting into the morning sunlight and Joanna Sinclair's smile. "As I've said, we Marches must always be doing," Diana replied as she returned to the rose bush she was transplanting, a little dazzled by the beauty of Joanna's smile on this spring morning.

"Why do you like gardening so?" Joanna settled herself on the lawn just to the left of Diana.

The question took Diana by surprise. "Well I . . . have an affinity for dirt, I suppose."

Joanna chuckled. "Why else?"

"I like creating life," Diana slowly replied as her fingers gently slid up to a tiny bud. "I like watching it grow, feeling it bloom in my hands."

Joanna stared at her hostess a moment, and in a flash of clarity understood that Diana was saying that she had met Death too often. But where? And how?

"Is Molly about?" Diana asked, resuming her work.

"She's on her morning run," Joanna replied, seeing and accepting the sudden wall. "Will you really give her a harem costume?"

Diana grinned. "If she wins."

"That is what worries me. I begin to believe that she *will* win."

"I can have a matching costume made for you if you like."

"Thank you, no."

"Faintheart," Diana chided.

Joanna smiled. "I'll not deny it."

There was a pause. Joanna decided to take up her habitual post at the marble bench and unpack her sketchcase. Then Diana cleared her throat.

"There is something that I must tell you," she said, turning slowly from the rose bush and looking across at Joanna. "Your brother called after you had left yesterday morning. He asked me to marry him. I refused. He took it very badly, I'm afraid."

"Yes, I'm sure that he did," Joanna said in amazement. "Hugo is not used to being denied what he wants. I did not know that he was in love with you."

"He is in love with my fortune and my title."

"Ah yes, that would explain it," Joanna calmly replied. "This might even explain why Hugo has taken it into his head to go to London."

"London?"

"Yes, he left early yesterday afternoon. Aunt Hampton

and I were surprised at the suddenness of the undertaking for Hugo had recently been consulting with Mr. Bartlett upon some new business venture and had shown no inclination for travel. Your confession explains much. Odd, I never thought of Hugo as a man unable to face the world after embarrassing himself. But then, I have never known Hugo to embarrass himself before this."

"How long will he be gone?"

"He did not say. Perhaps a fortnight. I really must express my gratitude. This is such a luxury, you know! A fortnight without Hugo!"

"Your cup runneth over?" Diana grinned.

"My cup, my saucer, my bowl. . . ."

They were interrupted as Molly breathlessly ran up to them in her gardening smock and demanded to know where she might find Bert. Directed to the thick bank of Sweet William on their right, Molly darted off to help her crusty idol.

Jennifer Hunt-Stevens strolled towards them from the nearby woods, a young man Joanna had never seen before holding Jennifer's hand securely in his own. Of medium height, he was possessed of a shock of dark red hair, freckles, and shining blue eyes that sparkled with particular intimacy whenever he looked into Jennifer's face, which was often.

"Peter! Jennifer! Over here!" Diana called out. "You must meet my newest boarder, Joanna," she said as the couple joined the two women. "Peter, darling, release poor Jen's hand for just a moment and say how do you do to Lady Joanna Sinclair. Joanna, this is Peter Elliot, second and most charming son to the Duke of Larkspur."

"Enchanted, Lady Sinclair," Mr. Elliot said with utmost sincerity as he raised Joanna's hand to his lips.

"As am I, sir," Joanna replied with a smile. "Have you newly arrived? I did not see you yesterday."

"I came with the dawn," Mr. Elliot replied grandly.

"And about time, too," Jennifer harrumphed. "I had been looking for you this last se'nnight, Peter."

"Sorry, Love." Peter grinned, tucking her arm back in his. "Family obligations and all that. A second son must not shirk even the lowliest of civilities where his parents are concerned."

"Oh bother," Jennifer retorted. "You've an uncle who's left you a tidy fortune. You're independent, Peter."

"Not until I am five and twenty and that is nearly a year away," her red-headed companion replied. "I must needs tread lightly, particularly after that set-to in October."

"Elliot!" Joanna gasped. "Of course! I thought your name was familiar. You cried off from a match to some German heiress. Over one hundred thousand pounds at stake and you cried off," she marvelled.

"There were extenuating circumstances," Jennifer said, looking up into Peter's sparkling eyes.

"So I see," Joanna murmured with a smile.

"The family doesn't know about Jenny yet," Peter said. "There's a good possibility they won't approve, you see. Jen hasn't got a royal ancestor to her name and her dowry is merely impressive. My parents have got it into their heads that I must marry a staggering fortune and unfortunately the Duke is powerful enough to block my inheritance should I announce an unsatisfactory sum as my bride. Jen and I may be in love, but we're not idiots. We like money. So we're waitin' 'em out. Once I inherit we'll post the banns, but until then it's all very hush-hush."

Joanna smiled. "I am the soul of discretion, I assure you."

"Knew so from the moment I clapped eyes on you," Peter said.

"And how does the second son of the powerful Duke of Larkspur come to know my all too eccentric neighbor?" Joanna inquired.

"Well, I was formally introduced to Diana four years ago in the Alexandrian municipal court. I was up on charges of drunk and disorderly conduct, assaulting an officer of the law, liberating a trader's camel, and soliciting the English Ambassador's wife for prostitution. I was guilty as sin, of course, but it was my Grand Tour, after all."

"And why was Lady Diana standing before the local magistrate?" Joanna demanded amid a gurgle of laughter.

'She was up on charges of drunk and disorderly conduct, assaulting an officer of the law, liberating a trader's camel, and soliciting the English Ambassador for prostitution."

"I was innocent as a newborn lamb," Diana assured Joanna.

"And I've got Cromwell's head on my bedpost for a souvenir," Peter retorted. "I bumped into Diana at a local cafe, French of all things," he explained to the highly amused Joanna. "We agreed to share a table when it became obvious that if left to our private resources we wouldn't get fed before midnight. We consumed a certain amount of surprisingly good wine and then went adventuring, having assured ourselves that we were, indeed, kindred spirits. We never discovered each other's names, however, until we were standing before that fat magistrate."

"In Alexandria one tends to forego the usual social introductions," Jennifer explained.

"The magistrate did not pardon us our youth, our innocence, or our playfulness, but he was softened by the two hundred pounds in my reticule," Diana said.

"My pockets were totally to let, you see," Peter said.

"I even had to pay for our dinner," Diana said, "and I've been feeding Peter ever since."

"You would wither and die if you could not constantly feed your friends," Jennifer stoutly declared, "and you know it, Diana."

"Our Diana adores playing the hostess," Peter explained.

"It fulfills all of her maternal yearnings."

"Ugh! Go away the both of you," Diana said with a grimace. "I will not have you disparage my character so early in the day."

Since their fondest wish was to be alone, Peter and Jennifer happily strolled off towards the meadows lying to the south of Waverly Manor.

"Maternal yearnings indeed," Diana grumbled as she began to dust off her trousers.

Joanna found it hard not to laugh. "I like your friends, Diana," she said impulsively. "They make me feel so very alive."

"I have been indebted to their peculiar talent on more than one occasion."

Joanna looked at Diana, but Diana was still attending to her trousers and so Joanna said nothing. Without a word they began to walk towards the Manor, Diana intending to change into attire more befitting an English gentlewoman, and Joanna to fetch her sketchcase from the marble bench. They were but halfway to the bench, however, when Joanna spied her brother-in-law and Geoffrey Hunt-Stevens emerge from the stables and walk towards a side entrance to the house. Their gestures, the bristling way they held themselves, indicated that a heated discussion was in progress.

"One of the benefits of Hugo's leaving just now," Joanna said, "is that I will not have to hear him complain about Richard's taking up lodging at Waverly rather than at Pembroke. Hugo doesn't like Richard, but his fear of unkind gossip overrules even that. Richard is a relation—he should be at Pembroke. Hugo is certain that Heddington gossips are saying they've had a row. What a bother it is. For myself, I am glad my brother-in-law was able to flee such unconvivial company. But it is a little odd, don't you think, that he should never mention the Colonel to me in all these years when they seem such particular friends," Joanna said, puzzlement crinkling her forehead.

"It is not so very odd. Some friendships seem never to come up in conversation. For example, we have known each other for well over three months and you have heard me rattle on and on about all of my impossible friends, but you never mention yours."

"That is because I have none," Joanna replied steadily.

Diana stared at her in surprise.

"Do not look at me so," Joanna protested. "It is not so very remarkable as you seem to think. I have no skill for ingratiating myself with those I admire. Being of a headstrong stamp I did not admire those people Father thought it appropriate that I know. When Colin was alive I entertained his friends, not mine. With his death and Molly's constant illnesses I have been unable to maintain those acquaintances that in general pleased me, and really I do not feel the loss. While you are very outgoing, I think my nature tends to be hermitic."

"I am sorry for you," Diana said quietly. There was something in her voice that made Joanna stare at her in turn. "Friendship, real friendship, is a very difficult article to acquire, but once you have it soundly in your possession it can carry you through those periods . . . when the world seems an Inferno. I think you are not a hermit, Joanna. I think you are a very sensible woman who is used to doing without."

Diana left her with those words and went quickly into the back of the house as Joanna gazed after her, seemingly rooted to the fragrant earth beneath her feet. She walked slowly on, her thoughts grappling with an image of Diana escaping Mr. Dante's hell.

Reaching the marble bench Joanna discovered not only her own sketchcase, but an additional case as well, lying beneath the bench. Puzzled, she drew the interloper out, placing it on the bench beside her own case. JGS was chiseled into the center of the lid. Curiosity getting the better of her, Joanna raised the top and stared at the myriad of colors. "Paint!" she breathed and then noticed a large assortment of brushes tucked into the side. "My God!"

"Marvelous, they've arrived I see," a brisk voice declared. Joanna spun around to discover Lady Hildegarde. "I'm glad to see they came so promptly. Diana has been pacing the floor these last few days. Impatience is one of her many faults."

"Diana bought these. . . ." Joanna asked, scarcely able to comprehend such a gift.

"Yes, of course. Who else?"

"But . . . but this is impossible! These paints are Italian. They must have cost a fortune."

"Diana has a fortune," Hildegarde pointed out. "She also has bought an easel and several canvases for you. I think she's put them in the Music Room for now."

"But this is insanity!" Joanna said with a shaky laugh. "Why would she do such a thing?"

"Diana wanted you to be able to paint Molly, or whatever else you take into your head to do."

"But I cannot accept so extravagant a gift," Joanna protested, mesmerized by the brilliant colors.

"Never refuse something you desire when it is given with a sincerity of thought and emotion," Hildegarde advised.

Joanna stared at the case once again. "How could she do such a thing?" she murmured.

Hildegarde smiled. "It is my understanding that Diana likes you."

Suddenly cognizant of the fact that she was standing in the company of a Notorious Woman, Joanna felt herself flush and tried to disguise it by bending down to close the lid on the paints. "I . . . did not see you yesterday. I thought you had left," she managed to say over her shoulder.

"Scurrying off, tail between my legs? That's not my way,

Lady Sinclair. I enjoy being at the center of a good scandal. It keeps the blood flowing. I spent yesterday morning attending to my correspondence. You've heard the rumors, I suppose.''

"How could I not?" Joanna replied, turning around. "There are hundreds of them flying about Heddington."

"Rest assured, Lady Sinclair, they are all true."

"I do not think that possible. You haven't tried to seduce Mrs. Hornby, have you?"

Lady Hildegarde erupted into a hoot of laughter. "Not that I recall," she replied.

Silence fell between them and Joanna found that she could look everywhere but into Hildegarde's eyes. There were so many questions she wanted to ask. Yesterday afternoon Tom Carroll had related the History of Hildegarde Dennison with such horror and in so hushed a voice that Joanna had felt the full import of what he had told her: Lady Dennison was an outcast of society and all who associated with her were tainted.

"Lady Sinclair, I think perhaps you would be more comfortable if I left you to your paints and sketchpad," Hildegarde said in a not unkind voice.

"Oh no, please!" Joanna cried, catching Hildegarde's arm. "Lady Dennison, you must forgive my rudeness. Having entered Lady Diana's world these last few months I find the ground swept quite out from under me. Nowadays I know not what to do or say and so muddle through as best I can. I have heard much of you these last two days, Lady Dennison, and I am amazed for I have never known anyone with such courage." As Hildegarde stared at her, Joanna pushed on, "I admire you, Lady Dennison. You had the strength to follow your own heart. So few of us possess such courage."

"You underestimate yourself, Lady Sinclair," Hildegarde said gently.

"No, no, it is not that." Joanna smiled a little sadly. "My

heart has not had anything of any import to say to me for many years now."

"Perhaps you should listen a little closer."

"Perhaps. . . ." Joanna said and then paused for a long moment. "How did you find it in yourself to stand up to the world as you did?"

"I fear my story is really rather prosaic," Hildegarde replied with another smile. "I was the eldest of several daughters in a family steeped in nobility. The rules you were taught as a child I also followed. It was decided by my parents that I should marry Lord Dennison, who was twenty years my senior and possessed of an impressive lineage, title, and fortune. I felt not the slightest regard for the gentleman but did as my family instructed. We were married. Five dreary years later Lord Dennison became an ambassador to the French court—this was before the revolution, you understand. And it was there that I met Celeste and discovered that love existed and that it meant something important in this world. But I had been well trained by my family. I could not leave my husband and bring scandal to both our houses. You must understand—at that time I was very young and very foolish. When the Paris uprisings began, Lord Dennison was transferred to Vienna. Celeste, determined creature that she is, followed me. Some would regard it as weakness to admit love when tied by God and State to someone else, but I could not deny myself the happiness Celeste offered. When Lord Dennison was transferred to Constantinople she followed again."

Hildegarde ran her fingers over the gleaming wood of Joanna's new paint case. "You will realize, Lady Sinclair, that my marriage to Lord Dennison was a mockery. He and I had quickly developed a disgust of each other. We detested every quality the other possessed. I had a particular abhorrence of his demands in the marriage bed."

She looked steadily at Joanna. "Twenty years after I had

met Celeste I left my husband. I was no longer young and therefore not as stupid as I had once been. I decided I disliked being a martyr to my family's pride and my husband's position. Really, that is all that happened."

"And where is Celeste now?"

"She is waiting rather impatiently for me to return to her in Vienna. After following me all over the world Celeste has a decided abhorrence of travel."

"But . . . if you love Celeste how could you come here and leave her in Vienna?"

"I love Diana as well and was worried about her."

"Worried? About Diana?"

"She seems strong and capable, I know. But she has been through a lot these last two years and has not yet recovered. Celeste and I took her from Constantinople and she lived with us for a year in Vienna. She had by then crawled into a shell, curled into a tight little ball, and refused to come out. She would not admit her friends into her apartments. She had become a recluse—something very unlike Diana. She still has that ruinous tendency, I'm afraid. I must seek her out two or three times a day and insist that she enjoy the company of her guests. Geoffrey and Jennifer and I, and a few others, have appointed ourselves her guardians, you see, until she gets over this worrisome episode."

"What happened two years ago, Lady Dennison?" Joanna asked, her heart pounding. "Why does she hide from . . . everyone?"

"You will not ruin your hands, Jorge, I promise you," Diana's voice carried to them.

Both women turned to see Diana and the Spaniard emerge onto the back terrace, Diana carrying a large canvas, her companion struggling with an easel. Joanna studied Diana, who was laughing with genuine mirth at the many complaints Jorge Morales seemed to be uttering. As they advanced across the lawn the sun radiated off Diana's blonde hair creating a soft halo. Joanna looked searchingly at Hildegarde for her answer, but Hildegarde shook her head. It was impossible to respond now.

Diana and Jorge reached them at last. Joanna expressed her heartfelt thanks for the paints. Diana brushed off her gratitude with a careless shrug and insisted that Joanna should start painting that very day. As this was Joanna's fondest wish, she began to set up her easel. After lunch, Joanna returned to her canvas and Bert and Molly to their gardening. The other guests dispersed, and Diana disappeared entirely.

As she outlined with charcoal the picture her brushes would bring to life on the canvas, this last fact troubled Joanna more and more. How did Diana spend her days when she was not riding or gardening or talking with her friends? Where did she hide herself, and why? An hour's curiosity got the better of Joanna. With a resolute squaring of her shoulders, she abandoned her easel and went in search of her hostess.

Upon entering the back of the Manor Joanna heard music—a pianoforte. Recollecting that the only known household musician had ridden off with Geoffrey, Joanna followed the musical trail through hallways and parlors until it led her to the partially closed door of the Music Room. With some timidity Joanna pushed the door open and stepped into the room.

Diana sat at the pianoforte, in profile to Joanna, her eyes closed, her long, slender fingers moving over the keyboard with a loving skill. The room swelled with the music that poured from Diana. The surprise Joanna felt was quickly supplanted by the beauty of the music which invaded Joanna's senses and left her feeling curiously exhilarated. Diana was not playing Bach or Handel or Beethoven, she was playing her soul. Joanna knew this with an unshakable certainty.

With this newfound knowledge Joanna listened all the harder and found at last the dark well at the heart of the music Diana was creating. Joanna felt her breath cease at the pain she heard, and at the sadness, couched in such beauty that Joanna felt herself tremble with the power of it. The music revealed its creatress, and awakened its listener, as words never had.

Slowly, softly, the music ended and Diana was motionless at the pianoforte, still mesmerized by the instrument. Joanna drew in a breath and felt it settle within her. A second breath came and with it she spoke. "That was . . . incredible. Why didn't you tell me you are so good?"

Diana swiveled to stare at Joanna with stunned eyes. "I . . . I thought you were painting."

"I was outlining, really, and I got curious about your whereabouts."

Joanna moved further into the room, thus upsetting Diana's equilibrium even more than she already had.

"I can still scarcely comprehend the magic you possess. I have heard many musicians before, Diana, but you are . . . brilliant. Why have I not heard you before?"

"I play for my own amusement and do not, as a rule, perform for others," Diana replied from her bench for she knew that to attempt to stand would only invite disaster.

"Why deny your friends the pleasure your music gives?"

"It seems . . . vanity to drag one's friends into a room and insist that they hear you play."

"Is it vanity for me to put my visions on canvas?"

"No, of course not, but—"

"Then it is not vain for you to share your musical visions with your friends," Joanna relentlessly pointed out. "Do you usually play just your own compositions?"

"How did you—I . . . only recently," Diana stammered. "I enjoy many composers but have felt the need to perform my own notes for a while."

Joanna smiled. "I should like to hear some more of your notes."

"That is impossible!"

"Then I won't let you see my painting of Molly."

"What?"

"It seems an equitable exchange to me. You let me hear your music and I will let you watch me dabble."

Diana stared at Joanna for a long moment and then began to chuckle. "This is famous," she declared. "You are as formidable as I once called you. Very well, you shall have your private concerts."

Joanna smiled. "Then I am content."

"But I am not. I do not understand why you must hear me play."

"Your music gives my heart things to say."

Diana regarded her blankly. "To whom?" she finally asked.

"To me, of course," Joanna said, grinning. "And I find I enjoy the listening. It is a startling development after all these years. I am very grateful to you."

"Are you?" Diana said weakly. "Then I wish you would repay me by translating everything that you have just said, for I did not understand a word of it."

But Joanna's only reply was to laugh and suggest that a walk in the May afternoon sunshine would do them both a world of good.

CHAPTER 15

The day set for Molly's long-looked-for run around Waverly Manor dawned with a clear sky, the wind slight, and a hawk circling above the building in a lazy manner before spying a mouse in the stableyard and speedily diving for its breakfast. Everyone felt the excitement of the day, Lady Hildegarde going so far as to express her willingness to view the athletic event, should her letter to Celeste be completed in time.

The hour approached, the letter was finished, and Lady Hildegarde, the Hunt-Stevenses, Jorge Morales, Richard Sinclair, and their hostess gathered around the pug-nosed

Atalanta and her mother. Advice, stratagems, and words of encouragement flowed freely from the throats of this gallery until Molly declared that the incessant babble wearied her, she would much rather run and know the satisfaction of success than stand beneath the sun feeling freckles pop out all over her face. The hint was taken and the contest begun.

Minutes later a breathless Molly hurtled herself into her mother's outstretched arms amidst the wild applause of her gallery and Diana's victory yell which set her dogs to barking in the stableyard.

"I win . . . I win!" Molly gasped in her mother's arms.

"Oh well done, my love, well done!" Joanna crowed, rocking Molly.

"I didn't . . . walk once. Not once! Did I Lady Diana?"

"I was hard pressed to keep up with her. Molly neither stopped nor slowed her pace for even a moment," Diana confirmed as she, too, caught her breath.

"Congratulations, Molly." Lady Dennison smiled, and the rest of the gallery quickly added their own praise.

Molly looked up at Diana. "Where's my prize?" she demanded, having regained full use of her lungs. "We had a wager and I won! Where's my prize?"

"Youth is always so impatient," Diana sighed as she turned to bellow for Mrs. Pratt. But the housekeeper was already moving towards them with befitting gravity, a housemaid trailing her. Each carried a tray.

"Congratulations, Miss Sinclair. I have always been confident of your success," the housekeeper declared, and placed her tray directly before Molly. On it rested a large, gaily wrapped box.

"Well don't just stand there. Open it!" Jennifer demanded.

Needing no further urging, Molly unceremoniously tore away the wrapping paper to reveal a red harem costume embroidered in gold. Molly lifted it from its resting place and held it up in the morning sunlight. Joanna's groan was overruled by Molly's delighted gasp. "It's perfect!" she breathed. "It's wonderful! It is just what I wanted! Oh, thank you Lady Diana!" Molly cried as she threw herself into her mentor's arms.

"You're very welcome, my little cub," Diana softly replied.

The housemaid moved through the group with her tray bearing lemonade and slices of celebratory cake while Diana's peacock strolled majestically across the grounds.

"I told you I could win," Molly exulted around a bite of cake. "I told you!"

"Very true," Diana gravely agreed. "But can you run around the house twice without stopping, in, say, another month's time?"

The challenge given and as quickly accepted, Molly's impromptu victory party continued for several hours during which the budding athlete put on her new costume and paraded about the back gardens thoroughly pleased with herself and the lavish praise heaped upon her. At last, however, the imminent departure of the sun beneath the horizon forced an end to the celebration. An additional half hour was required before the leavetaking could be accomplished to the satisfaction of all and then Molly and Joanna reclaimed their barouche and made their way back to Pembroke Park.

Talking quietly they began to mount the Grand Staircase when from the library a familiar voice greeted them: "So, you have returned at last."

"Hugo!" Joanna turned to discover her brother emerging from the room, a scowl marring his features. "How is it that you have come back. . . . That is . . . I did not expect you so soon."

"That much is apparent."

"We have had no word from you in the twelve days that you have been gone," Joanna said, defensive in reaction to her brother's tone.

"Where were you today?" Hugo demanded.

A steadying chill settled upon Joanna. "We have been visiting Lady March at Waverly Manor as you very well know, Hugo," she said.

A strained silence ensued in which her brother seemed to struggle with his emotions. "I wish to speak with you in my library, Joanna. At once!"

Recognizing the futility of protesting so tyrannical an edict, Joanna handed the box containing Molly's treasured harem costume to her daughter and bid her go up to her room. Without another word, Joanna and Hugo entered the library.

"How could you, Joanna? How *could* you?" Hugo exploded, slamming the library door shut.

"Molly and I both enjoy visiting Lady March very much," Joanna calmly replied as she turned to face her brother. He stared at her as if he could not credit what he had just heard.

"Enjoy?" he gasped. "How can you—Joanna, Tom Carroll told you what Lady Dennison is and has done, did he not?"

"With many exclamations of horror, yes."

"And still you went. *Still* you lent your countenance to the woman who freely houses that creature?"

"You have it exactly, Hugo."

"Are you mad? Have you lost all sense of decency? All sense of honor?"

'Not that I am aware of," Joanna replied, amazed at her own calm in the face of a fury that would have left her shuddering not six months earlier.

Scarcely able to comprehend so measured a response, Hugo took several turns around the room before he could trust himself to speak. "What Lady Dennison is, what she has done must be abhorrent to anyone of understanding," he declared, stopping before Joanna. "Her very nature opposes the word of God and the laws of the State. She is unclean, Joanna. By bringing both yourself and your daughter into her presence you have polluted yourselves and have sullied the Garfield name!"

"I disagree—" Joanna began.

"You enjoy Lady March's company, do you?" Hugo seethed. "Did it ever occur to you, Joanna, did you ever once consider that she provides shelter and support to Lady Dennison because she is guilty of the same crimes?"

"I will not stand here and allow you to give vent to speculation and gossip," Joanna stiffly replied.

"This is not speculation, Joanna, I've proof of what I say. Why else would I go to London? Lady March's deeds are known to many. In her youth she was *twice* expelled from institutions of feminine instruction because of her avid pursuit of members of her own sex! In Constantinople it was well known that she was engaged in an adulterous liaison with a Miss McFadden for nearly five years. Do you understand me, Joanna? Their heinous affection for one another was common knowledge in the highest circles of society! Had it not been for the plague mercifully claiming her paramour's life, Lady March might even today be involved in so corrupt an acquaintance."

There was a moment of silence as Joanna calmly regarded her brother. "You speak as if this news were of some moment. Pray, Hugo, how should it affect me?"

Hugo gaped at his sister. "How?" he sputtered. "Surely, Joanna, you comprehend what I have just said?"

"Perfectly."

"Are you not appalled?"

"Not at all. To be blunt, Hugo, I am glad to learn that Lady March has known at least some love in her lifetime. Now, before you continue with that ranting and raving that you do so well, permit me to inform you that, however critical your view of Lady March, I think myself fortunate to count her as my friend and will continue to enjoy the pleasure of her company, and allow my daughter to enjoy the healthful environs of Waverly Manor, until I remove to Kent in six weeks' time."

"I warn you, Joanna, do not associate with that woman," Hugo retorted, his fury barely harnessed. "I am determined to see her ruined and exiled from this country. I will not have your name dragged through the mud with hers."

"As for that, the choice is entirely your own, Hugo. I have already told you of my decision," Joanna replied in a level voice, turning and quitting the room before her brother could dismiss her. He was left to stare after her, utterly confounded.

Slowly Joanna mounted the Grand Staircase unmindful of the front doorbell and her aunt's strident calls to her to come down at once. "Caroline Humphrey is to join us for dinner. Joanna! I will not tolerate your snubbing our guest!" And still Joanna climbed. Her brother's low-voiced greeting and Caroline's perfectly modulated reply were but discordant patterns in the back of her mind. She gained the door of her room without knowing how she had got there and locked the door behind her. With a weary sigh Joanna eased herself into the rocking chair placed before the fire crackling fiercely in the grate. Her hazel eyes drank in the undulating flames of orange tipped in blue until the heat of the fire stole over her and the numbness left her heart and mind and body.

Miss McFadden. What a very prosaic sort of a name. Scotch, of course. Joanna imagined a very practical woman, so different from Diana's madcap gaiety. Had she and Diana known love as Hugo had said? Had they shared passion? Blushing at her thoughts Joanna attempted to turn her mind in another direction. But her mind would not be schooled. It insisted on forming a picture of Diana lying with indecorous abandon in Miss McFadden's arms.

Understanding came amidst Joanna's fevered flush. The

sadness she had sometimes glimpsed in Diana's green eyes, the pain she had heard in her music, were now explained in the death of a lover.

Lady Diana March, for all the walls she used to surround herself, had loved. Had loved so deeply and openly that an entire city had known of it. Joanna trembled at this. What would it be like to know, to feel the full force of such a love? To be held in the embrace of such passion?

Joanna wrapped her arms around herself. She had known only two passions in her life: her art and her daughter. Never had she known that passion that could touch her woman's soul. Never had another being inflamed her heart with desire and love. Colin had been an excellent husband: kind, gentle, loving. When he visited her bed at night he would touch her with tenderness and create within her a warmth, but never heat. It had been enough then. Before she had married Colin Sinclair she had not known the possibility of so tender a regard. She had been grateful to feel his love, to be held in his arms. Yet when these gifts had been taken from her, when Colin had died, her heart had not been broken. She had wept, she had mourned—but for a brother, not a lover.

How had Diana mourned when Miss McFadden died? Did she mourn still?

The log in the grate snapped in two amidst a shower of golden sparks. Joanna leaned forward and placed another log in the fire, the sudden flame lighting her face, banishing the shadows. Slowly Joanna leaned back in the rocking chair, her toes keeping the chair in gentle motion. She looked deep within the flames, now orange, now gold, and remembered Diana's hair and how it shone in the morning sunlight, remembered when she and Molly had gone to tea and she had had to continually stop herself from reaching out to run her hands through the honey waves to discover if they were truly as soft as they seemed.

Thinking of that day Joanna could not banish the image

from her mind of Diana stretched out on her side across from her, her flesh so open to contemplation. And Joanna had gazed far more avidly than she cared to remember. Even now she could picture every inch of Diana's languorous form: the surprisingly small feet, the muscular calves and thighs molded by the gossamer material of Diana's costume. She let her memory linger once again upon Diana's rounded belly before it recalled breasts that seemed succulent, like some lush tropical fruit. Joanna was shaken with a sudden longing to feast there, to taste the richness that Diana promised. Her heart thudding within her, Joanna's imagination summoned Diana's long, slender throat and called forth Diana's wide mouth and lips so full that Joanna's own mouth hungered to taste them, devour them. A murmured phrase stole unbidden into her thoughts: At last!

More than a little disconcerted by this reverie Joanna stood up suddenly, wanting to flee. But her eyes scanned the room that had been hers since childhood, her mind searched through every room in Pembroke, and she knew that none could offer her sanctuary.

Exhausted, Joanna methodically drew off her clothes, exchanging them for her nightdress, and then crawled between the sheets that seemed cold to her flesh. And still her mind would not be quiet. Tears began to slip from her closed eyes. Colin had given her warmth. What would it be like to know heat?

CHAPTER 16

Lady Hildegarde Dennison walked with her usual composure out of the woods and into the back gardens of Waverly Manor, permitting herself to revel in the feel of the sun on her head, firmly ignoring the little voice within her that was Celeste insisting that if she did not wear a bonnet and carry a parasol when out of doors she would become a withered hag and not at all the inspiration for *amour* that Celeste had always proclaimed her to be. With a smile, Hildegarde shook her head. Celeste. She had sent a letter to Vienna only yesterday. Another fit of literary passion seemed imminent.

Hildegarde observed with what she considered com-
mendable dispassion the sight of Molly Sinclair engaged in a
rollicking game of tag with Jennifer and Peter, Molly's
delighted shrieks ringing in the late morning air. A gurgle of
laughter caught Hildegarde's ear and she turned to see Diana
kneeling behind Joanna Sinclair and peering over her
shoulder. They sat on the lawn, Diana looking at the sketches
Joanna was rapidly drawing of her daughter's rambunctious
play with the two adults. Joanna's creative intensity left her
unaware that Diana gazed at her with open pleasure.

Hildegarde's pleasure was nearly as great. It had been over
two years since she had seen such happiness radiating from
Diana. She had watched that expression grow daily as Diana
took pleasure in Joanna Sinclair's company. The widow had
woven a spell of which Diana seemed unconscious, yet
Hildegarde, with her greater years of experience, understood
the spell all too well. She would be able to return to Vienna
much sooner than she had initially anticipated, it seemed.

"There, you see? Peter wins again and I win our bet!"
Diana crowed. "I warned you, Joanna. I know my champion's
skills all too well. You should not let sentiment blind you.
Come," she said, standing up and holding out her hand, "you
have now lost thrice in a row and must pay our wager."

"Couldn't I at least use a sidesaddle?" Joanna complained
as she took Diana's hand and rose to her feet.

"Don't be absurd. None of my horses would tolerate that
torturous contraption."

"But to wear turkish trousers! What if someone should
see us?"

"We shall keep well within Waverly's borders, I promise
you. Now come along and stop being such a dreadful
stick-in-the-mud. Think of this as an adventure."

"But I don't like adventures."

"That is because you have not yet been on enough of
them," Diana sagely remarked. Still holding Joanna's hand,

she pulled her into Waverly Manor.

Thirty minutes later both women emerged in costumes similar to the one Diana had worn when they first met, although today Diana was clad primarily in green that made her eyes seem luminous, despite the soft shadow beneath them, while Joanna wore red and brown.

"Do you mean to blush during the whole of our ride?" Diana inquired as they walked toward the stable.

"I feel perfectly wanton," Joanna replied.

A ripple of laughter escaped Diana as she led them into the stableyard where a straw-haired lad of fifteen years held in one hand the reins of Diana's favorite bay mare and in the other the reins of a tall, dappled mare.

"She's beautiful!" Joanna breathed.

"I've only had her a fortnight but I assure you she's as prettily behaved as any horse in Britain. I think you will enjoy her."

"But where's the mounting block?"

Diana stared at her companion with what she hoped was one of her more severe frowns and then informed the stableboy that he could throw Lady Sinclair into the saddle. Thoroughly chastened, Joanna placed her left foot in the youth's clasped hands and was vaulted into the air, the saddle catching her neatly. Years of habit, however, left both of her legs on the left side of the horse. To make another attempt did not bear thinking of, particularly with Diana cackling from atop her own mount. Her teeth gritted with true English determination, Joanna swung her right leg over the horse's neck, gasping at so unique an exercise.

"I feel like a fish who has suddenly had its tail split in two. It feels so very odd!" Joanna exclaimed as they left the stable.

The two rode north, weaving through fields of carefullly cultivated crops that were already arching towards the June sun, and then turned to the east, cantering easily across pastures of thick green grass, startling a small flock of long-tailed sheep.

As they slowed their horses to a walk to enable conversation once again, Diana grinned. "What thinks the fish of its newly designed tail?"

"It has begun to wonder how it ever tolerated its old-fashioned style. This is really rather fun!" Joanna confessed.

"Think of it as yet one more way to shock your brother."

"Oh, Hugo has given up being shocked in favor of a more murderous state of mind."

"It must be very difficult for you," Diana said.

"Really, it is not so very terrible," Joanna reassured her. "Hugo spends his days courting Caroline Humphrey and I spend my days at Waverly Manor. We only meet when Aunt Hampton insists on giving one of her all too formal dinner parties, and then we are separated by guests so that we are limited to sniping at each other over our raspberry trifles."

"Still, it has not been a pleasant week for you."

"No," Joanna conceded, "it has not. I've worried so about. . . . Has Hugo. . . . Has he taken any action against you, Diana?"

"He has tried to break the sale of Waverly Manor."

"He what? How?"

"He claims that I did not honor the letter of the sale when I fenced in the northern pastureland and planted corn and oats, thus ruining any hunting party's forays across my land. Unfortunately for your brother, his solicitor brought the case up before a London magistrate who happens to be an old family friend. The case was thrown out with not a few comments on the sanctity of private property."

"That would explain Hugo's foul mood."

"I was informed yesterday by my solicitor that Mr. Garfield has brought more . . . more personal charges to stand against me." Diana paused, knowing that Joanna would understand her perfectly. Hugo would not be reticent about divulging so colorful a past to his sister. "He can only harm himself by pursuing the suit."

"But Diana—"

"Joanna," Diana firmly interrupted, "your brother cannot conceive of the influence my family and fortune carry. All his efforts will come to nothing, I promise you."

They rode quietly together for some minutes, enjoying the warm fresh air and the soft breeze that teased their hair and their horses' manes, then they turned south, cantering over rolling hills, racing each other to the crest of one, and arguing over who had won the match as they headed west and entered the woods that would lead them back to Waverly Manor.

"How beautiful it is in this park," Joanna said with a sigh. "I have always wanted to paint this wood, but I could never devise a means of bringing my paints and canvas here without causing a royal set-to amongst my family."

"Whyever would your family permit you to develop the skill to paint and then deny you its use?" Diana asked.

"It was my governess who discovered that I had a facility for drawing. As she had some talent herself, she began to teach me. Miss Gibson knew nothing of paint, only pencils and watercolors, the only skills my parents approved, and I was restricted to their use. When I married, however, I acquired a freedom of decision and chose to study the use of oils with the masters then in residence in London. Colin had no real eye for art himself, but he knew it gave me pleasure and he loved me enough to take his happiness for me from that."

"A most remarkable man," Diana murmured.

They rode on in companionable silence, each lost in her own reverie. Diana's revolved around the late Lord Sinclair. In every respect he seemed an exemplary specimen of the male sex, but this reflection served only to agitate her thoughts.

Did you truly love her? Diana demanded of the late Lord. *Did she know pleasure in your arms? Did you honor her talent and glory in her laughter as I have?*

And what had Joanna really felt for her husband? Had she showered him with the love that Diana knew to swell her heart? Had she felt safe within his embrace? Had she laughed and joked with him as she had with Diana? Had Molly's birth forged a bond that no other could equal?

Diana tortured herself with these questions as she often had in her bed at night when her dreams brought her little rest and much torment. With an angry shake of her head Diana gave up this silent examination, drawing several deep breaths into her lungs as if to cleanse herself of so disturbing a train of thought.

Seeking a more enjoyable pastime, Diana chose to study Joanna, who rode slightly ahead of her in the thickly wooded park. This decision succeeded admirably; Diana's eyes were caught by the thick, dark brown hair pulled off Joanna's face and allowed to fall to her shoulders, and the grace of Joanna's back sweeping into the full swell of hips and buttocks, their gentle rocking motion setting Diana's heart to pounding. Joanna's legs, pressed confidently against the sides of her horse, were long and tapered filling Diana with the overwhelming desire to feel their strength wrapped around her. Blushing at a turn of mind she did not normally permit herself, Diana allowed her gaze to trail back up to Joanna's mane of hair. She drank in the highlights brought out by sudden patches of sunlight, her breath catching as a dark wisp caressed Joanna's cheek.

Thus diverted, Diana was wholly unprepared when her mare reared at a rabbit that had dashed out onto the path, only to find itself beneath the horse's hooves.

Joanna turned to see Diana tumble backwards off the bay

to land with a sickening thud, her horse dancing around her and seemingly intent upon trampling her at any moment.

"Diana!" Joanna screamed. She lunged for the reins of the mare and at last brought her to a standstill.

Hastily looping the reins of both horses over a scraggly bush, Joanna slid from her saddle and ran to Diana's crumpled form. She knelt and ran her hands over Diana's body, finding no obvious broken bones. She pulled Diana into her arms, and swept a hand up under Diana's green shirt to come to rest against the gentle swell of her left breast. She held her breath for one shuddering moment and then felt the strong, steady beat of Diana's heart.

Her hand still pressed beneath Diana's soft breast as if to a lifeline, Joanna tenderly placed Diana's head in her lap and brushed the blonde wisps from Diana's chalk-white face. "Oh wake up, wake up, can't you?" she urged, her fear at Diana's unconscious state increasing with each passing moment. Diana groaned and this comforting sound so thrilled Joanna that she fervently kissed Diana's dusty forehead.

Diana groaned again and slowly opened her eyes. It took a moment to focus her gaze and to recall sensation into her limbs. Two things struck her forcibly: Joanna's hand clasped to her breast, and the hideous throbbing of her head.

"What the hell happened?" she mumbled.

"You fell off your horse," Joanna softly replied.

"Don't be ridiculous." Diana closed her eyes against the pain that speech inspired.

"Sorry." Joanna smiled as relief washed over her in great waves. "Does anything hurt?"

"Everything."

"Do you think you could stand?"

Diana moaned.

"Let's give it a try anyway," Joanna insisted, the need of getting Diana to a doctor firing her determination. Murmuring encouragement, Joanna spent the next several minutes getting Diana to her feet. Diana leaning heavily on her, Joanna led her to the horses who were happily munching on the grass where they were tethered. Somehow Joanna got Diana back onto her mare where she promptly sprawled over the neck of the horse. Hurriedly Joanna gathered the reins of both horses before mounting the bay behind Diana and pulling Diana up against her.

Whether she swooned from the pleasure of having Joanna's breasts pressed against her back, or from the pain the continual movement of the horse sent spiraling through her, Diana was never able afterwards to accurately recall. She only knew that she reopened her eyes to blinding sunlight and a series of anxious shouts.

"Hildegarde! Send for the doctor. Quickly!"

"Dear God, what has happened?"

"Lady Sinclair, is she badly hurt?"

Diana felt herself begin to fall and cried out. "Don't worry, Diana," Geoffrey said softly as he finished pulling her down into his arms. "I've got you safe. You'll be fine now."

With long strides, Geoffrey carried Diana through the gardens and into Waverly Manor. Joanna slid from the mare.

"I've sent that tow-headed stableboy for the doctor," Hildegarde announced as she came up to the group clustered around Joanna and the horses. "He should come soon. Now, will someone kindly tell me what happened?"

Briefly Joanna described the accident and watched disbelief cloud the faces of her audience.

"But Diana is a superb horsewoman," Jennifer protested. "I've never known her to fall. What could have happened?"

"I daresay she was distracted by something," Hildegarde replied, casting a swift glance towards Joanna that Jennifer did not miss.

The doctor appeared at last, refused to allow anyone but himself into the sickroom, stayed with his patient for a full half hour, and then adjourned to the front parlor to announce that Lady March had acquired a dandy concussion and several assorted bruises that would undoubtedly be quite colorful in the days to come. A good deal of rest and she would be well in no time, he assured his anxious questioners; and then he departed.

Relief at this report was vast and immediate. All wanted to visit Diana at once but this Mrs. Pratt, with a martial air, would not permit. Her ladyship required rest, something none of her guests knew how to provide.

Still shaken by the accident and by Diana's pallor as Geoffrey had pulled her from her arms, Joanna reluctantly returned with Molly to Pembroke Park. Molly voluntarily elected to retire to bed early and Joanna was able to escape to the sanctuary of her own room.

Slowly she eased herself into her rocking chair. Knowing that sleep would not come soon, she rocked slowly back and forth, her mind replaying over and over the terrified rearing of the bay mare, Diana's fall recalled in slow motion, the horse's hooves dancing closer and closer to her tender body. "She might have been killed," Joanna whispered hoarsely. "Dear Lord, I might have lost her."

After a night that knew only anxiety, Joanna descended once again upon Waverly Manor. Mrs. Pratt greeted her and Molly at the door and informed the Sinclairs that Lady March was indeed up and receiving visitors. To their surprise she led them not upstairs to Diana's bedroom, but out to the back terrace. There a chaise lounge had been placed beneath a shady fruit tree and on the chaise lay Diana, her face still pale, a blanket tucked securely around her.

"She insisted," was Mrs. Pratt's frosty comment before she returned to the house.

"Lady Diana are you all right?" Molly gravely inquired as she advanced towards the chaise.

"Of course I'm all right," Diana replied, the animation of her words bringing some color to her cheeks. "You don't think I can be hurt by a silly fall, do you?"

"Well . . ." Molly said dubiously, "you seemed very ill yesterday. I was scared."

"Poor little cub." Diana smiled warmly as she held out her arms. Eagerly Molly moved into them and received a kiss on both cheeks. "Thank you for worrying about me, but I really am much better. Now off you go to Bert. He is already peevish because I've cried off gardening for a few days. If you were to be late I shudder to think to what heights his temper would climb."

Molly dashed off into the gardens. Diana and Joanna were left to silently regard each other.

"Good morning my resourceful Knight Errant," Diana quipped with a sudden grin. "I've never before had to play a damsel in distress. I am not at all certain that I like the role."

"I am certain that I hate it," Joanna frankly replied as she took the chair beside Diana's chaise. "Should you be out of bed so soon? You are still so very pale."

"The doctor says that I must deny myself all my romps for a few days, but I would not permit him to deny me the pleasures of a June morning. I detest sickbeds."

"Still," Joanna said with a smile, "you should not be walking down stairs and through manor houses."

"Oh, but I didn't walk," Diana ingenuously replied. "Geoffrey carried me. He carries me everywhere now. My feet have begun to forget what the ground feels like."

Joanna laughed at this but still could not hide her concern. "You are so pale," she said, "and there are circles under your eyes. Could you not sleep? Was the pain so very great?"

Diana shrugged. "Insomnia is an old malady. Now do stop worrying about me. I'll not have you moping about prophesying doom on such a lovely day. Get thee out into the sunshine and paint!"

Joanna smiled, impetuously squeezed Diana's hand, and

then adjourned to the easel already set up by Mrs. Pratt in the garden where Molly and Bert were working. Diana contentedly watched her go, admiring the easy grace of Joanna's movements and the play of sunlight on her brown hair. That such admiration had been the cause of her most recent misadventure troubled Diana not at all.

"You should never send her away, Diana," a low voice declared. "She's the best thing in the world for you." Diana turned to observe Geoffrey drop into the chair Joanna had so recently vacated. "Call Lady Sinclair into your arms, Diana," he advised. "She'll make you happy."

"I can't," Diana said softly. "My courage died with Gwen. I don't want someone else. I can't let myself. . . . *You* should call Richard Sinclair into *your* arms. He's the best thing for you, you know."

"Yes," Geoffrey replied with a sad smile as he looked out towards the northern fields. "But I can't do it. I'm frightened, Diana."

"No more than I," came her soft reply.

CHAPTER 17

"What do you mean it can't be done!" Hugo demanded, setting down his wine with such force that the stem of his glass all but snapped in two. He sat behind his desk in his library, his narrowed brown eyes confronting the two men seated on leather wing chairs before him.

"Mr. Garfield," Acton, his solicitor, calmly replied, "there is no precedent for the action you wish taken."

"Then we shall set the precedent!"

"No sir, you will not," Lord Barthwaite bluntly replied. "As magistrate of this shire I won't permit it. 'Tis folly, sir, and I'll have no hand in such a scheme."

"You will allow this deviant woman free rein in Herefordshire?" Hugo exclaimed in a choked voice.

"I will not allow you to dictate to me," Lord Barthwaite corrected him, the corset surrounding his large bulk creaking in protest as he leaned forward to refill his glass with his host's excellent port.

"May I remind you, my lord, that it is your duty to protect and defend the laws of this land *and* the word of God, both of which this woman has desecrated!" Hugo cried.

"Mr. Garfield, you must try to understnd," Acton broke in quickly in an attempt to forestall the magistrate's clearly mounting fury. "The deeds of which you accuse Lady March occurred in her youth and in a foreign nation that is not even a British colony. According to the exact letter of the law, she has as yet committed no crime on English soil."

"Good God, man, where is your sense of Christian duty?" Hugo bitterly demanded.

"Did not Christ say, 'cast not the first stone,' Mr. Garfield?" Lord Barthwaite held up a hand to forestall Hugo's angry reply. "For some reason of your own devising you have taken it into your head to dislike this woman. Far be it for me to question your motives. However, I will not allow you to make a mockery of the law in your fevered attempt to ruin Lady Diana March. And that is all that I will ever have to say on the subject." Lord Barthwaite moved ponderously to his feet. "Thank ye for the port. I still say you've the best wine cellar in all of Herefordshire."

"And is that all?" Hugo demanded in a thunderous voice. "You refuse to bring to trial a woman who commits atrocities with her own sex, who defies the natural rule of man, who usurps the very fabric of a moral society in search of her heinous pleasure?"

"I will say this to you only once, Mr. Garfield." Lord Barthwaite paused at the door of the library. "Lady March is a noblewoman of excellent birth. Her connections with every level of British government, her friends at the highest level of English society, and her vast fortune make any move against her sheer lunacy. No sir, I will not allow you to charge her before me. No noblewoman has ever suffered such an indignity and I will not be the first to permit such scandal to enter an English court. Perhaps, not being of noble blood yourself, you cannot fully comprehend the power and impregnability of Lady March's position. I suggest you ruminate on just that fact at your leisure. Good day sir!" Lord Barthwaite quit the room and shortly thereafter, Pembroke itself.

With this painful reminder of his position Hugo Garfield's hopes were not merely dashed, they were shattered. Every action he had taken against Diana March had, at every hand, been decisively blocked. The influence of this woman who had spent most of her life abroad was staggering; he could still scarcely comprehend it. It had stretched even into his own household. Daily—nay, hourly he did battle with Joanna, and still she and Molly went to Waverly Manor. To deny her the use of his carriages and horses was useless for she had her own barouche and cattle. Often he had thought of locking her into her room until she came to her senses, but Hugo did not dare commit an act that would cause instant comment amongst his servants and thus all of Heddington.

Never had he known such obstinancy in his sister. Never had she so actively and successfully defied his commands. Because of the influence of one foul woman the power, the order, the control over his life which he had always enjoyed was slipping from his grasp.

* * *

Three days later on a rainy night in the second week of June, as Hugo sat before his desk in the library staring moodily at the wall of books before him, he made a decision.

He might not be able to defeat Diana March—but Lady Joanna was another matter entirely. He would bring *her* to her senses. She would return to the proper sentiments and actions of a Garfield woman. The question was, how to do it? To this Hugo could devise no answer, but he went up to his bed feeling on the precipice of the solution to his problems.

On the following morning he made what was now his daily call on Lady Caroline Humphrey. As he sat opposite her in the Humphrey Morning Parlor watching Caroline stir her tea with a leisurely grace, as she spoke of the dinner party she had attended at the Chesterfield's the night before, once again he noted her beauty, and approved of it. Caroline held herself with a superiority and ease that few women could imitate or attain. The opinions she gave of the dinner and what was said there were ones he might have uttered himself.

That he and Caroline would marry had been an inevitability both had taken for granted. Diana March had temporarily distracted him, but now he felt himself back on course and, in the wake of the recent fit of feminine opposition he had suffered from both Lady March and Joanna, he had begun to see Caroline with newly appreciative eyes. In every way she seemed perfectly suited to his life and his needs. Her fortune and her title would give him leverage to claim a title for the Garfield name at last. Her views matched his own. Her actions never shocked, her words never embarrassed. She would be an exemplary wife, doing all she could to further, not hamper, his own ends. Nor, Hugo thought looking across at her, would he feel the slightest reluctance at sharing such a wife's bed—as he most assuredly would have, had he married the hideously plain Diana March.

The softness of Lady Humphrey's beautifully modulated speech, her concern for his kind regard of her, her attention to his comfort were like a balm after so many weeks of female vexations. In this gentled frame of mind, Hugo was brought to speak his mind to Caroline.

With a gravity befitting the forthcoming proposal Hugo reminded Caroline of the many ways in which their families and fortunes complemented each other. He recalled for her the three times in the last four hundred years when their families had been united in marriage. He went so far as to mention the expectations of their neighbors regarding any future connection of Humphrey to Garfield. Judging her sufficiently prepared Hugo proceeded. "In short, Caroline, it would seem mutually beneficial to us two to marry."

The grave smile and the hand she offered him with her acceptance were all he could have wished. He kissed the proffered fingers with all of the pleasure her response had given, and sat down beside her on the ice blue couch to discuss their decision in greater detail.

A long engagement, they discovered, was desirable to them both; a honeymoon trip held no allure. A large wedding with every possible noble lord and lady in attendance suited both admirably. Mrs. Hampton was quickly demoted and relegated to the position of a charity relation, an unattached woman with no viable means of support other than her nephew's good will. This train of thought naturally led the newly affianced pair to the problem of Joanna.

Both decried her wayward behavior, her inattention to her daughter's moral environment, her seeming insistence on ruining her reputation in Heddington with her frequent and open association with Lady Diana March. Both asked the question that had plagued Hugo three nights before: What was to be done about Joanna?

"Hugo," Caroline said with gentle urgency, "I have always looked upon and loved Joanna as a sister. Perhaps if I were to speak with her. . . ."

"No," Hugo said. "If Joanna will attend neither the words of her brother nor her aunt she will not be influenced by you. No, I fear the time for kind persuasion has passed. More definitive action is required."

"The power you hold over her is great, though untried," Caroline tentatively offered.

"To threaten Joanna's material well-being has often occurred to me, but I think it wisest to withhold the use of such power until all other efforts have failed."

Both reflected on the problem in silence.

"It appears to me," Caroline began slowly, "that Joanna's waywardness stems from the fact that the natural order of her life has been disrupted."

"What do you mean?"

"She spent her childhood in her father's house and had his hand to guide her. She then entered her husband's house and once again knew a manly rule. But with Lord Sinclair's death Joanna suddenly found herself without that masculine guidance that had protected her all of her life. She began to exhibit a woeful independence uncurbed by her occasional visits with you, for your influence could only be temporary based upon the time she spent under your roof. Four years spent in such a fashion would naturally lead to the willfulness she now displays."

"I begin to understand you. But have you thought of some remedy to so distressing a situation?"

"I believe that I have," Caroline replied with a smile. "Joanna requires the permanent rule of a man over her life."

"I have asked her often to spend each day of every year with me, but she refuses."

"But you are her brother. Joanna could not refuse to spend each day of every year with a husband who would quickly end her infatuation with Lady March."

"Very true," Hugo replied slowly. "But Joanna has as yet shown no inclination to remarry."

"Then it will be our task to convince her of its necessity. There are many ways that this may be done."

"Indeed. But before we come to that, whom might she marry? To serve our purpose he must not be a rattlepate for

Joanna is surprisingly intelligent for a woman and could easily rule *him* which is contrary to our goal. Nor may he be a dandy for he would spend more time looking into his mirror than after Joanna, and again she might easily stray onto her own path."

"We require for our purpose a gentleman who would have a high regard for Joanna so that he might, of his own choosing, always keep an eye on her and keep her from those errors of judgment that have already led her so close to ruin," Caroline affirmed.

"He must also be a man of property and one sufficiently elevated in society to bring further honor to the Garfield name," Hugo said decisively.

"I believe the gentleman we require," his fiance calmly stated, "is Lord Thomas Carroll."

Hugo stared at her, unable to voice the tumult of emotions and thoughts Caroline's words created.

"Think on it, Hugo," she urged, taking his hands in hers, an action perhaps more forward than he would normally approve in his betrothed, but his concentration on the matter at hand was such that he forebore to notice Caroline's lapse of propriety. "Lord Carroll is a man of character and understanding whose views match our own on every point. His marriage with Joanna would unite two noble houses with the Garfield name. More importantly, he has already formed a *tendre* for your sister. If she were but a little more inviting he could easily be brought to his knee of his own accord."

"Lord Carroll is a brilliant choice," Hugo warmly declared. "He possesses the strength to rule Joanna with a firm hand. His wealth and position make a match with him wholly attractive to any woman, even my sister. And he has the further advantage of long friendship that must have instilled within Joanna's heart an affection for him. She cannot help but marry him."

Caroline and Hugo had soon mapped out a campaign to

get Joanna to the altar before autumn. The first step of their plan required the presence of Tom Carroll, in tandem with a few judicial hints from Hugo to set him on the course to matrimony. To this end Hugo wrote instantly to his old friend and invited him for a lengthy stay at Pembroke Park, specifically mentioning the pleasure Joanna would assuredly take in his company.

Two days after Hugo had proposed to Caroline, the Carroll coach, laden with luggage, bowled up the drive to Pembroke Park.

CHAPTER 18

Hildegarde buttered a muffin and began to munch on it. "I begin to feel as if I had innocently wandered onto the field of Waterloo only to find myself trapped between Mr. Wellington and Monsieur Bonaparte."

Listening to the furious voices emanating from the parlor next door, Diana could only agree to this statement with a sigh as she brought her cup of breakfast tea to her lips.

"Even the most devoted of lovers turn surly when trapped together under one roof for three days of rain," Jennifer said.

"Celeste and I never do," Hildegarde retorted.

"That is because you are both paragons," Jennifer said with a smile. "We mere mortals drive each other to distraction under such lamentable conditions."

"In the end they will either kill each other or declare their undying love," Peter prophesied. "Either way we will have an end to their endless battles."

"Optimism in youth is always so charming," Hildegarde drily stated and won a grin from Peter.

"Where is Jorge?" Jennifer asked. "He is not one to miss breakfast like this."

"He is hiding in the Music Room, as always," Diana replied. "I do pity him. He never bargained for hysterics and high drama when he came with Geoffrey to England. It doesn't seem fair."

"Fairness? Bah!" Hildegarde said. "He was a fool to get involved with Geoff in the first place."

"I beg your pardon?" Jennifer said stiffly, sibling devotion causing her black eyes to sparkle dangerously.

"Please," Diana implored, "let us not follow their example by bickering amongst ourselves. Our nerves are all frayed by this damned rain. The least we can do is try to remain on civil terms with one another."

"Poor Diana," Peter said sympathetically. "Three days without a word from Joanna Sinclair have begun to take their toll, haven't they?"

"Word from Joanna, or lack thereof, is neither here nor there! All I am asking is that you stop snapping at each other!" Diana threw down her napkin, pushed back her chair, and stormed from the room.

"Poor Diana," Jennifer said, echoing Peter. "I don't think even Gwen McFadden left her this muddled."

"Perhaps she is not as recovered from her concussion as she would like to think," Peter offered.

"Have you no romantic sensibilities whatsoever?" his

beloved demanded in exasperation.

Diana, meanwhile, stalked into the library, threw herself into her favorite chair, picked up the book she had started to read the night before when her disturbed dreams had once again brought her awake. A few minutes later she tossed the volume aside; none of the letters had managed to form themselves into coherent words. The fury of the two men in the parlor between the library and the breakfast room reached its zenith in the house-rattling slam of the parlor door and the infuriated stomping of boots up the main staircase.

Unnerved by the silence, Diana rose and went to the door that joined the library to the parlor and timidly peered within. Richard Sinclair stood at the large bay window, a hand pressed against one wall as he stared out at the rain.

Quietly Diana entered the room and closed the door behind her. "Poor boy," she said softly. "Where has Geoff gone?"

"He has taken Jorge back to bed to prove how much he does not need me," Richard replied in a dead voice as he continued to stare out the window.

"Hildegarde was wrong," Diana said as she advanced into the room. "Jorge is not the fool, Geoffrey is."

"No, I am the fool." Richard collapsed onto the windowseat, defeated. "I should never have come. I should have known it was impossible to win Geoff's love."

"You won it years ago, Richard." Diana sat on the floor before him, gazing earnestly up into his face. "Why else has he run from you these last five years? Why else does he fight you with such passion now?"

"A funny kind of love to be always denying it," Richard sadly observed.

"Geoffrey is a funny kind of man," Diana replied with a soft smile. "Think on it, Richard. He is a man of good background with a solid, if not overwhelming, fortune behind him, possessing intelligence, talent, wit, beauty, knowing adulation every day of his life from his nurse, his mother—and lust from every stableboy and prince from here to Russia. Because he has taken each physical offering made him he believes that he cannot be faithful. Because he has known only adulation he believes that he cannot be loved. Geoffrey defines himself in terms of his beauty. He cannot be brought to acknowledge his heart—for in all of his thirty years that has never been praised."

"I understand him, Diana. Really I do. But in all honesty, my fair Amazon, how much of this pain must I withstand?"

"He will come round, Richard. I know it!"

"How long am I expected to wait until this miracle occurs?"

"How much do you love him?"

Richard paused and then smiled. "Enough to almost believe that miracles can happen."

"Then stay," Diana urged, clasping his hand firmly in her own. "Often that which we want most in life is that which we most strenuously struggle against."

"You begin to understand yourself, then."

"I was speaking of Geoff." Diana's voice was stiff.

Richard smiled. "Sorry, my mistake."

Diana would not be baited nor allow her train of thought to be disrupted. "I have spoken with Geoffrey often this last fortnight," she said. "He knows he's behaving like an idiot, Richard. I think the ferocity of his reaction to you these last few days stems from the hope, the desire, that you stay because your love is strong enough to put up with him even at his worst. Geoff will crack, I know he will. You two cannot help but post the banns."

"Dear Diana," Richard said, cupping her face and giving her an affectionate kiss on the nose. "Truly, you are the best of friends. I will stay, for I suspect that you would tie me to my bed in order to keep me here if I ever threatened flight."

"Clever boy." Diana grinned as she stood up. "Now have some breakfast before Mrs. Pratt swoops down and rings a peal over your head for slighting the efforts of her household and Juan Carlos's kitchen."

"An amazing woman, your Mrs. Pratt," Richard said with an answering grin. "How ever does she put up with the histrionics and the highly improper relations of your guests?"

"Didn't I ever tell you? For years she was the paramour of a volatile Italian contessa. By comparison, our displays serve only to amuse her."

* * *

The rain continued another two days before it finally ceased shortly after midnight. Jorge Morales greeted the morning sun with a sigh of relief only the Spanish can understand, and began to pack his bags, a task soon completed for he had been preparing for this departure for many days. He then went in search of his hostess, finding Diana at her dressing table, still clad in her nightclothes as her very pregnant maid, Annie, braided her hair in preparation for a morning ride denied Diana for too many days.

Diana's surprise at so early a guest was trebled when the Spaniard announced his intention of catching the morning post for London. "You're leaving?"

"Thank the good Lord, yes!" Jorge exclaimed as Annie discreetly left the room. "Diana, you are a good woman and I am very fond of you, but this house and this country I can no longer tolerate!"

"It has been very hard for you these last few weeks, I know, but—"

"Diana, I have been trapped in this house with a madman!" Jorge began to pace the room. "When Geoffrey is not arguing with Lord Sinclair about nothing at all he is making the calf eyes at the fellow when he thinks no one is seeing him. And when he is doing neither of those things he is pulling me into his bed! The other night, Diana, when Geoffrey and I were in the throes of passion he actually called out Sinclair's name!"

Diana clamped her hand to her mouth to stifle her hoot of laughter.

"Fidelity I do not concern myself with, but this obsession with the English lord invades my peace of mind. I am an artist, Diana, a musician. I cannot live under these conditions. Not even Geoffrey's skilled lovemaking can convince me to stay a moment longer!"

Diana, after a slight struggle, regained her composure, expressed the pleasure she had had in Jorge's company and his music while at Waverly Manor, and her sorrow at his abrupt departure. She then set about arranging immediate transportation to carry him to London; she would permit no guest of hers to travel on a common stage. Cheerfully waving Jorge adios, Diana returned to the house, trotted happily upstairs, rapped once upon the third door of the second landing, and entered before she could receive a reply. Richard was but half dressed, the lower half having fortunately attained this desirable state.

"Pack your bags, Dick," she commanded, grinning at the blush that flooded her startled guest's face, "you're moving."

"Throwing me out?" Richard managed to inquire as he manfully stifled the urge to hold a sheet in front of his naked breast.

"In a manner of speaking. Another room has suddenly become available at the Hotel Waverly. A guest has vacated the premises and I am now at liberty to install you in the bedroom adjoining that of one Geoffrey Hunt-Stevens. I hope you don't mind."

The ecstatic smile on Richard's face answered her. Quickly he summoned his valet and together they transported his many personal belongings to the bedroom Jorge Morales had so recently given up. In order to get his man out of the room, Richard handed him a large stack of cravats to starch and iron, then cheerfully set about reorganizing his things in the wardrobes and drawers.

A groggy Geoff, clad in an haphazardly fastened dressing gown, entered through an adjoining door without knocking, yawned, and said: "Jorge, what the devil do you mean by making all this racket?"

"Just settling in." Richard smiled as Geoffrey belatedly realized to whom he had just spoken. "Jorge has fled your arms, old fellow. But have no fear," Richard continued with a wicked grin, "I intend to stay."

Geoffrey turned and ran back into his room, slamming the door behind him. He sat down on the foot of his bed and stared at the door leading to Richard Sinclair's room. A wave of trembling seized him.

Richard, unperturbed by the actions of the man he loved, finished dressing and then went downstairs to enjoy the first hearty breakfast he had known in nearly a week.

A few hours later, both men elected to stroll within nature's wonderland and revel in the glories of the unclouded sky. Their separate serpentine wanderings brought them unexpectedly together in the woods to the east of Waverly Manor, the two coming upon each other with such suddenness that neither realized what had happened until they stood staring hungrily into each other's face. Geoffrey ran an unsteady hand through his black hair, tried to speak, could not.

"We meet again," Richard murmured with a soft smile as he began to move slowly towards the stunned Geoffrey. "Do you remember the first time we made love? It was on a day very much like this. We were on a picnic in the deserted hills just oustide of Rome. Do you remember?" Richard held Geoffrey's gaze trapped within his own. 'The sun was so hot, nearly blinding. I found that the only place I could look at with ease was into your eyes and that was how I discovered that you truly wanted me. I had been kissed by striplings in my schoolyears," Richard said as his arms slid around the mesmerized Geoff, "but never had I known a man until the moment you leaned forward and kissed me," he whispered before his mouth found Geoff's.

With a groan that might have been Richard's name, Geoffrey's mouth devoured the lips he had dreamt of so many nights when Jorge Morales had lain in his arms. His tongue plundered Richard's mouth while his hands raked over Richard's back and thighs and buttocks, the beating of their hearts racing out of control.

Sanity finally returned. Geoff wrenched himself from Richard's strong arms. He stood staring at his tormentor as he struggled to draw air into his lungs. 'Damn you," he said in a voice filled with pain. "Damn you!" he shouted again, and turned and for the second time that morning ran from Richard Sinclair.

It was several minutes before Richard collected himself. For one brief moment he had known happiness. To do without it once again seemed impossible. Slowly he began to walk back to Waverly Manor, taking the path along which Geoffrey had fled. He emerged into the back gardens and saw in the distance old Bert lovingly tending his flowers, Molly Sinclair at his side.

"There you are, Richard. I've been looking all over for you!"

Richard turned to stare down at the woman who had come to his side. "Joanna," he said as if from far away.

"Richard, what is wrong?"

"It is . . . nothing."

"I cannot believe you when I see such misery in your eyes," Joanna gently countered. "Come," she said, taking his arm.

Richard obediently followed his sister-in-law, her firm grip on his arm, and her many worried glances up into his face gradually returning him to his senses.

"Will you sit?" she asked when they had reached the shaded marble bench under an ancient oak tree.

"I . . . cannot." Richard began to pace restlessly before her.

Joanna stood watching him in silence as he seemed to wrestle with some difficult decision, until concern and curiosity would allow her to remain mute no longer. "Richard, what is wrong? I beg you tell me what it is."

Richard stopped his pacing and moved in front of her, capturing her hands in his. "Joanna," he said, his voice unsteady, "there is something I must tell you. I should have told you of it long before this but. . . . Has no one mentioned. . . . Have you not guessed?"

"What should I guess, Richard? What should I have heard?"

"That I am in love with Geoffrey Hunt-Stevens."

Joanna sat down abruptly on the bench behind her. Hurriedly Richard sat down beside her and looked anxiously into her eyes, awaiting her response. She stared at him a little dazedly and then cleared her throat and said, "Does no one at Waverly Manor love members of the opposite sex?"

"We love those that bring us the greatest happiness."

"Then why do I see such pain in your eyes?"

"This is nothing compared to what I do to Geoff."

"I do not understand you," Joanna said, slowly shaking her head.

"Then I will be plain," Richard replied. "Geoffrey will be my life's partner. He merely insists on struggling against the inevitability of his future."

Joanna turned and stared straight ahead of her, digesting this information.

"Joanna?"

"Richard, you are my brother more surely than Hugo can ever hope to be. I love you. It is just . . . this is a little outside my sphere of experience. Do you truly love each other?"

Richard smiled. "Truly."

"Well then, I am happy for you, if the Colonel will ever consent to making you happy."

"I'm wearing him down," Richard assured her.

"Oh but Richard, is it wise?" Joanna suddenly cried. "If your love for the Colonel should become known outside this circle you might be thrown in gaol, or flogged, or worse!"

"Geoffrey is more than worth the risk, Joanna. More to the point, living as you yourself have, perhaps you will understand when I say that my life has been spent perfecting the art of deception."

"I understand you," Joanna murmured.

"Then have no fears on my account," Richard said, warmly squeezing her hand.

"Richard, does Lady Diana . . . know about all of this?"

"Know about it? She's been our go-between ever since I arrived."

"I should have known," Joanna murmured.

"Indeed you should. Now tell me why you were looking for me earlier."

"Oh no, Richard, it is not important."

"It must be important for you to abandon your paints after being denied them for five days in a row in order to search me out," Richard insisted. "Tell me what has happened."

"It seems so silly to speak of it, but Richard, the oddest things have been happening! Aunt Hampton and Hugo have suddenly begun to plague me at every turn with a recitation of all my inadequacies as a mother. They speak of my inability to reason soundly, they belabor every defect of my character. And Tom . . . I told you Lord Carroll had come on an extended visit?"

"Just before the rains came, yes."

"With the change in the weather came the most extraordinary change in his conduct towards me! He has begun . . . Richard, I think Tom Carroll is courting me!"

Richard was silent for a moment and then he regarded his sister-in-law. "This is not unexpected, but there is more, I think, or you would not have sought me out."

"Richard," Joanna said slowly as she took one of his hands in both of hers and looked anxiously up into his face, "you know Hugo and Aunt Hampton and Tom Carroll better than anyone else in my acquaintance. Is it possible. . . . Could they actually be plotting to get me married?"

CHAPTER 19

"I noticed that Molly did not seem to be feeling well during lunch," Mrs. Hampton commented as she placidly worked on her needlepoint. "She appeared flushed with fever."

"Her cheeks have a rosy glow brought on by fresh air and exercise. It is a pleasure to no longer see her skin looking so sallow," Joanna replied, turning a page of Mr. Fielding's *Tom Jones*.

"She is becoming bloated."

"She is gaining weight," Joanna countered, looking up from her book. "For the first time in Molly's life I am unable to count her ribs when she undresses for bed."

"You appear to take a most cavalier attitude towards the well-being of your only child," Mrs. Hampton observed. "A father would take more care of Molly's health."

"A father would rejoice at the improvement in her constitution," Joanna retorted, snapping shut her book.

"Her running up and down the halls and yelling like a banshee is hardly progress," Mrs. Hampton intoned. "Her father would not tolerate such atrocious behavior."

"Her father is dead."

"I was speaking generally. Any father would take a firmer hand in Molly's upbringing and end these lunatic exercises you have started her on."

"We must leave that to the realm of conjecture, for Molly is not going to have another father. She will, therefore, have to make do with my hand in her upbringing."

"Not have a father? What can you be thinking of, Joanna? A child needs both parents, a mother *and* a father, if she is to have any hope of growing into a mature and healthy young woman free from that willfullness of spirit that fatherless girls are wont to develop under the lax hand of a mother's care. You are too tender, Joanna, too generous and too lenient for Molly's own good."

"I am an excellent mother!" Joanna exclaimed.

"Indeed. But you make a very poor father. Without a husband to guide you, Joanna, you have fallen prey to errors in judgment that cannot but harm your daughter in the end."

Outraged, Joanna took up her book and stalked from the Drawing Room, leaving Mrs. Hampton to complacently return to her needlepoint. Joanna went up to her room and attempted to return to her novel, but her agitation was too great to permit this pleasure. She tossed the book onto her bed, drew a shawl from her wardrobe, tied a bonnet to her head, and started back downstairs, ignoring an impulse to call Molly from her schoolroom for a walk outdoors. She would not prove herself lenient to Mrs. Hampton so soon after being charged with the crime.

Joanna walked through the conservatory and out into the late afternoon sunlight, the air cool and welcome on her skin. Taking a deep breath she let it out in a long sigh that did much to cleanse her of the unpleasantness of Mrs. Hampton's company. Aimlessly, she wandered through the formal gardens behind Pembroke, admiring a rose here, the bloom of a chrysanthemum there, and thinking all the while how much she preferred the lush, seemingly untamed gardens of Waverly Manor. So lost was she in thought that she was unaware of the footsteps drawing near until she looked up and spied Lord Carroll almost upon her. Wishing she might swear, but not having quite the temerity to do so, Joanna instead waited unsmiling for one of her oldest acquaintances to join her.

"How charming you look in that bonnet," Lord Carroll declared as he smiled down at her. "Your beauty but enhances Nature's offerings in this garden."

"Do not, I beg you Tom, begin another of your hymns to my beauty," Joanna implored, "for I could not tolerate it!"

"How can I not speak when my heart is swelled with your loveliness, Joanna," Lord Carroll said fervently, drawing closer. "You cannot be unaware of my feelings for you. I find that if I sleep I must dream of you, if I am awake I must think of you. Joanna, I loved you long before you married Colin Sinclair. I have been faithful to you all these years. Surely by now you have ceased to mourn your husband and may look unencumbered to your future. Let me be a part of that future, Joanna. Say that you will marry me."

"Oh Tom, why must you bring this to a head?" Joanna sighed miserably. "You know that I am fond of you, but I regard you as a brother, not a husband."

"I can change that regard into love!" Lord Carroll cried, grasping her arms.

"No, Tom, you cannot," Joanna insisted, carefully disengaging herself.

"Let me try, Joanna, please. I love you! You *can* and *shall* love me!" Lord Carroll pulled Joanna into his arms and kissed her.

She felt neither revulsion nor pleasure. She felt nothing whatsoever. And so she remained calmly in Lord Carroll's arms until he at last released her. "Can you now deny your feelings for me?" he demanded with a ragged breath.

"I have spoken honestly of my feelings for you from first to last, Tom. I do not love you. I will not marry you. My decision is irrevocable."

"No!" Again he tried to pull her into his grasp. But Joanna easily darted out of his reach and ran through the gardens, unmindful of Lord Carroll's infuriated shouts that she stop where she was and start behaving sensibly. Her actions, Joanna told herself, were perfectly sensible.

She ran for nearly a quarter of a mile and then slowed to a walk for she had not yet taken up Molly's daily exercise and lacked her stamina. But she continued to walk quickly through the park and emerged at last on the lane that led to Heddington. A further twenty minutes led her to a fork in the road and she turned to the left, towards Waverly Manor. Before she could fully realize how it had happened, Joanna found herself knocking on the front door and gaining admittance into the house through the momentarily startled Mrs. Pratt who could not discover where Lady Sinclair had left her carriage. The housekeeper led Joanna to the dining room where Diana, Hildegarde, and Jennifer were just sitting down to their evening meal.

"Good God, what has happened?" Diana cried, which was not a surprising reaction for, in her dusty shoes, her shawl hanging at her elbows, her bonnet slightly askew, her cheeks flushed, Joanna looked very much as if something had happened.

"Might I . . . speak with you a moment?" Joanna inquired somewhat breathlessly.

"Of course you may, child," Hildegarde said soothingly as she rose and led Joanna to the chair beside her own. "Come, have some supper with us."

"Oh, I couldn't possibly eat!"

"Then sit down and have a little wine," Hildegarde commanded. "It will do you a world of good, I promise."

After a few obedient sips, Joanna had to agree that the wine did indeed make her feel better. "Where are the others?" she asked, setting the goblet down.

"The men have gone off to carouse in the local inn," Jennifer sardonically replied, "so we may all sit here and have a private female coze."

"Thank heaven," Joanna said, and sighed in relief. "I think I have just created a good deal of trouble for myself." In as few words as possible she proceeded to relate the last fortnight's events at Pembroke Park: her family's insistence that she marry, and Lord Carroll's insistence today that she marry him.

"I think you have shown great fortitude," Jennifer stoutly declared from the end of the table.

"And I concur," Hildegarde said. "To defy such a united force shows much courage and great strength of character."

"But what if . . . I have it wrong, somehow?" Joanna worried. "My family's concern is perfectly natural. And Tom is an old acquaintance. He would make me a comfortable husband, I suppose. Oh dear," she sighed, "I am beginning to feel singularly pig-headed and childish."

"Now don't go falling into that trap," Hildegarde counseled. "They are trying to wear you down to have their own way and you mustn't let them."

"But why don't I want to marry Tom? Why don't I want to marry at all?"

"How would you describe your first marriage?" Hildegarde

inquired. "Were you happy?"

"Did your husband make you laugh?" Diana asked, speaking for the first time since her initial outburst and with such an intensity that Joanna found herself unable to pull her gaze from Diana's eyes.

She said softly, "Colin was not given to levity."

"Did he please you in bed?" Hildegarde asked.

"Lady Dennison!"

"Is something wrong?" Hildegarde asked, clearly puzzled by Joanna's outrage.

"Women do not speak of such things!" Joanna declared with utter moral certainty.

"Horsefeathers!" Hildegarde retorted. "Women speak of such things all the time. I certainly do, don't you, Diana?"

"Constantly," Diana affirmed, which set Jennifer to giggling and Joanna to staring at them all in amazement.

"But it isn't proper," she stammered.

"That *vile* word again," Hildegarde said in disgust. "Propriety, my dear Lady Sinclair, was invented by men solely to keep women in ignorance of even the most elemental human rights and needs. I, for example, never realized that a woman could derive pleasure from the sexual act until I had been married three years and a cousin of mine regaled me with the many delights she took in her dalliances with several of her husband's business associates. I was stunned by this new knowledge as you may well imagine."

Diana and Jennifer rocked with laughter while Joanna could only stare at Hildegarde, a blush stealing over her cheeks.

"My dear," Hildegarde said gently as she patted Joanna's hand, "if we women do not talk of such things we will only remain in ignorance, convinced that we are alone in our feelings and beliefs. Now tell me, did Lord Sinclair give you pleasure in bed?"

"He . . . treated me with great . . . tenderness," Joanna

managed to reply, her blush deepening. "He regarded . . . it . . . with much reverence."

"Oh good God," Diana could not help but say, "you must have been bored to tears!"

"I gather Lord Sinclair was singularly lacking in that passion which his brother so easily displays?" Hildegarde said.

"Colin was a man of most moderate temperament," Joanna said.

"That is all very well at the dinner table but it will not *do* in bed," Hildegarde declared.

"But Colin was an excellent husband to me. Really, I do not see that such things are of very great importance," Joanna insisted.

"Don't you?" Diana said with a softness that left Joanna's entire being hanging upon her words. "Did your husband never teach you that lovemaking is the greatest gift to any union? To express love physically unites the heart, the mind, and the body with your very soul."

"Heavens, Gwen must have been good," Hildegarde marveled.

"Hildegarde. . . ." Diana seethed.

"Certainly I know Celeste is," the older woman calmly continued.

"We are straying from the point," Diana said, attempting to ignore Joanna's piercing gaze. "Grant us please that sex *is* important; that making love should be highly pleasurable; and that passion must be present occasionally both in and out of bed. With such premises, Joanna, and what little you have told me of Lord Sinclair, it is my opinion that your marriage was rather dull. This casts no aspersions on you. You simply did not have the right material to work with."

"Which brings us back to Lord Carroll," Hildegarde said before Joanna could make any sort of response. "From what little I have heard and seen of him it is my opinion that he would make you a much worse husband than Lord Sinclair. He exhibits the common allotment of male arrogance and egotism that will overrule any opinion or plan you may have that runs contrary to his own. He seems to me a man who will claim his role as your head, your guardian, your master, once the ring is on your finger, with all of the force and authority that Christianity and English law confer upon him. He sounds a very poor bargain."

"Look at the state you are in now," Jennifer interrupted. "Do you think you could continue to stand up to Lord Carroll for what might easily be decades of marriage?"

Joanna's pained expression clearly indicated that she did not.

"Thus we very neatly dispose of Lord Carroll," Hildegarde said with obvious satisfaction.

"But this does not explain why I am so adamantly opposed to remarrying," Joanna said. "Colin and Tom are but two men. Their faults are not universal."

"I wouldn't be too sure about that," was Hildegarde's rejoinder.

"Why do I fear reentering a lawful, church-blessed union?" Joanna wondered.

"Perhaps," Diana quietly suggested, "you prefer in its place independence and the exercise of your free will . . . and heart."

Joanna regarded Diana for a moment and then a smile stole across her face. "Perhaps I do," she said softly.

* * *

An hour later Joanna returned to Pembroke Park in Diana's barouche enjoying a much calmer frame of mind than when she had left her ancestral home.

She had no sooner gone through the front door, however, than her brother grasped her by the arm and dragged her into the nearest parlor demanding to know where she had been these last three hours.

"I have been out walking," Joanna stiffly replied as she struggled without success to free herself from her brother's painful grip.

"Indeed," he sneeered. "And you return in Lady March's coach!"

"Where I went and how I returned can be of no concern to you, Hugo," Joanna angrily retorted, freeing herself at last and backing away from her brother. "How dare you treat me in such a brutish fashion!"

"And how dare you spurn so coldly the proposal of a gentleman and a friend!"

"Is this the cause of your insulting conduct?" Joanna hurled at him. "You abuse me merely because I will not marry Tom Carroll?"

"Merely?" Hugo raged. "Cannot you, even in your blindness, see the importance of such a match?"

"Importance to whom, Hugo?"

"To us all!" Hugo shouted. "You need the firm rule of a man, Joanna! And the financial peace of mind marriage with Tom Carroll would bring. Your daughter needs the guiding hand of a father. Are not these reasons enough to marry?"

"They are your reasons, not mine. They are your opinions of my life, not my own. I need no husband. I'll marry no man, particularly Tom Carroll."

Hugo turned abruptly away from his sister and stalked to a window that looked out across Pembroke's eastern gardens, a hand clenching and unclenching behind his back. Finally he turned back to Joanna, his face stiff, his eyes cold, his words clipped and under the sternest control. "You *will* marry Tom, Joanna. If you do not I shall disown you. Never again will you be allowed to visit Pembroke Park. You'll know neither my protection nor my aid. I shall withhold the monies you were to inherit from our grandmother upon your thirtieth birthday. You know that I can do this, Joanna. You know you cannot survive without my help. Think again, Joanna. You *will* marry Tom Carroll. I insist on it."

"You are the male head of this family and may do with our money as you think fit, Hugo. I can easily live year round in Kent on the money Colin left me and the income I would derive from my house in London. As for the rest," Joanna said, her voice choked with fury, "I shall bless the day I need not step foot in this mausoleum again. Goodnight Hugo!"

"Joanna!" Hugo's voice caught her at the door of the parlor. "If you have not placed your name beside Tom's on a marriage license by noon this Friday I shall have Lord Barthwaite declare you an unfit guardian of your daughter and have him place Molly in my custody until the day she marries! And I shall do more. If you persist in this insane obstinancy I shall have you committed to some safe place so that we need never be embarrassed by your words or your actions again. By Friday, Joanna, you will do as I say or feel the full force of my wrath bow you down!"

Joanna waited to hear no more but turned and fled the room and the house itself, running out into the night.

The cold evening air slowly brought a return to rational thought. She stood beneath the thick stars and knew with a certainty as dark as the night itself that her brother could and would do all that he had threatened. Molly, in Hugo's care, would wither and die. And what would she herself do, locked away in some airless prison, denied her daughter, her art, her life?

The chill of the evening air finally making itself felt, Joanna returned to Pembroke through a side door and made her way up back staircases to her room. Slowly, methodically, she locked her door, changed into her nightclothes, and then lowered herself into her rocking chair, allowing its gentle motion to soothe the tumult of her mind. She was faced with a crisis of unlooked for proportions. Only calm, rational thought could aid her now.

The dawn found Joanna dressed in her riding habit and impatiently rousing one of the Garfield grooms. Her ancient mare was saddled, Joanna tossed upon her back, and the groom forbidden to accompany her as propriety demanded. Joanna set the somnolent horse on a ragged canter towards Waverly Manor, her purpose firm: if Hugo insisted on using his influence to destroy her she had no recourse but to enlist her own sphere of influence to counter so vicious an attack.

The Manor gained, her horse tethered, entrance was attained into the house and then the parlor where all of the denizens of Waverly Manor had gathered after breakfast. Quickly Joanna told her friends of what had occurred. All were silent at her story's end.

Unable to control her fury, Diana jumped up and went to lean one hand against the mantle of the fireplace as she stared into the dancing flames below.

"The monster!" Jennifer cried at last. "Can he really do all that he threatens?"

"Depend upon it," Hildegarde said bitterly. "You forget, Jennifer, that we women are nonentities in English law. Mr. Garfield has every legal precedent behind him. Such things have occurred too many times for him not to succeed on his threats."

"He will not, however, be given the opportunity," Diana declared in a cold voice as she turned to face the others.

"No, he will not," Richard agreed as he sat down beside his sister-in-law. "Joanna, the money is nothing. You know I will help you in every possible way. More than that, if Hugo does indeed carry through on his threats I shall take him instantly to court. I've a greater legal claim to Molly's custody. Rest assured, Joanna, you'll not lose your daughter."

"But she could still lose her freedom," Peter pointed out. "It's no good, Richard. Garfield's got to be stopped before he even gets started."

"He might meet with an untimely accident," Geoffrey suggested.

"An admirable scheme, but one to be used only as a last resort," Hildegarde replied with a smile.

"You are all talking nonsense and I wish you would stop," Diana declared in a calm voice that drew all eyes to her. "Mr. Garfield has kindly given us three days in which to defeat this horrendous scheme and I suggest we use them wisely. Joanna," she said, her green eyes locked on Joanna, "can you and Molly be ready to leave Pembroke by Friday?"

"Yes, of course. But it will do no good to run," Joanna replied. "Hugo will only find us."

"When I am through with your brother he will be glad to forget your very existence I promise you, Joanna."

"What do you have in mind, Diana?" Richard asked.

"Mr. Garfield enjoys issuing threats. I will counter them with some of my own," Diana replied.

"But how?" Joanna asked.

"What do you know of your brother's investments?"

"Why . . . almost nothing."

"What can you learn by noon tomorrow?" Diana asked.

"Anything you need to know, my friend," Joanna declared with her old strength.

"What is wending its way through that devious mind of yours?" Jennifer demanded.

Diana regarded the young woman with an ingenuous smile. "I am curious to discover," she replied, "if it is possible to completely ruin someone in forty-eight hours' time."

CHAPTER 20

With a calm Joanna found remarkable, she advanced down Pembroke's Grand Staircase, smoothing her traveling dress as she went. Reaching the Entrance Hall, she turned, stuck her tongue out at the gargoyle leering at her, and then made her way to the Pembroke breakfast room. She entered to find—as she had hoped—her brother, her aunt, and Lord Carroll already seated at the table.

"Joanna!" Mrs. Hampton barked. "You are late. Why are you dressed in such a fashion?"

"I've come to say goodbye," Joanna announced in a firm voice as she returned her brother's dark gaze. "I am leaving

194

Pembroke and intend never to return. I realize it is not yet noon, Hugo, but I trust that you will forgive my feminine impetuosity in exchange for a prompt and unequivocal response to your ultimatum. I shall not bow down to your command now or at any time in the future. But I thank you for this opportunity to flee a home I have detested from birth."

"You think I will allow the tender feelings of a brother to overrule me, but you are mistaken, Joanna," Hugo replied, his voice murderous. "I swear to you that I shall carry out every threat I have made. I will disown you. I shall take your daughter from you and have Lord Barthwaite declare you insane!"

"You must, of course, do as you think best, Hugo. Goodbye Aunt Hampton, Tom, Hugo. This has, I fear, been an entirely unpleasant visit," Joanna said.

Turning on her heel, she quit the room and, a moment later, Pembroke itself, forever.

Joanna entered a world of warm June sunshine radiating across a clear blue sky. She drew in a deep breath of the fragrant air and smiled despite all the difficulty of her present actions. Then she walked up to her barouche, settled herself beside Molly and opposite Miss Anthony and her maid, Ellen, and then informed her coachman that he could drive them out of Pembroke Park.

Hugo, meanwhile, was pacing the breakfast room in increasing agitation.

"I warned you, Hugo. I warned you not to press her too hard! But you would not heed me and this is the result," Lord Carroll cried. "All our plans are for nought because of your heavy-handedness."

"How could she do this?" Mrs. Hampton moaned. "Does she not realize what a scandal this will cause?"

"Be quiet the both of you!" Hugo thundered. "I will not have you jabbering like magpies when I am trying to think."

There was silence for a moment and then Hugo bellowed for Winston, his butler, and when that beleaguered servant appeared, ordered him to have his chestnut gelding saddled at once.

"Hugo, what are you going to do?" Lord Carroll asked. "She is gone. It is ended."

"Hardly that," Hugo seethed. "I gave my word to Joanna and I intend to keep it! I shall have Lord Barthwaite's men after them before the hour is out."

Hugo stormed from the room and upstairs to change into his riding breeches and boots. Ten minutes were all that were required before he was stepping into the saddle and spurring his horse down the gravel drive of Pembroke.

He emerged onto the lane fronting Pembroke Park at a hard canter, his mind churning with all he had suffered at his mad sister's hands. He dwelled upon her intractibility, her ingratitude, her willful disobedience. He recalled every instance in which she had set herself in opposition to his expressed wishes. Joanna might have been taken in hand and shown the error of her ways had she not come under the damnable influence of that wretched Lady March.

All of his difficulties had stemmed from That Woman's entrance into Herefordshire. Joanna had been drawn to her like a moth to a flame, already she was burned beyond recognition. Lady March had corrupted her.

Hugo's heart seemed to stop. How far had the corruption gone?

His vision blurred by his fury at such a thought, Hugo was only dimly aware of a horse suddenly emerging from the side of the road and stopping directly before him. Hugo jerked back on his reins causing his horse to rear hysterically from the pain of his mouth.

"Blast you!" Hugo shouted. "Have you no more sense than to—" He finally recognized the rider who had so unceremoniously interrupted his journey. "Lady March! I might have known."

"And how well your sister knows you," Diana remarked pleasantly. "She said that you would set out for Lord Barthwaite before too many minutes had passed. You must be on a mission of some importance to cause your horse's sides to bleed so profusely."

"I'll see you in hell!" Hugo raised his riding crop to strike Diana.

"It would be my very great pleasure to send you there," a low, masculine voice offered from behind Hugo. "You could be our welcoming committee."

Hugo wheeled his horse to discover Richard Sinclair seated upon a fine black gelding, smiling at him, a pistol resting casually on the pommel of his saddle. "Have you become highwaymen then?" Hugo sneered.

"On the contrary," Diana returned in an amused voice, "think of us as counselors, sibyls, servants to your future. We've come to advise you, Mr. Garfield."

"You can have nothing to say that would interest me," Hugo declared. "Now out of my way!"

"Don't be so rash, Mr. Garfield," Diana said soothingly as she blocked his path. "Lord Barthwaite will wait. It will do you no harm to listen to what we have to say. Richard, I fear, would be forced to shoot you in some nonvital limb should you try to abscond without benefiting from our pearls of wisdom."

"Sinclair?" Hugo laughed. "He wouldn't dare!"

"I should like you to put me to the test, old fellow. Really I would." Richard smiled engagingly.

Hugo regarded him, and for the first time that morning began to know fear. "Very well," he said. "What have you to say to me?"

Richard grinned. "Obliging fellow, ain't he?"

"Top notch," Diana agreed. "Tell me, Mr. Garfield, do the names Ainsbury Coal, Waterbury Incorporated, and

Danby and Fine mean anything to you? No? Then permit me to remind you, Mr. Garfield, that they are companies in which you have invested quite heavily in recent years. Now I am certain that you will recall the Chinese Star and the Imperial Lady, for they are ships you have but recently purchased and outfitted. They are the base, I believe, upon which you intend to build a merchantile fleet to rival anything seen in London or Southampton. An ambitious scheme, Mr. Garfield, and an expensive one as I am certain you are all too aware. Your finances are in a precarious state just at the present. Neither Lord Sinclair nor I wish to see you place them in any greater danger."

"What do you mean?" Hugo demanded. "What are you saying? I tire of these games. Tell me what you have to say and then leave me be!"

"Gladly," Diana replied. "I have just acquired a controlling share of stock in Ainsbury Coal, Waterbury Incorporated, and Danby and Fine. Also, I have bought out your partner, Mr. Bartlett, and now own fifty-three percent of the Chinese Star and the Imperial Lady. I've even acquired the mortgage you made on Pembroke Park to finance your investments. Let me be blunt, Mr. Garfield: I own you. If you make one move against Joanna or Molly I will crush you as I would some loathsome insect."

"And if financial ruin does not frighten you," Richard cheerfully offered as Hugo began rhythmically rapping his riding crop against his own boot, "allow me to remind you that I am a man of some influence at Court. If you ever threaten or harass my sister-in-law again, if you dare to challenge her reputation, if you attempt to separate her from her daughter I shall see to it that you are forever denied the peerage you have dreamt of for so long."

Hugo regarded these two and felt the blood pounding in his ears. "What do you want me to do?" he asked at last.

"Nothing," Diana replied amiably, "that is the beauty of

it. Do nothing, Mr. Garfield, and you will be allowed to continue just as you are. Do anything to upset Joanna, however, and we will destroy you. It's all quite simple, really."

"I'll not be the puppet to dance to your tune!" Hugo cried.

"Then you are lost," Richard replied.

Silence hung over them as Hugo sat upon his horse suffering the turmoil of conflicting emotions.

"You must decide your future now, Mr. Garfield," Diana declared, breaking into his maelstrom of thought. "You may either ride on to Lord Barthwaite, or turn your horse and return to Pembroke like a sensible man. The choice is entirely your own."

Hugo looked from Diana to Richard and then to Diana again. "Damn you!" he hissed. "Damn you!"

Hugo wheeled his horse and spurred him down the road back to Pembroke Park.

"I thought he took that very well," Richard said with a grin.

Diana smiled in turn. "Really, the man is a pleasure to deal with." Together they set their horses to a gentle canter towards Waverly Manor.

Joanna's barouche stood in front of the house. The Hunt-Stevenses, Peter, and Hildegarde stood clustered around Molly and Joanna in the front drive. All were anxiously peering down the road.

"There they are!" Molly shouted a moment before everyone else could detect the two riders coming towards them.

"Well it is about time," Hildegarde harrumphed. "I could have managed the whole affair in a far more expeditious manner."

Diana and Richard jumped from their horses and handed the reins to the groom who had come running towards them.

"Not a shot fired," Richard declared with a grin as he strode up to his sister-in-law and kissed her cheek, unaware of Geoffrey's sigh of relief.

"Thank God," Joanna breathed. "It went well?"

"It couldn't have gone better," Diana assured Joanna from her position some ten feet away for she could not bring herself to draw any nearer. It required, in fact, all her concentration just to speak in a normal voice. The Sinclair barouche, laden with trunks, was an all too clear reminder of the leave-taking she had yet to endure. "You may go to Kent without fear of pursuit or persecution. Hugo Garfield has been made to see sense and will trouble you no more."

"It seems scarcely possible," Joanna murmured.

"I've notified the staff at Laurelwood to expect their former mistress," Richard said, slipping an arm around his sister-in-law's waist. "Think of it as your home, Joanna, until your tenants have removed from Hetchley Place and you may retire, at last to your own estblishment."

Joanna smiled. "You'll not be our outrider?"

"I've some unfinished business to attend to in Herefordshire first. I'll join you as soon as I am able."

"I've no wish to be the humbug," Jennifer broke in, "but the hour is advancing and Lady Sinclair has a long journey before her. She should be off."

"Yes, she should," Joanna said with a sigh, "and she finds it nearly impossible to do. I've known you all for such a short time, yet I feel closer to you than to anyone else in my life. How can I leave?"

"Because you have no desire to live within a hundred miles of your brother," Peter replied.

"Too true!" Joanna laughed. "The voice of reason amidst so much madness. Thank you, Mr. Elliot," she said, extending her hand which Peter raised to his lips. With Molly trailing sadly behind her, Joanna slowly moved around the circle offering a kiss or a handshake as she insisted that everyone visit her that summer.

Finally mother and daughter turned to regard Diana who stood rooted to the spot where she had jumped from her horse. Joanna thought that she had never seen Diana look more beautiful. Diana stood so still, so silent in the brown trousers and vest and the blue shirt in which she had first met Joanna, the June sunshine dancing through the honeyed gold of her hair, her eyes unwillingly held by Joanna's gaze. Joanna felt a sudden urge to rush into her arms and never let her go. Molly, however, circumvented this impulse by hurtling herself in a flood of tears into her mentor's arms, insisting that she could not possibly leave when the roses were blooming so profusely.

Gently Diana calmed her apprentice, imploring her to stop such weeping. "Now come, you would not have me remember you with red eyes and a runny nose, would you?" she asked. Molly bravely shook her head and hurriedly wiped her eyes with the back of her hand. "That's my little cub." Diana smiled. "Mrs. Pratt and Bert and Joy and Harmony and that wretched peacock are all waiting to say goodbye to you and it would not do to keep them waiting. Off you go!"

Molly obediently ran off in search of her five friends as Diana slowly straightened and returned her eyes at last to the hazel gaze that had never left her. A sound like thunder roared in her ears, a tremor began deep within Diana's breast as Joanna came to her, a hand reaching out and gently brushing her cheek.

"How can I thank you for all that you have done for me?" Joanna softly asked.

"You played the Knight Errant for me once. I was glad to return the favor," Diana managed to reply.

"But there is so much more than what you have done for me today. . . . In seven and twenty years you are the first, my best friend. It seems madness to leave you, and madness to stay. Hetchley is not so large and grand as Waverly but I can promise you only the best company. Will you come? Will you visit?"

"It is difficult," Diana said hesitantly. "There are so many things that claim my attention. It hardly seems—"

"Diana, please. You must," Joanna insisted.

"I. . . ."

"Please."

"I'll come," Diana whispered, closing her eyes against the pain of the moment and thus leaving her unprepared as Joanna's lips softly brushed her own. Shock waves rocked through Diana.

"Thank you, my friend," Joanna said into Diana's stunned eyes before she turned with the last ounce of purpose she possessed and made her final goodbyes.

Molly came running from the house carrying a small basket bearing the cinnamon muffins Mrs. Pratt had herself taken from Juan Carlos's oven. Goodbyes were hurriedly called to the small group gathered in front of Waverly Manor as Joanna helped Molly back into the barouche and then sat beside her, her eyes caught by the intensity of Diana's gaze. The coachman lifted his whip and set the barouche moving easily down the road.

Caring not what the others might think, Diana turned and fled into Waverly Manor, running up the main staircase and stopping only when she had reached the eastern window of her bedroom. From there she could follow the path of the Sinclair barouche, a dull, aching throb in her heart increasing with each breath she took. "She's gone," echoed within her mind, repeating over and over again until Diana thought she would go mad. "She's gone, she's gone."

Unable to watch the coach any longer, Diana spun around, an arm smashing into a Greek vase resting on the lacquered table by the window, sending it crashing to the floor. One sob and then another broke from her throat until she was racked with weeping. She wrapped her arms around herself and still the choking sobs came until she could scarcely breathe and did not care if she ever did so again.

Drawn by the sound of the shattering vase, Hildegarde and Jennifer ran into the room.

"Go away!" Diana sobbed. "Please, I beg of you leave me alone!"

"Oh my poor child," Hildegarde crooned, pulling Diana into her arms. "Don't be afraid to weep for her."

"Oh Hildy," Diana sobbed, ceasing her struggle and collapsing into the older woman's arms, "why must everyone that I love leave me?"

Hildegarde and Jennifer looked at each other as Diana was once again overcome by her tears.

"What is wrong? What has happened?" Geoffrey demanded as he joined Richard in Diana's doorway. Richard took the taller man's arm and pulled him down the hall.

"Diana has admitted to herself the true scope of her feelings for Joanna," he replied. "She is mourning the loss of the woman she loves."

"Poor Diana," Geoffrey sighed. "I should go to her. I might help—"

"Help *me,* damn it!" Richard exploded. "I need you! I love you. My God Geoff, if Diana can love Joanna, can love at all after everything she's been through, why the devil can't you admit the depth of your own feelings and come to me?"

Geoffrey's eyes anxiously scanned the taut lines of Richard's face, seeing at last the pain and hunger. A sigh broke from him as he stepped into Richard's arms, murmuring love and need, his mouth ending its long famine as his lips eagerly found Richard's own.

CHAPTER 21

To be a scavenger of a beach in Cornwall in the month of August would not, as a rule, recommend itself as an occupation worthy of the undivided attention of a surprisingly well-educated English noblewoman, but this did not concern Diana. To walk barefoot across the sand on this day, the waves lapping and chilling her toes as a fine mist turned to drizzle and thence to rain, would have struck even the most casual observer as a rather lunatic thing to do, but Diana did not regard it so. She was hunting for shells as she did every day, or so she told herself. Shells to send to Molly Sinclair. Diana entertained herself by imagining the pleasure they

would bring to the freckled eight-year-old and the praise that
their beauty would elicit . . . from anyone else who chose to
study them.

Already she had a fine collection to send, for she walked
this beach for several hours each day. She had forgotten how
well Cornwall suited her. The harshness of the coast, the
passion of its weather, the beauty of the land itself
reverberated within her and had prolonged what was to have
been a visit of only a few days into a stay of over a fortnight.
Perhaps, Diana thought as she wrested a pink shell from its
thickly embedded sandy prison, she would move back here
once the sale of Waverly Manor was completed. Perhaps, she
thought as the rain began to fall in earnest, this was where
she was meant to be all along.

How quickly Waverly, and Herefordshire itself, had palled
on her. Even her garden had failed to provide any pleasure.
Hugo Garfield had seen to it that no one called on her, and
that no one sent her an invitation to a ball or a dinner. She
and her guests had been left to their own amusements and
these had quickly failed to amuse, or so it had seemed to
Diana.

Noticing at last how heavy her gown had become in the
rain, Diana turned and began the long walk back to Marwick,
her ancestral home.

The March family had inhabited this Cornish estate for
some six hundred years and had had the sense to permit the
ancient structure to remain unmarred by the architectural
fashions of succeeding years. It had been the scene, for
Diana, of much happiness in her childhood. Odd that it did
not provide the same sensation now. Diana's fingers sifted
through the shells in the basket held in the crook of her arm.
Yes, Molly would be pleased with this gift. She might make a
necklace of them as Diana once had for Gwen when they had
visited Crete . . . but that had been such a long time ago. . . .

"Diana, are you mad?" Jennifer shrieked. "You'll catch

pneumonia in this downpour. And if that doesn't do you in, Hildy will have your head!"

'I'm fine, Jennifer. Really," Diana replied as she allowed her anxious friend to pull her through Marwick's front door and into the small Entry Hall where she proceeded to drip on the flagstone floor.

"Of course you're fine," Jennifer scoffed, "and I'm the Grand Duchess of Budapest."

"Good heavens, Diana, what have you done to yourself now?" Hildegarde demanded as she emerged from the front parlor.

"It's raining," Diana replied as she began to mount the staircase. "I'm going to change."

"You're going to have a hot bath and get right into bed with a good cup of tea!" Hildegarde said resoundingly. "Pratt! Mrs. Pratt! Oh where *is* that woman when you need her?"

"I'm fine, Hildegarde. Don't upset yourself."

"Fine, are you?" Hildegarde snorted. "When was the last time you ate a decent meal? When was the last time you had a full night's sleep? When was the last time—"

"Enough, Hildy," Diana broke in wearily. "I am going upstairs to change."

"You are going to have a hot bath," Hildegarde countered. "Mrs. Pratt, where the devil are you?"

Mrs. Pratt, capable woman that she was, had observed her mistress approaching Marwick and had already seen to it that a bath was installed in her ladyship's bedroom. She listened impassively to Diana's protests, then calmly stripped the frigid gown from her employer and threatened her with castor oil and gruel if she did not get into the tub at once.

Jennifer, meanwhile, had searched out Peter. Together they sat down to a council of war with Hildegarde in the front parlor. They argued passionately for several hours over the best course to take and adjourned at last, their plot simmering and ready to spring upon their unsuspecting victim with the evening meal.

"You're what?" Diana choked, and then coughed as her sip of turtle soup, the first course of Juan Carlos's dinner, went down her windpipe.

"Going to Kent," Hildegarde carefully enunciated from the opposite end of the dinner table.

"But . . . but . . . but . . . " Diana sputtered.

"It has been nearly two months since we last saw Lady Sinclair and we find that we miss her company very much," Peter calmly informed his hostess.

"You're leaving me?" Diana asked in a small voice.

"En masse." Jennifer smiled.

"But you can't!"

"Of course we can," Hildegarde said. "My dear Diana, we have accompanied you to the Lake Country with the Lamberts. Amidst so much natural splendor you remained mute and miserable, and depressed the Lamberts so much that they fled to Denmark. We then toured Derbyshire with both you and that snooty Italian Countessa whose acidic acquaintance you continue to court for no good reason that I can recall. Even she could not tolerate your wan expression and had the very good sense to return to Rome. We have come with you to Cornwall where it has rained every day for the last fortnight and frankly, Diana, none of us can tolerate another minute of such misery. We are going to Kent where the sun reputedly shines all summer long and where we may be warmed at least by the beauty of Joanna Sinclair's smile."

A flicker of pain crossed Diana's face. "I bore you then," she said dully.

"Frankly, yes," Jennifer replied. "Geoff and Richard billing and cooing every minute of the day was bad enough, and we were well rid of them. But watching you waste away because you have not the temerity to pursue Joanna Sinclair is by far the worst way of spending a summer that I can think

208

of."

"How can I pursue Joanna?" Diana demanded with sudden anger. "She is a gentlewoman of the strictest upbringing who feels for me only the kind regard of a friend."

"She also writes to you at least three times a week," Peter pointed out.

"And begs you to visit her," Jennifer added.

"And closes each letter with a warmth that only a dimwit like yourself could fail to understand," Hildegarde stated.

"Oh stop it, all of you!" Diana demanded in a voice very near to shouting. "It is preposterous. Joanna cannot love me."

"How do you know this?" Hildegarde inquired. "Have you ever asked her?"

"Are you mad? And lose her forever?"

"You have been behaving as if Lady Sinclair had been swept away with the tide never to return," Hildegarde snapped. "She is alive, Diana, and begging you to come to her. Why not go with all the love in your heart to find, perhaps, that her heart is as large and as full as your own?"

"It is impossible," Diana whispered. "She cannot love me."

Peter smiled. "How can she not love you when we all adore you?"

"Then why are you leaving?"

"Because we can't stand the sight of you anymore," Jennifer replied. "You've lost weight, you can't sleep, you don't laugh, you never even smile. You've not sat at your pianoforte in two months. There is just so much unhappiness a friend can withstand, after all."

"I cannot go to Kent. Not now," Diana pleaded. "Perhaps in another week or two—"

"You have been saying that for the whole this summer," Hildegarde broke in. "I have never in my life aided and abetted procrastination and cowardice and I'll not start now. I came to England to look after you, Diana. I have left Celeste all alone for the last six months in a city noted for its passionate and predatory women. Celeste is by nature faithful, but there is just so much temptation a woman can withstand. I therefore wash my hands of you. If you refuse to take care of yourself, why should I do the job for you?"

"I thought you were my friend," Diana said bitterly.

"I am. And as your friend I advise you to go to Kent and throw yourself at Joanna Sinclair's feet. She'll make you happier than Gwen ever dreamt of doing."

"I'll not have you run my life, Hildegarde," Diana seethed.

Hildegarde shrugged. "As you will. We leave for Kent tomorrow."

Despite Diana's firm belief that this was some jest, a practical joke at best, blackmail at worst, and that nothing would come of it, Hildegarde, Peter, and Jennifer loaded their various trunks, valises, and servants into their carriages and departed before the sun had been but three hours risen in the partly cloudy sky. Diana watched them go in utter amazement; never had she believed that they would desert her, much less without a backward glance. Slowly she returned to the house. She felt the sudden stillness of Marwick surround her until she thought she would suffocate.

Without her friends to distract her, Diana found that she could not be still. She took to prowling the large stone home where centuries of mad March women had dwelt, and to riding about the countryside for hours on end. And still she could not escape the pain of her thoughts and her heart. The incessant rain that had suited her mood so well began to irritate. And worse, each day brought a new letter from Joanna detailing the many means of entertainment she and her brother-in-law and all of their guests were devising for themselves in Kent. Diana had not known that the woman she loved could be so cruel.

Ten days after her friends had deserted her Diana sat curled up in a chair before the fireplace in her room, another of Joanna's letters in her hand. How easy it was to see Molly high up in an apple tree and to hear Joanna's voice tinged with anger and amusement as she demanded for the third time that Molly come down at once. Diana could imagine the way Joanna would smile at one of Hildegarde's caustic remarks over dinner, the corners of those full lips turning up and then parting to reveal even white teeth, and a throaty laugh that made Diana shiver.

Diana sat in her chair for hours, until the warmth of the fire and several glasses of wine lulled her slowly to sleep, the letter slipping from her fingers.

Diana dreamt that she lay naked beneath cool silk sheets in the heat of midafternoon. She knew of nothing ouside this room with its drawn curtains that left it shadowed, expectant. The sheets caressed her thighs, her belly, her breasts, and she hungered for the hands, so like silk, yet skilled in the art of passion.

The door opened. Joanna entered clothed only in a white chemise. Entered and waited until Diana held out her hand. "Please," she whispered.

Joanna smiled and then the chemise slipped lazily to the ground allowing Diana to feast on the sight of those full breasts and large brown nipples, the rounded belly, the curling mass of dark hair that set her heart to shuddering.

Slowly Joanna came to her. She took Diana's outstretched hand and kissed the fingertips and then the palm, allowing her tongue to circle the fevered center. Diana's need poured from her throat in a long strained moan. "Please," she whispered again, "it has been so long."

Joanna nodded, and Diana quickly slid to the center of the bed, the silk teasing her body. But when she looked up Joanna was gone, vanished, with nothing remaining but the chemise crumpled upon the floor and Hildegarde's voice saying over and over: "She hasn't been swept away with the tide. She's in Kent, she's in Kent, she's in Kent."

With a strangled cry Diana dragged herself from sleep, pushed herself from her chair, and began to pace the room. "She's in Kent, she's in Kent, she's in Kent," continued ringing in her mind. Suddenly Diana grasped her wine glass and sent it hurtling into the fireplace.

"Damn you all!" she shouted. "I give up. I concede. Just let me be. I'll go to Kent!"

CHAPTER 22

"Will she never come?" Joanna said as she let the curtain fall and once again began to roam around the room.

Hildegarde smiled. "Such impatience. It is not yet ten by your own clock on that mantle you have just passed. She will be here shortly. Diana has many faults, but she is always punctual."

"How I wish you were staying, Hildegarde."

"You have no need of my services, but Celeste most emphatically does."

Joanna stopped and was silent for a moment. "Hildegarde," she said tentatively, "what is it like . . . loving

212

Celeste?" Instantly would she have called back so outrageous a question, but her voice died away as Hildegarde gazed at her knowingly from over the rim of her book. A blush burned Joanna's face.

"It is the greatest joy and the greatest pain I have ever known in my life," Hildegarde slowly replied. "Celeste can fill me with such passion or happiness or fury and all in the span of three minutes."

"Is it hard to live your lives as outcasts?" Joanna asked, a desperation she could not name pressing her on.

"We aren't really outcasts, you know. We enjoy a large acquaintance and Celeste is a woman of some power in Vienna. We are shunned by a few people, certainly, but I have never been disturbed by that. You forget, my dear, that I have known what it is to move in the most proper and noble of circles. I can think of nothing to recommend it. Hard to be outcast? Not at all. But impossible to live without Celeste."

Joanna took this in and then wandered around the room again. "This last fortnight has been so very difficult," she said as she idly shook out a pillow.

"Has it?"

"I am forever forced to observe Cupid capering through my gardens," Joanna complained as she began to rearrange six yellow roses in a vase. "Richard and Geoffrey seem incapable of doing anything save gazing into each other's eyes; Jennifer and Peter grow more forward in their attentions to each other with each passing day; and you keep speaking of all these infernally steamy letters you receive from Celeste! It is really quite trying at times."

Hildegarde smiled. "I daresay it is."

Joanna, suspecting collusion amongst these new friends of hers, was silent as she went once again to look out the front window. "Why won't you tell me about Gwen McFadden?" she asked without looking around.

"That is something for Diana to do."

"Diana has never even mentioned her to me."

"Then you must bring her to do so."

"What right have I?"

"As much right as Celeste has to ask me of my marriage to Lord Dennison."

Joanna turned and stared at the older woman, a blush inflaming her face once again, her mind in so tumultuous a state that she did not even hear Molly shriek "She's here! She's here!" until her daughter burst into the parlor, captured her hand, and began to drag her from the room. Desperately Joanna tried to collect herself as she was pulled inexorably towards the front door and her first glimpse of Diana March in ten weeks.

Her entrance into the cool September morning air steadied Joanna and she was able to take in the green and gold barouche pulling to a stop in the circular drive, as well as note the startling absence of Hildegarde, Peter, Jennifer, Richard and Geoffrey, all of whom, she knew, had been awaiting this arrival with much anticipation. Nor could she ignore the thudding of her own heart and the quickening of her pulse as the coach door opened and Diana jumped lightly, gracefully to the ground.

Joanna drank her in, all of her: the mass of honey hair like a halo in the morning sunlight; the green eyes darkened with shadow; the wide mouth grinning as Molly hurtled herself into her arms with a screech. Joanna's eyes feasted on Diana's smaller form, sweeping over the gentle swell of her breasts and the soft rounding of hips that had haunted too many of her dreams.

Diana looked up and their eyes met and held. "Hullo, Joanna," she said softly.

Her voice brought every nerve in Joanna's body back to life. She found herself grinning like a giddy schoolgirl and running down the front steps to pull Diana into a quick hug.

"Oh, I am so glad you have come!" she exclaimed. "Never have five days passed so slowly. Why could you not have come with your letter? You think me ridiculous, I know, but it is annoying how much I have missed you!"

Diana threw back her head and laughed. "With such a welcome I was mad to stay away so long."

"Yes you were," Molly solemnly agreed. "I don't know why you stayed in Cornwall. It must be an awful place for now you look just as I used to before I began to garden. Don't they have any gardens in Cornwall?"

"None whatsoever," Diana replied, flushing. "Come, show me this Kentish haven of yours and then feed me, I am suddenly famished."

Instantly Joanna looped her arm through Diana's and felt a sudden stiffness, a resistance; then Molly feverishly clasped Diana's other hand and led them all into the two-story Tudor house. They toured a large parlor, a small salon, a small library, a dining room, and a breakfast room on the first floor, while Molly told Diana all the work she had done in the back garden and in the flowered border that surrounded the house, promising to show her everything.

Joanna felt Diana slowly relax under these ministrations and knew a relief of such proportions that her own voice joined that of Molly in describing what had come with them from Laurelwood after Colin Sinclair's death. Journeying to the second floor they surveyed five bedrooms, Molly's schoolroom, and Joanna's studio, Molly still chattering away with an occasional comment from Joanna.

As Diana's tension eased she began to comment on Joanna's paintings which hung throughout the house, and Joanna's blushes grew more heated and the pounding of her heart more painful as she watched Diana devour these works with her green eyes, and praise and analyze and praise them again. All that Joanna had hoped to capture in paint was seen somehow by Diana and admired in a rush of words and exclamations that left Diana constantly breathless and Joanna reeling with an hitherto unknown pleasure.

Their tour ended in Joanna's bedroom and there the sunlight from a southern window streamed in on the painting Joanna had completed several weeks earlier of Molly in Waverly's gardens. She had placed a blooming rose bush in the foreground with Molly rapturously nestling her nose amongst its soft pink petals. Lush vegetation surrounded them with riotous abandon.

Molly declared that she looked very silly posed like that, but Diana shook her head. "You are wrong, little cub," she murmured as she gazed at the painting from the doorway. "Very wrong. It is brilliant, Joanna, truly."

"If you admire my work so very much you must allow me to paint you," Joanna impulsively declared.

"Oh yes!" Molly cried.

"No! It is impossible!" Diana stammered, drawing her arm from Joanna's and taking a step back from the room.

"Whyever not?" Joanna asked, puzzled by such sudden vehemence.

"I . . . am too plain for your paints," Diana replied as a hand that trembled slightly smoothed the skirt of her traveling dress.

"Don't be absurd," Joanna said, her body yearning for a return of that closeness they had shared but a moment earlier. "You are lovely, fascinating. I have wanted to paint you since we first met. It would give me such pleasure. . . . Why don't you want me to paint you?"

"You must not. Your eyes are too piercing," Diana replied in a low voice, a blush once again stealing over her cheeks. "It would be unendurable. As an artist you must see into your subject and understand it thoroughly in order to paint it well and if you look into me . . . you might see things that would disturb you. I wear . . . masks, Joanna. I shall feel naked if you paint me."

The air seemed to crackle with Diana's tension and Joanna realized, with astonishment, that the other woman was terrified . . . of her! Unable to comprehend this revelation she spoke without thinking. "I do not, as a rule, do nudes. However, if I were to paint you in the nude I would see no more of you than I do now. Your masks are perhaps not so effective as you would wish."

"There's a frightening thought for you," Diana said softly, looking everywhere but at Joanna.

"It is frightening only for someone who does not want to be seen for what she is, and what you are, Diana, is a beautiful woman comprised of intelligence, wit, strength, and a fragility that will take all of my talent to capture."

"May I watch you paint Lady Diana, Mama?" Molly asked eagerly.

"On occasion."

"But I haven't . . ." Diana began to protest. "Very well," she sighed, "you have a new subject for your paints, though it will undoubtedly drive me to drink."

"I have a small but ample wine cellar," Joanna assured her with a grin. She led Diana to her room and bid her wash and change for lunch.

Diana entered the Hetchley dining room twenty minutes later to discover everyone seated before her. "Well, well, well," she said jauntily as she advanced to the only remaining empty chair, "I thought I'd been deserted once again yet here you all are. And where, might I ask, have you been hiding yourselves?"

"We've been rambling amidst the wonders of a Kentish autumn," Peter volunteered.

"I see. You're looking well, Colonel," Diana politely remarked to her luncheon partner.

"It's *Mr.* Hunt-Stevens now, Diana. I've been cashiered, you see. The cavalry has a nasty habit of separating a man from the object of his devotion. And love does wonders for the complexion."

"You'd never know it by Diana," Hildegarde observed. "You look absolutely white, child."

"It has been raining a good deal at Marwick," Diana grimly replied. "And how are you, Hildy?"

"Splendid, thank you. I leave tomorrow for Dover and sail on the evening tide."

"You're leaving? But . . . but I've just arrived!"

"And it has put my mind at ease. Joanna can provide all that you require much better than I could ever hope to do. I may go now with a clear conscience. Celeste has written me a most impassioned letter. I don't dare delay my return for even one day."

"And Geoff and I are off tomorrow for a tour of Wales," Richard broke in. "I like to think of it as a long-overdue wedding tour."

"Now that you mention it," Peter said, suppressing a grin, "my doting parents have been most earnestly entreating my return. I might as well join you and Geoff on the road west."

"If that is the case," Jennifer said, her black eyes sparkling with barely controlled laughter, "I've an aunt in Northamptonshire that Geoff and I have been neglecting shamefully. If Peter and Geoff are leaving I might as well visit her now as later."

"But . . . but . . . but . . ." Diana sputtered as a thunderstruck Joanna regarded her guests, "you can't leave me all alone when I've just arrived!"

"You won't be alone, Diana," Hildegarde replied, wholly unperturbed. "You will have Joanna and Molly to keep you company."

Diana, already pale, blanched, and Joanna felt her own heart begin to beat an odd staccato rhythm that left her curiously lightheaded and eager to discover what the next day would bring.

* * *

The next day brought, true to their words, the departure of all of the guests of Hetchley Place and Laurelwood who had arrived before Diana.

With the absence of so boisterous a crowd Joanna began to sense for the first time a tension that seemed to pulsate between herself and Diana. It was there when they stood in the gardens admiring Molly's work; it flickered over Joanna as she listened to Diana play the pianoforte in the small parlor, the dark beauty of the music a tangible force between them; and it left a roaring in her ears when they gazed at each other from across the dining table on their first night alone together.

In the days following Diana's arrival Joanna's perceptions seemed to have been suddenly heightened. She knew whenever Diana had entered a room before she turned or Diana greeted her, and she knew whenever Diana looked up from a book to gaze at her. Joanna's breath would suddenly catch in her throat, as if she were waiting for something to happen, for something to be said, but always she was disappointed. She would stand beside Diana in the formal back gardens at dusk and feel a sudden longing to have Diana in her arms, the need so great that she trembled with it. And yet she did nothing.

During the weeks of their separation Joanna had come to understand her own heart; but even so, she was not prepared for this odd fever that only grew in intensity whenever she was near Diana. In her most private moments Joanna secretly admitted to herself that she liked the sensation very much indeed . . . and wondered if Diana felt it as well. But Diana held her thoughts back, kept her emotions in check, until Joanna was left baffled and a little angry at such reticence. It seemed that she would have to take matters into her own hands.

Accordingly, three days following the mass exodus from Hetchley Place, Joanna ordered Diana into her riding togs, for she would begin work immediately upon the portrait that, despite all Diana's protests, would have its subject on horseback. To have Diana sitting demurely amidst a field of daisies did not seem at all appropriate to so vibrant a woman, Joanna contended, and her conviction held sway at last. Diana entered Joanna's studio dressed in riding trousers, vest, and shirt, her hair still held in the tight knot she had created that morning.

Joanna's studio was a potpourri of color; three of the walls were cluttered with her most recent works, there being not a single space left in the rest of the house to hold them. A large oak table held a variety of palettes, brushes, paint rags, and her many jars of pigment. It was here that Joanna felt most in control of her life, and she allowed no scruple to arise that would prohibit her from using such power to her own advantage.

"Very well," Diana said as one being led to the stake, "I'm here."

"I think I want you standing before that bare wall," Joanna replied, struggling not to smile at such reluctance.

"One sits a horse, one does not *stand* a horse," Diana said severely.

'I am merely going to do a few sketches to get the feel of your body," Joanna said, which sent Diana into a violent fit of coughing. Recovering at last Diana moved to the position indicated to her and stood facing Joanna who was seated on her stool, sketchpad in hand.

"Where is Molly?" Diana inquired through an immobile mouth as Joanna quickly set to work.

"In her schoolroom and you may talk to me, you know. You may even move your lips. I wish you would not hold yourself so stiffly," Joanna continued. "You needn't look so grim, either. Why must you seem so uncomfortable?"

"Because I *am* uncomfortable!" Diana exploded. "I have never posed in my life."

"That's just my point. I don't want you to pose. I want you to hold yourself naturally," Joanna replied, startled by so violent a reaction.

"I do not naturally stand before a wall and have myself drawn," Diana said witheringly.

"Pretend that you are at Waverly in the spring studying the blossoms of your fruit trees."

Diana opened her mouth as if to make some other objection but then seemed to think better of it, and, sighing heavily, concentrated on the image of a cherry tree as Joanna ordered her to present first her left profile and then her right. Joanna's heart began to pound, and her hand to tremble as she luxuriated in the freedom of being able to study Diana with a hungry gaze too long denied such pleasure. Noticing, at last, the almost indecipherable scribbles on her sketchpad, Joanna took a deep breath and brought herself in order. Half an hour after they had begun she asked to see Diana's back.

"What on earth for?"

"I have to have a complete understanding of your body if I am to paint it and your body includes your back."

"But I will be sitting my horse facing out towards the multitudinous audience. You won't be painting my backside. I have a *hideous* backside!"

"Be a brave girl and turn around," Joanna said, chuckling. "I am sure that it is not half so bad as you think it is and this *is* necessary. Show a little March spirit and turn!"

Diana grudgingly did so and Joanna's mouth went dry at the sight of her slender back tapering into rounded hips and full buttocks which the trousers seemed only to accentuate. Summoning all of her self control, Joanna began to draw once again as she teasingly lauded the many excellent qualities of Diana's back until her model was trembling with laughter. Ten minutes of work brought Joanna to declare herself satisfied, and she ordered Diana to face her once again for further work on her head and shoulders. She then spent the next five minutes gazing intently at Diana's face.

"You are going to put me to the blush!" her beleaguered model finally hissed.

"Sorry." Joanna smiled as she slipped off of her stool and moved towards Diana. "I cannot decide about your hair. May I experiment?"

"If it means that you will leave off with your odious staring, yes!"

"Such truculence." Joanna chuckled as she undid the thick knot of blonde hair at the back of Diana's head. A sigh escaped her. "Your hair is so soft," she murmured. "I knew that it would be." Her fingers stroked the honeyed waves, her breath coming in quick gasps as her heart began to increase is pace. "To hide such beauty would be criminal," she said softly as her fingers brushed Diana's hair back from her forehead and temples to tumble down to her shoulders. "Yes," she said, studying her handiwork as her intoxicated fingers wound the curling ends of silken honey around themselves, "I prefer this." Suddenly her hand reached up, cupping Diana's face, as her thumb slowly caressed the violet shadow beneath Diana's eyes. "What has caused this?"

"I . . . have not been sleeping well," Diana managed to reply, her body rigid.

"Insomnia?"

"No. . . . Nightmares."

"What haunts you, Diana?" Joanna whispered as the fingers of both hands caressed Diana's cheeks before sliding to her long slender throat, winning a moan from Diana as her eyes closed with the tenderness of the touch.

"Don't, please!" Diana implored, jerking away.

"What is wrong?" Joanna asked, stunned by the sharp

pain that had stabbed through her at this rejection and by the hunger her hands felt now that they were denied the warmth of Diana's skin.

"You mustn't.... I cannot..." Diana's voice faltered and she stopped. "I should not have come," she said at last. "I was insane to think that I could do this."

"Do what?" Joanna said with sudden anger. "Hide from me as you have done from the day we met? I am tired of my enforced ignorance, Diana. I want to know you, all of you. I want to know everything about you: your family, your friends, your past. I want to know why you have nightmares, and why you stayed from me for over two months, and why you have never told me about Gwen McFadden when I have told you of my husband!"

The color drained from Diana's face and she took a step back as if she had been struck. The pain and the fear in her green eyes steadied Joanna; she felt the fury drain from her. Amazed at her own temerity, Joanna nonetheless knew that she could not take back the words that had hovered in her throat for so many months now. She could only press forward.

"Why have you never told me about Gwen McFadden?" she repeated softly.

"I did not think that you would understand," Diana replied, her eyes intent on the knot her hands had made before her.

"How should I not understand love?"

Diana looked up with astonished eyes into Joanna's face.

"Diana, you have known what I have never experienced. I envy you that joy, and ache with the pain I know you feel. Can you not tell me of her? Can you not even tell me what she looked like?"

"She was so unlike you," Diana said, her hand reaching out as if to touch Joanna's cheek and then abruptly dropping away. "Gwen was a slender fairy sprite with strawberry blonde hair and blue eyes that were always so serious and a face dotted with freckles. Her hands were tiny and yet incredibly strong. Everything about Gwen was small, except her heart. My hand could easily cover one of her breasts or encircle an ankle. She was Scotch and quite fierce at times and a little dour at others, and always so alive."

"And you loved her."

"Yes."

"And she died."

"Yes."

"And you have let yourself love no one since her loss."

"I have not the courage to . . . claim love again," Diana whispered.

"You are wrong."

"Then your eyes are not as piercing as I thought them."

CHAPTER 23

The clock in the hall had struck midnight long ago and still Joanna could not sleep for her head was too full of Diana's portrait. Her head was too full of Diana, she wearily conceded. She felt as if she were at war with a woman she wanted only to love.

In the eight days since their row in Joanna's studio Diana had become even more reclusive, avoiding any private conversation with Joanna, insisting that Molly be with them as they worked in the studio. When not being painted Diana spent her days gardening with Molly or teaching the increasingly rambunctious youngster to ride. But even when she and Diana were surrounded by a room full of servants there still existed a cord, seemingly invisible to all but herself, that would draw the two of them closer and closer until only a breath separated them. How Joanna longed to eradicate that distance—but Diana held herself stiffly back. She would not yield, even though there were times that Joanna believed she saw her own need burning deep in Diana's green eyes.

The shadows beneath those eyes had darkened, Diana's appetite had disappeared entirely. Try as she might Joanna could not touch the source of such unhappiness, could not understand the withdrawal of a woman who had been so close a friend but a few months earlier. She could only believe that Diana's time in Herefordshire had been but a respite from the pain she still felt at the death of Gwen McFadden. This thought did nothing to improve Joanna's spirits.

Joanna had come to know her heart soon after she and Molly had returned to Kent. She had come to know her hunger in the following weeks. The discovery amazed her for never had she believed her heart capable of such emotions. Since Diana's coming to Hetchley Place Joanna had been forced to confront a need of such intensity that she was left shaken and dazed. How could one woman stir such heat within her when so many men had failed? She felt herself trapped in longing for another woman and she simply did not know what to do.

Always before it had been she who was ardently pursued by determined suitors, she had never set her cap for anyone in her life, saving Colin, of course, but that was another matter entirely—she had not known what love could be. And now. . . . How did one initiate a courtship of another woman, make one's feelings known, when her heart's desire might well still be mourning the death of another lover?

"Damn!" Joanna said aloud as she threw back the covers, intending to pace the room as she had last night and the night before that.

She heard Diana cry out.

Heedless of her lack of slippers and dressing gown Joanna ran from her room and down the hall, another cry reaching her as she pushed open Diana's bedroom door and entered the blackness, automatically closing the door behind her.

"Gwen!" Diana cried in a voice of such agony that Joanna felt her own heart frozen within her breast.

Every fear had been realized. Pushing away her own despair Joanna quickly gained the bed and sat on it, her hands holding Diana's shoulders. Gently she shook her, her voice imploring Diana to awaken. Diana clutched the arms that held her and seemed to struggle to pull herself back from the nightmarish world that imprisoned her.

"Diana, it's me. It's Joanna. You're safe now. Safe." With a gasp, Diana opened her eyes and stared uncomprehendingly up into Joanna's face. "It's all right now, Diana. I'm here," Joanna murmured. "You're not alone."

With a moan Diana sat up into Joanna's arms where she was held fast as sob after sob shuddered through her body. Joanna rocked her slowly and said she knew not what to soothe, to quiet, to erase the terror that still gripped the woman in her arms.

"Don't go. Please don't go," Diana wept over and over again.

"I won't," Joanna whispered fiercely. "I won't leave you. I swear it." For hours she held Diana until at last Diana slipped into the sleep of exhaustion, her arms still clenched around Joanna as Joanna, too, permitted herself to sleep after pulling the bedclothes over them both.

She awoke to a room left in shadow by the heavy curtains though the clock on the mantle above the fireplace proclaimed the hour to be a little after eight. She looked down at the woman curled against her and thought she had never known such sweetness. Unable to stop herself, Joanna allowed her fingers to brush honeyed wisps of hair from Diana's cheek and this gentle touch brought Diana's eyes open.

"Good morning," Joanna murmured.

"Good morning," Diana replied as Joanna eased her arm free and leaned on an elbow gazing down at the woman she loved.

"Were you able to get any sleep?" Joanna asked.

"Hours," Diana sighed and then took Joanna's hand and kissed her fingertips with a whispered caress. "Thank you for staying with me last night, Joanna."

"There is no need to thank me," Joanna replied as she tried without success to cool the fever Diana had flamed within her. "I wanted to stay with you."

"You should go back to your own room," Diana said, abruptly sitting up. "I'm fine now, really."

"No."

"But—"

"I have spent over a se'night watching you waste away and not understanding why you are so haunted. When I came to you last night you were calling for Gwen McFadden and then I knew. You still love her, don't you, Diana? She has been dead nearly three years and you can't let her go." Joanna tried to keep the anguish from her voice but failed miserably.

"I love her, yes. I will always love her. But you are wrong in what you think. I—"

"How am I wrong? You called to her. You wanted her."

"Shall I tell you of my nightmare?" Diana demanded, her voice unsteady, her eyes feverish as she gazed across at Joanna. "I dreamt of the plague that swept through Constantinople almost three years ago. Have you ever seen the plague disfigure and destroy the people you love? I watched them all die, Joanna: my sister, Rebecca; my father; my mother; my brother, Sam; Gwen last of all. My brother

Tony was in Jamaica knowing nothing of what had happened. And I was alone, so terribly alone. Don't you see? Gwen was the last one I saw die. In my dream I do not call out to her only, but to all that was taken from me . . . and all that I cannot have."

"My poor Diana," Joanna said softly as her hand brushed the tears from Diana's face before her lips gently caressed Diana's mouth.

"Don't!" Diana shouted furiously as she tumbled off the bed and stood on the cold floor, her hair disheveled, her breast rising and falling with her quick breaths.

"Diana, what is wrong?" Joanna demanded, shocked and frightened.

"Oh God, I must have been mad to have stayed this long," Diana said, a hand raking her hair. "I've got to get out of here now, this morning." She turned to flee but in the next moment Joanna, to her own amazement, lunged across the bed, caught Diana's arm, and pulled her forcibly back.

"What on earth do you think you're doing?" Joanna hissed, stunned by her own fury but too caught up to stop now.

"I'm running away you little fool!"

"From what?"

"From *you*!"

Joanna stared at Diana, wholly nonplussed. "From . . . me?" she managed to say at last, her heart racing out of control.

"I love you," Diana said, sagging as if defeated. "I adore you. I need you so much I ache with it every minute of the day . . . and I can't have you."

"Why can't you have me?" Joanna demanded, feeling quite as insane as Diana declared herself to be and not caring a jot.

The question was apparently unexpected for Diana stopped her struggle to free herself and stared at her captor.

"Because you . . . couldn't. . . ." she faltered and then ground to a halt, her green eyes helplessly regarding Joanna.

"How can you love me and yet know so little of me?" Joanna asked in a soft voice.

The color, raised by their recent struggle, drained from Diana's face. Silence stood between them for a long moment and then slowly Joanna released Diana's arm.

"If you run away from me now," Joanna said, "you will assuredly be the greatest lunatic ever bred in England."

"Why?" Diana croaked.

"Because only a lunatic would run away from love and happiness when she has only to reach out . . . and they are hers."

Joanna felt the world drop away leaving only herself and Diana and this cord that throbbed between them, and a roaring in her ears that suddenly ceased as Diana's hand reached out, her fingers gliding over Joanna's cheek. Joanna heard herself sigh at the touch and then she felt Diana's fingers slide through her hair until they cupped the back of her head.

Joanna knew that her heart would explode, it had to. Nothing could withstand such violent pounding as Diana drew her nearer and nearer like a spring slowly being tightened. Her eyes held Joanna's prisoner before the light lashes hid her green gaze and then Diana's warm lips brushed Joanna's mouth with addictive softness. Joanna felt every muscle in her body harden with desire as Diana's mouth came again and again to her lips in a gentle sampling of them.

Joanna's hands went around Diana's back and with a sob she pulled her against her with a need she could deny no longer. Where Diana's caress had been tender, Joanna's mouth was ravenous, devouring the lips pressed to her own, sucking Diana's lower lip before her tongue expored the inner warmth. Diana's moan made Joanna tremble as she felt Diana's arms clutch at her back, heard Diana murmur her name with such desire that Joanna felt her heart shudder. Diana's warm, sweet tongue began an intoxicating dance over her lips, moving slowly, surely, into her mouth where her own tongue eagerly sought Diana's. This joining flooded Joanna's core with a wet heat. She felt her muscles abandon her as she collapsed into Diana's strong arms, Diana's tongue sinking farther and farther into her.

Diana pulled away at last and Joanna nearly cried aloud her anguish until she felt Diana's lips caress her forehead, her eyes, her lips once again, and then they were pressed to her throat leaving Joanna unable to hold back her gasp, her hands pulling Diana's mouth hard against her. "Yes!" she whispered.

"Joanna, sweet Joanna," Diana moaned, her lips finding the pulse at Joanna's throat as her hands swept up over thighs and buttocks that convulsed at her touch. "Tell me," she demanded, her mouth moving to the side of Joanna's throat as Joanna's head fell back, inviting this touch that was so like fire. "I love you, Joanna. Love you! Tell me," Diana demanded again, her lips claiming Joanna's mouth once more, then murmuring against Joanna's lips, "Tell me that you want me as much as I want you. Tell me that you love me. I must hear it, Joanna. I must. . . ."

"Love you?" Joanna's hands cupped Diana's face; she pulled slightly away so that Diana must look at her. "I've been in an agony for you!" Her lips explored Diana's pale face with feathery caresses that left Diana trembling against her. "You are a fever in my heart, a thirst, a hunger. Love me, Diana, for I do love you!"

She pulled Diana's mouth back to her own, her lips capturing Diana's; her tongue, growing bold, flicked out and into Diana's mouth, tasting a new sweetness, discovering a new need. Diana's moan of pleasure poured into Joanna's throat, her hands sweeping up under Joanna's nightdress. The shock of flesh against flesh sent a shuddering through Joanna and she pulled her lips from Diana's mouth. "Please," she whispered.

Diana stepped back. Her eyes never leaving Joanna's, she began to untie the ribbons that held her nightdress together at her shoulders. Slowly the white material slid to the floor. Joanna drank in the creamy shoulders and rounded breasts whose small brown nipples were hard, seeming to reach out for the attention Joanna's mouth longed to give them. But she held herself back as her eyes feasted on Diana's gently rounded belly and slim, curved hips. The lush, dark blonde triangle made Joanna flame with desire. Her gaze fed itself on muscular legs, then rose to the mane of golden hair that cascaded over Diana's shoulders and halfway down her back.

Slowly, tentatively, her hands reached out to touch those strong thighs, to slide up over hips and belly, and around to the smooth, slim back, marveling at the feel of warm female flesh molding itself to her caress. Her mouth tasted shoulders and the pulsing hollow of Diana's throat, before lazily working its way down to Diana's gently rounded breasts. Her tongue flicked across one stiffened nipple before, with a groan, her mouth captured it, enveloped it as Diana cried aloud.

"Oh come to bed, woman. Come to bed," Joanna whispered as her mouth drank in Diana's other breast. "I want to feel you. . . ."

"Then why are you still in your nightshift?" Diana managed to gasp as she arched into Joanna's caress.

With one deft movement Joanna drew her nightdress up and off and tossed it as far away from the bed as she could.

"You are so beautiful," Diana breathed.

Many men had said this to Joanna, but never with such frank admiration or desire, and none had been able to make her blush as she did now. "Come to me, then," Joanna murmured as she sank down on the bed.

Joanna watched, her heart pounding, as Diana knelt above her, her green eyes gazing down into her own before she slowly lowered herself, molding herself to Joanna, her mouth gently meeting and teasing her lips.

Nothing had prepared Joanna for how right this merging of satiny flesh, this connecting of bodies, felt. Her skin absorbed Diana, her breasts sank into Diana's ribs, her hips rested against her belly, her legs clung to Diana's leg placed between them. "It's so good," she gasped as Diana's hands began to explore her with a hunger that tightened the spring within Joanna's breast.

"And you feel . . . delicious," Diana murmured, her eyes seemingly hypnotized by the contours of round, golden brown flesh beneath her hands. "So beautiful," she murmured again before her mouth sank into Joanna's hip, and Joanna gasped her shock and her pleasure.

Slowly Diana's tongue traced Joanna's hip and glided across that round belly to taste and explore the other hip as Joanna shuddered beneath her. Her tongue moved up, her teeth gently sank into side, into belly as her hands created whirlpools of fire in Joanna's thighs. Never had Joanna known such heat, such desperation. Her body was besieged with desire under Diana's fevered caresses, a throbbing need Joanna had never before experienced. She arched into Diana, wanting to feel all of her.

She trembled as Diana's tongue circled her left breast, around and around, before it flicked across the large, taut nipple and came back and back again until her lips suddenly drew it into her mouth. Her arms clutched Diana to her as Diana sucked first gently, and then harder and harder upon that engorged nipple until Joanna's body began to move rhythmically beneath her. A low moan escaped her as the center of the fire that raged within her slid across Diana's strong thigh.

"I need you, Joanna. Need you," Diana gasped, her hand sliding down over Joanna's belly to the black, curly hair below. Slowly, deliberately her fingers crept through that ineffectual barrier to touch silken engorged flesh. "You're so wet!" Diana moaned, her fingers circling Joanna's heat. "So very wet!"

Joanna was unable to make any articulate reply for never had she known such a touch, never had she felt this tempestuous wave that rolled through her as her wet flesh was pressed against the smooth hard bone of Diana's mons. Joanna's hips rose again and again of their own accord to meet those wickedly skilled fingers, her hands buried in Diana's mane of golden hair as she pulled Diana's mouth down to her own.

"Touch me," Diana implored. "I need to feel you touch me!"

Eagerly Joanna brought her hands down to explore Diana's smooth back, her fingers wending their way down to the full, round buttocks that had tantalized her for so long. "Please," she sobbed as her touch drew a moan from Diana. "Please."

"My love, anything," Diana murmured against her throat as she slid long fingers into Joanna's heat. Their cries at this union merged, and tightened even more the spring within Joanna's breast. The intensity of this lovemaking, unlike any she had known, terrified Joanna, but Diana's flesh, her hand, had become necessary to Joanna's every breath, every heartbeat. Her hands stroked Diana's back and thighs only to clutch Diana's shoulders as she felt Diana's fingers sink farther and farther into her, then draw themselves nearly out, before plunging into her once again.

"Oh God, Diana," she gasped. "It's . . . I can't. . . ." She arched against Diana as the spring wound tighter and tighter within her. Her mouth found Diana's breast and drank it in.

"Yes!" Diana shouted as her fingers thrust again into Joanna's hot core, her cries driving Joanna to the edge. Their wet bodies moved against each other as Joanna's hungry mouth sucked Diana's breast harder and harder, mirroring the power of Diana's fingers as they pressed into her again and again, pushing into her very soul until Joanna lunged up into the woman above her, the spring exploding within her. Her head fell away from Diana's breast, and she cried out this shattering of her very being as Diana shuddered uncontrollably against her. She clutched Diana to her, refusing to release those fingers, needing this total merging of flesh as spasm after spasm rocked her.

Gentle silence finally spread over them as Joanna's breathing and heartbeat began to return to a slower pace; her arms and hands and legs loosened their fierce grip. Even in her newly languorous state she felt Diana's tears against her cheek and opened her eyes to see Diana smiling at her with such wonder in her green gaze that Joanna felt herself tremble.

"Tell me again," Diana whispered.

"I love you."

Diana drew in her breath, and then began to chuckle as she curled herself against Joanna.

"Is my abject adoration so amusing, then?"

Diana grinned, tilting her head up so that their eyes could meet. "I am laughing because Hildegarde was right as always. You *do* make me happier than Gwen ever dreamt of doing."

CHAPTER 24

The room was white and gold with a high ceiling bearing a mural of pudgy cupids capering in an Olympian garden. Thick white curtains held back street noises but could not, however, dispel the noise emanating from within the room itself.

"There was a young lass from Vienna," Diana was lustily singing half-submerged in her bathtub as she scrubbed the bottom of one foot, *"who darkened her unmentionables with henna. She reportedly said, 'Tis not for my head, I've a lover who lusts for magenta!"*

"The songs you know." Joanna chuckled as she turned

from adjusting her gown of pale yellow before the full-length mirror.

"Comes from foreign travel." Diana grinned as she stood up, water running in rivulets down the body that stirred within Joanna a hunger that two years of lovemaking had not satiated. "Aren't you going to help me dry off?"

"The last time I did that we both ended up in the bathtub."

"And a wonderful time we had, too." Diana grinned wickedly as she stepped out of the bath.

"You are incorrigible and I will not be led astray. . . ."

"That sounds suspiciously like locking the barn door after the horses have bolted," Diana observed as she wrapped a towel around herself.

"Beast!"

"Why are you dressed so soon?" Diana complained.

"Because Celeste will have our heads if we are late for breakfast one more time this week."

"One must take pleasure when one finds it. Speaking of which. . . ." Diana said as her hand ran caressingly up Joanna's spine.

"Think of breakfast!" Joanna implored.

"Oh I am, I am. I was just thinking of how hungry I am," Diana said as her lips brushed the base of Joanna's neck.

"Behave!" Joanna commanded despite the soft moan that escaped her lips.

"Oh I am, I am," Diana murmured as her lips found Joanna's sensitive ear before progressing to her cheek and slightly parted mouth.

"Beast," Joanna said with little conviction a long moment later.

"I can't help it," Diana said with a grin, her arms wrapped around Joanna's waist. "I am enamored of you. I love you. I adore you. I want to marry you and have your children."

"Idiot!" Joanna gurgled.

"I want to grow old and grey and crotchety with you."

"And I with you," Joanna murmured as her lips found Diana's once again.

"Engraved invitations," Diana stammered as Joanna's hands began to sweep over her, removing the towel, and delving into the heat between her legs as her mouth claimed one of Diana's breasts. "I. . . want engraved invitations . . . in gold. . . ." An aching groan escaped her. ". . . on cream stationery."

* * *

An hour later Joanna and Diana at last repaired to the breakfast salon of the stately town home Lady Hildegarde Dennison shared with Celeste Marie-Therese Sauvatin in the supremely elegant city of Vienna. They had been guests of their two friends for nearly a month while Joanna's works were exhibited in the gallery of one of Hildegarde's childhood friends, enriching the purses of both artist and exhibitor in a manner that Joanna had begun to accept as familiar. She was a success—in many cities a sensation—and still she found it difficult to comprehend the fact.

Chuckling together over their latest indiscretion, Diana and Joanna entered the breakfast salon.

"So, *mes amis,* you come at last," Celeste greeted them from the head of the table, her black eyes snapping. "And do you expect that I should feed you when all of the food we have eaten?"

Diana looked guiltily at the silver-haired Parisienne, at the grimly pinched lips. "I'm so sorry, Celeste. It was all my fault. I . . . dawdled too long in my bath," Diana said as she slid surreptitiously into her place at the table.

"And yesterday it was Joanna who could not get her hair to behave properly. Perhaps if you do not eat a breakfast or two the weakness that would result would end these activities that make you late to my table."

"We really are very sorry, Celeste," Joanna replied, trying not to grin.

"You seem to be under the misapprehension that I run one of your grubby English inns, *mes enfants,* but I wish to point out that such is not the case."

"Our inns are not grubby," ten-year-old Molly cried with patriotic fervor. "They are very clean and have good food and jolly people!"

"Pardonnez-moi," Celeste murmured, unsuccessfully struggling against a smile.

"You will both be on time for tonight's opera, I trust?" Hildegarde broke in. Joanna and Diana hurriedly assured her that they would.

"Bien," Celeste said and, with a gracious inclination of her head, allowed Hildegarde to ring for the servants to bring the breakfast dishes back to the table. "I have received a letter from Madame Verdoux, Joanna," she said when the two had quieted the rumbling within their bellies. "She wishes to sponsor yet another exhibition for you before you return to England."

"How marvelous!" Diana exclaimed.

"It is impossible," Joanna said. "I have no more than six paintings left at best. The others have all been sold."

"Then you will have to work quickly, eh?" Celeste replied.

"You paint very quickly, you know you do," Molly said eagerly. "Oh Mama—Paris!"

"Perhaps we could rent the same house along the river," Diana said. "Do you remember the many pleasures we enjoyed there?"

"It would be lovely," Joanna conceded, with a sidelong glance at her lover. "But it has only been a year since we were in Paris. The critics might easily develop a disgust of me."

"My dear Joanna," Hildegarde said, "your work has undergone such growth and change in this last year of touring that those idiot French critics will stumble all over themselves to claim that no one possesses such skill as you, not even David or Gericault."

"Don't be absurd, Hildy. Their disapprobation is a very real possibility. And I was looking forward to returning to Kent next month," Joanna complained.

"Nonsense," Celeste sniffed. "Why would anyone wish to return to that backwater?"

"Because it is my home," Joanna said with a smile.

"And mine," Diana said.

"And mine," Molly stoutly added.

"And we miss it," Joanna concluded.

"The French could swell your purse to twice the size the Italians and Viennese have made it," Celeste pointed out.

"To triumph twice in the span of a year would be something," Joanna mused.

"It is settled then. I shall write to Madame Verdoux at once," Celeste declared.

Knowing it futile to protest a decision already settled in Celeste's mind, Joanna shrugged and returned to her trout as Diana ordered Molly off to her schoolroom, a scheme requiring nearly ten minutes of artful persuasion before the freckled youngster finally acceded. With youth no longer in their presence Hildegarde and Celeste sat opposite each other, one with her tea, the other with her cocoa, and both with newspapers from their respective homelands propped in their hands.

"Caroline's dropped her foal at last, I see," Hildegarde commented from behind her paper.

"May I take that to mean that I have been made an aunt?" Joanna inquired as Diana choked on a piece of cold ham.

"A boy, of course. Garfield would produce nothing less," Hildegarde continued.

"The poor child, I do pity him," Joanna said.

"It might work out for the best, you know," Diana offered, having recovered from her earlier distress. "He might one day marry Peter and Jennifer's daughter and in that way gain some pleasure from life."

Joanna grinned. "It is a thought."

"And one apropos to a situation which both Celeste and I have recently discussed at great length," Hildegarde said, setting down her newspaper. "Children, although often obnoxious, are just as often to be found quite necessary in the scheme of things. A gentleman such as Richard for example, must have an heir to shoulder the burdens of fortune and property left upon his father's deathbed." Hildegarde stopped, as if that was all she intended to say on so grim a topic.

"Very true," Diana ventured, casting a puzzled glance at Joanna. "But why speak of children and inheritances on this perfectly wonderful summer morning in Vienna? You do not even like children and have more money than you know what to do with. Have you an offspring tucked away somewhere that you have not revealed to us?"

"Were you not attending?"

"I heard every word, Hildegarde, I assure you."

"But you did not comprehend," Celeste observed disapprovingly. "Richard Sinclair is a wealthy man with no heir."

"The Sinclair estate is entailed to the male line and Richard has no son, he has no fruit from his own loins," Hildegarde said flatly.

"My aren't we blunt this morning?" Diana said with a grin.

"Hildegarde is always blunt," Celeste said. "It is her nature to be so."

"Why this sudden interest in Richard's lack of children?" Joanna asked. "Have you just discovered so glaring an absence or had you some point to make?"

"There is a point to every remark I make," Hildegarde declared. "Richard has no male heir, no wife, nothing to mark him as the usual sort of English gentleman—but he does have Geoff. Thus he is viewed with some suspicion by his peers and neighbors. Now we come to the two of you."

"I *have* the fruit of my own loins," Joanna reminded her.

"True," Hildegarde conceded. "You also have the fruit of your own labors." She ignored Diana's guffaw. "With your newfound fame, England is not the safest place to reside, Joanna. I have received letters from many friends reporting that nothing so delights the bastions of English society as gossiping about your 'companion.' You might easily be vilified if you return to your homeland, particularly if you exhibit in London."

Joanna said stubbornly, "I do not care for others' opinions, I want to go home."

"I expected as much." Hildegarde sighed. "Very well, if you are firm in this decision I must demand that you at least give yourself the trappings of propriety to ward off the certain difficulties you would otherwise encounter."

"What had you in mind, Hildy?" Joanna inquired.

"An English gentlewoman requires a family to insure her reputation."

"We *are* a family," Diana protested, her eyes glinting dangerously, "and a good one."

"It is not my nature to shilly-shally," Hildegarde declared. "Joanna, Diana, you should both be married . . . to men."

"What?" they both squeaked.

"Hildegarde is right," Celeste said. "This acquiring of the husbands is of much importance."

"Are you both mad?" Diana demanded. "Marry? *Us?* Why on earth should we do so foolhardy a thing? You two never did."

"That is because we had the very good sense not to live in England—*and* we created a social circle that effectively shields us from the rest of the world," Hildegarde replied. "You two have chosen to move in the public realm. Joanna is famous now throughout Europe and even you, Diana, are becoming known for your music. Two independent women living and traveling together with a child are but red capes before the maddened bull of propriety. At least one of you must marry."

"And whom do you have in mind as prospective husband material?" Joanna dryly inquired.

"Hildy! Celeste! Are you there?" a cheerful masculine voice shouted.

Geoffrey Hunt-Stevens and Richard Sinclair burst into the room. "There you are!" Richard said. "What? Still at breakfast? For shame! My dear ladies, the sun has been up these four hours and more. Arise, I say, and come with us to stroll down the boulevard on this beautiful summer morning. We've only a se'night before our return to England and Geoff and I intend to imbibe fully from every Viennese pleasure that is available. Arise, I say, and lead us into merriment!"

"You have your answer," Celeste said with a smile.

"Them?" Diana choked.

Joanna began to laugh. "You must be mad."

"Not at all," Hildegarde said. "Richard has Geoff but no direct heir; you have Molly and fame but no husband. What could be simpler?"

"I beg your pardon?" Richard said politely as he and Geoff looked at the women in utter confusion.

"It is for the good of Richard and Geoffrey as well," Celeste pointed out. "The two men always in each other's company has created talk, even in Vienna. Think of what it will stir in England. For their own safety they must have wives."

"These females are bandying about inflammatory phrases and hideous schemes, Richard. Let us flee while we can," Geoffrey urged.

"No wait, what they say makes sense," Richard said. "Think on it, Geoff. We can't wander around in a pink cloud of love forever, someone is bound to notice and attempt to ruin us all. Besides, I need a son to carry on the Sinclair line. However unfair it may be, the estate is entailed solely to male heirs. If I have no son, Laurelwood will pass to my dreadful cousin Collins. I cannot let that happen."

"You were always a most sensible man, Richard," Celeste commended him.

Richard bowed.

"But . . . but marriage? To a woman? Is such a thing possible?" Geoffrey dazedly inquired.

"The practice is carried out in a few remote places on earth, I believe," Joanna said with a smile.

"Oh God," Geoff groaned.

"Resign yourself to a wife, Geoffrey," Hildegarde commanded. "She may well save your lovely hide from a flogging."

"But I don't want to get married!" Geoffrey wailed.

"There, there," Richard said, patting his shoulder, "try to put a brave face on it, old fellow."

"I weary of these histrionics,"Celeste announced. "Hildegarde, let us leave these young fools to resolve the matter amongst themselves."

Hildegarde quickly took her lover's arm and together they swept regally from the room.

"I will not have those two dictate to me!" Diana said furiously once the door had closed behind Hildegarde and Celeste.

"Be reasonable, my love," Joanna implored. "We are in danger every day of our lives living as we do. I have felt it, and I know that you have too. Marriage is a reasonable—nay, a necesary precaution. And there is your fortune to consider. As it stands, there is no one to inherit it once you pass away. Were you to have a child—"

"Children again, Richard!" Geoffrey shuddered. "They're talking about children! Such a thing isn't possible, is it? Oh I couldn't . . . couldn't possibly consider—"

"It's all right, Geoff," Joanna said dryly, "we shan't tie you to the bed."

"Personally, I find the mere suggestion of a man in my bed appalling," Diana said with great dignity.

"You are too kind," Richard replied, a grin tugging at his lips. "But one generally begets the fruit of one's loins in bed with the opposite sex."

"Speaking for both Joanna and myself, Richard," Diana said grimly, "you will never get your loins near either of us!"

"But if not from the marriage bed," Richard countered, "how shall you get a child? By the stork?"

"Men are so unimaginative," Diana said with a sigh.

"Under a cabbage leaf then," Richard suggested.

"Brilliant, really," Diana said witheringly. "There are thousands of unwanted children born in England each year. Only think what would have happened to my poor maid, Annie, if I had not taken her in. It would be a simple thing, I should think, to find another Annie and adopt the child she bears with the world none the wiser to our little plot."

"A much more suitable suggestion," Geoffrey said, sighing in relief.

"Very well, we adopt," Richard said. "I don't suppose it's the blood that makes the gentleman anyway."

"Are we resolved, then, to marry each other?" Joanna asked.

The four stared at each other.

"If only for the look of shock on our friends' faces when they hear the news," Diana said at last, "it will be worth it."

"The lads at the Rose and Crown will never believe it,"

Geoffrey said and began to laugh.

"It appears," Richard said, smiling, "that we are resolved."

"There is just one sticking point," Joanna said. "Who is to marry whom?"

There was a frozen silence.

"I think I need a drink," Diana said, rising hurriedly from her chair.

"I think I need two," Geoffrey moaned.

"I'll not be the one to start a row by choosing one fair damsel over the other," Richard said.

They all looked to Geoffrey, who promptly choked on his wine.

"Having never intended to marry," he said hastily, "I can hardly be left to make such a decision."

"Men, as I've frequently remarked, are of no earthly use," Diana said disgustedly. "Very well, Joanna, which stalwart male shall you call husband?"

"It is only reasonable that I marry Richard and you marry Geoff," Joanna stated.

"Why is it reasonable?" Diana demanded, refilling her wine glass as well as Geoff's.

"I have known Richard longer than you and you have known Geoff longer than I," Joanna replied.

"Where is your imagination?" Diana demanded. "It would be far better if you and Geoff were swept away by each other's beauty, and Richard and I were swept away by each other's good sense."

Joanna forgot herself so much as to laugh at this. "My dearest love," she said, "it is perfectly natural that I marry a brother-in-law who has protected me through all the years of my widowhood and that you marry one of your oldest friends."

"But I don't want to marry Geoff!"

"Whyever not?" Joanna asked.

"He is too beautiful for me," Diana replied. 'Everyone

will think he married me for my fortune and that is a terrible reputation for one as plain as me. No, I should marry Richard. Neither of us are remarkably beautiful and our fortunes are similar."

"But I could not marry Geoff!" Joanna exclaimed.

"Why the hell not?" Geoffrey exploded, outraged that he should be shunned by two women in less than a minute.

"You know that I am very fond of you Geoff," Joanna said placatingly. "But I can't imagine myself married to you."

"This is only a formality, Joanna," Diana said. "You won't find yourself acting out cozy little scenes by the fire."

"You and Geoff are flamboyant, and Richard and I are the retiring types," Joanna said. "These are much more sensible matches."

"Geoff is perfect for you," Diana insisted.

"He is perfect for you," Joanna countered.

"I deal very well with Richard."

"So do I!"

The two women glared at each other as the men looked on, bemused.

"Diana," Joanna said with a sigh, "I do not want to fight with you and I certainly will not marry unless you do, but we must come to an equitable decision. . . . We could draw straws."

"Blindman's Bluff," Diana countered. "Whichever one we catch we marry."

"We could toss a coin," Joanna said.

"Never!" Diana insisted. "I'll not call heads for any man."

Geoffrey fell into a violent coughing fit.

"Diana, my head is dizzy with arguing," Joanna said. "I leave the matter entirely in your hands. You shall choose Molly's stepfather."

"There you have it, Diana. You must decide," Richard

said. "Which one of us is to be your lord and master?"

Diana stared at Richard and Geoffrey.

"Beauty or fortune," Geoffrey said amiably, "you've only to say the word."

Diana, looking helplessly from one man to the other, opted for a third glass of wine.

A very few of the more than 70 books available from
THE NAIAD PRESS, INC.
P.O. Box 10543 • Tallahassee, Florida 32302
Mail orders welcome. Please include 15% postage.

Pembroke Park by Michelle Martin. A Regency novel. 256 pp.
ISBN 0-930044-77-0 $7.95

The Long Trail by Penny Hayes. A western novel. 248 pp.
ISBN 0-930044-76-2 $8.95

Horizon of the Heart by Shelley Smith. A novel. 192 pp.
ISBN 0-930044-75-4 $7.95

An Emergence of Green by Katherine V. Forrest. A novel.
288 pp. ISBN 0-930044-69-X $8.95

Spring Forward/Fall Back by Sheila Ortiz Taylor. A novel.
288 pp. ISBN 0-930044-70-3 $7.95

For Keeps by Elisabeth C. Nonas. A novel. 144 pp.
ISBN 0-930044-71-1 $7.95

Torchlight of Valhalla by Gail Wilhelm. A novel. 128 pp.
ISBN 0-930044-68-1 $7.95

Lesbian Nuns: Breaking Silence edited by Rosemary Curb and
Nancy Manahan. Autobiographies. 432 pp.
ISBN 0-930044-62-2 $9.95

The Swashbuckler by Lee Lynch. A novel. 288 pp.
ISBN 0-930044-66-5 $7.95

Misfortune's Friend by Sarah Aldridge. A novel. 320 pp.
ISBN 0-930044-67-3 $7.95

A Studio of One's Own by Ann Stokes. Edited by Dolores
Klaich. Autobiography. 128 pp. ISBN 0-930044-64-9 $7.95

We Too Are Drifting by Gale Wilhelm. A novel. 128 pp.
ISBN 0-930044-61-4 $6.95

Amateur City by Katherine V. Forrest. A mystery novel. 224 pp.
ISBN 0-930044-55-X $7.95

The Sophie Horowitz Story by Sarah Schulman. A novel. 176 pp.
ISBN 0-930044-54-1 $7.95

The Young in One Another's Arms by Jane Rule. A novel.
224 pp. ISBN 0-930044-53-3 $7.95

The Burnton Widows by Vicki P. McConnell. A mystery novel.
272 pp. ISBN 0-930044-52-5 $7.95

Old Dyke Tales by Lee Lynch. Short stories. 224 pp.
ISBN 0-930044-51-7 $7.95

Daughters of a Coral Dawn by Katherine V. Forrest. Science
fiction. 240 pp. ISBN 0-930044-50-9 $7.95

The Price of Salt by Claire Morgan. A novel. 288 pp.
ISBN 0-930044-49-5 $7.95

Against the Season by Jane Rule. A novel. 224 pp.
ISBN 0-930044-48-7 $7.95

Curious Wine by Katherine V. Forrest. A novel. 176 pp.
ISBN 0-930044-43-6 $7.50

Mrs. Porter's Letter by Vicki P. McConnell. A mystery novel.
224 pp. ISBN 0-930044-29-0 $6.95

Faultline by Sheila Ortiz Taylor. A novel. 140 pp.
ISBN 0-930044-24-X $6.95

Anna's Country by Elizabeth Lang. A novel. 208 pp.
ISBN 0-930044-19-3 $6.95

Prism by Valerie Taylor. A novel. 158 pp.
ISBN 0-930044-18-5 $6.95

The Marquise and the Novice by Victoria Ramstetter. A novel.
108 pp. ISBN 0-930044-16-9 $4.95

Outlander by Jane Rule. Short stories, essays. 207 pp.
ISBN 0-930044-17-7 $6.95

Sapphistry: The Book of Lesbian Sexuality by Pat Califia. 2nd
edition, revised. 195 pp. ISBN 0-930044-47-9 $7.95

All True Lovers by Sarah Aldridge. A novel. 292 pp.
ISBN 0-930044-10-X $6.95

A Woman Appeared to Me by Renee Vivien. Translated by
Jeannette H. Foster. A novel. xxxi, 65 pp.
ISBN 0-930044-06-1 $5.00

Cytherea's Breath by Sarah Aldridge. A novel. 240 pp.
ISBN 0-930044-02-9 $6.95

Tottie by Sarah Aldridge. A novel. 181 pp.
ISBN 0-930044-01-0 $6.95

The Latecomer by Sarah Aldridge. A novel. 107 pp.
ISBN 0-930044-00-2 $5.00

9-2 (